TWO FOR THE MONEY

BLAIR HOWARD

Two for the Money

A Harry Starke Novel
By
Blair Howard

TWO FOR THE MONEY
A Harry Starke Novel

ISBN-13: 978-1518653988

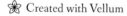 Created with Vellum

Chapter One

The call came out of the blue on a Tuesday evening in the middle of August at around nine-thirty.

"Harry, this is Tom, Tom Sattler." *Tom Sattler? I don't know any... oh, him.*

I hadn't heard from him in almost five years. I hadn't thought of him in almost as long.

"Hey, Tom. Wow, it's been a long time. How the hell are you?"

I went to school with Tom. We graduated from McCallie together in '92.

"Yeah, Harry. I know it's been a long time, but... well... I need some help, some of your expertise. I need to see you."

"Sure. Why don't you call my office in the morning and tell Jacque I said to set something up."

"*No!* Sorry, Harry, but that won't work. I'm in trouble, and I need to see you, now, tonight."

"Tom, it's almost ten, and I've had a long day. Can we not do it at my office first thing tomorrow?"

"No. I need to see you tonight. Please, Harry. I wouldn't ask if it weren't important."

"Well... okay, I suppose. Where are you?"

"I'm at home. I have a place on Royal Mountain Drive."

"That's off Banks Road, right?"

"Yes."

"I need to get fixed up a little first... that and the drive over, say ten-thirty. Okay?"

"Yes, I'll be waiting." He gave me the address and then disconnected. *What the hell could be so urgent?*

It took a little longer than I figured. I arrived outside his home just before 10:45. I parked in the driveway in front of the garage and walked around to the front door of a rambling two-story house with a single story wing on either end, one of which housed a three-car garage; a high-end home in an expensive sub-division. It had to have cost something in the range of eight or nine hundred thousand.

I rang the front doorbell and waited. The lights were on inside, but no one seemed to be about. I rang it again. Nothing. I wandered back to my car, looked around, and then walked to the door beside the garage. I rang that bell, and again I waited. I tried the doorknob. When it turned, I pushed the door open.

"Hey, Tom. You there?" No answer. *Dammit.*

Silence. I walked slowly through the mudroom, then the kitchen, and then the foyer, which opened up into a vast open space with a cathedral ceiling dominated by a two-story high picture window. Tom Sattler lay on his side, his face in a pool of blood. The black, terry-cloth robe and the crimson lake that surrounded his head made a stark contrast against the white carpet.

The living room – I assumed that's what it was – was accented by an imposing, floor-to-ceiling stone fireplace with tightly-packed bookshelves on either side. The rest of the room was sparsely but tastefully furnished: just a black leather sofa, three matching easy chairs, and a baby grand piano. There was also an expensive walnut partner's desk set against the wall to the left of the window. Carefully, I stepped across the carpet and knelt at Tom's side and felt his neck for a pulse; there was none. My old school friend was dead, still warm, but dead. Blood still oozed from a gunshot wound to the right side of his head. A Ruger .22 LCR revolver lay close to his right hand. *Suicide? If he was going to do that, why the hell did he call me?*

I eased carefully back to the foyer, turned, looked around the room once more, and started to punch 911 into my iPhone. Then I stopped, turned and looked around the room once more. It seemed tidy enough.... *What? Am I missing something?*

I shook my head, finished punching in the number, gave the dispatch operator my name and the address, and then I called Kate Gazzara. I looked around one more time, and then went outside to wait.

Kate's a long-time friend and a lieutenant in the major crimes unit of the Chattanooga PD. I've known her for more than fifteen years, since she was a rookie cop. Until recently, we were in a fairly serious relationship, until I screwed it up, that is, but that's another story. We're still friends, at least I think we are, and we still work together, now and then. I was a cop long before I was a private investigator, and I still enjoy a semi-official standing as a consultant to Kate, unpaid of course. She makes good use of my freedom, and I have access, though limited, to her resources. We have faith in each other, Kate and I. We support each other. Always have, and I hope we always will.

She arrived not more than ten minutes later, with Sergeant Lonnie Guest in tow, only minutes after the first cruiser had arrived.

"Harry, Harry, Harry," she said, shaking her head. "What is it this time?"

Kate's a beautiful woman: almost six feet tall, with a slender, muscular figure, tawny blond hair, an oval face with high cheekbones, huge hazel eyes and a high forehead. Her hair was tied in a ponytail that covered her right ear. She wore lightweight black pants, black shoes with flat heels, a white tee under a tan buckskin vest, and a Glock 26 in a holster on her right hip. As always, she looked amazing.

Detective Sergeant Lonnie Guest is an enigma, an eminently stupid individual given to rare bursts of brilliance that can shock and amaze; a big man...no, dammit, he's fat. He could do with losing fifty, maybe even sixty pounds. Obnoxious, arrogant, always trying to be something he never could be, he shambled along behind Kate like a giant sloth. Oh hell, maybe I'm being too hard on the man. He had managed to clean himself up a little since I last saw him, and I think he may even have lost a little weight, although his gut still hung over his belly like a deflated basketball. As always, he was sporting an intensely annoying, shit-eating grin.

"Hey, Kate. How are you, Lonnie?"

"Not so well as you, you ugly–"

"That's enough, Lonnie," Kate said. "Keep it civil or go sit in the car and wait."

He continued to stand there and grin at me. The fat bastard hates my guts. We were at the police academy together, and he never got over how I was fast-tracked for promotion and he wasn't. *Tough shit, Lonnie.*

"It's a friend of mine, Kate. Well, not really a friend. We were at school together. Long time ago. I haven't seen him in years. Looks like he shot himself."

"So what are you doing here, Harry?"

"He called me. Asked me to come over. Said he needed help. I told him to come to the office tomorrow, but he insisted. I got the call around 9:30, give or take five minutes. I arrived at a little after 10:45, which means–"

"He hasn't been dead long, right?" she interrupted.

I nodded. "No more than an hour at most, I'd say. Is Doc Sheddon on the way?"

"Yup. He should be here in a few minutes. Let's take a quick look. Lonnie, you stay out here and get the tapes up. Don't look at me like that; just do it."

And he did, though with a great deal of mumbling and gesturing.

Not a pretty sight when he's pissed off, Lonnie Guest.

I followed Kate into the house through the side door. We retraced my short journey through the kitchen, but stopped short of the living room. She looked at Tom and shook her head. "Sure does look like suicide, but why call you and then shoot himself in the head? Is there something you're not telling me, Harry?"

"No, he sounded fine on the phone. A little agitated, but not upset."

We could hear sirens; more cruisers were arriving, along with an ambulance and a fire truck, for God's sake.

Two minutes later, Doc Sheddon, the M.E., joined us in the foyer. He waddled in, puffing, his big black case hanging heavily in his right hand, the bottom of it only a few inches above the floor.

"Good evening, Lieutenant. You wanna tell me why these things always happen late at night? I was just about to go to bed, for God's sake. How's it hanging, Harry?" *Same tired old greeting.*

He set his case down on the polished wood floor and surveyed the living room, humming and huffing to himself like some modern-day Bilbo Baggins.

"Whew. Nasty one," he said, as he dropped to one knee beside his case. He opened it and put on a pair of latex gloves and Tyvek boot covers, before stepping gingerly into the room. He knelt beside the body, felt for a pulse, shook his head, examined the wound, shook his head again, and withdrew a small camera from his jacket pocket. He shot twenty or thirty images, and then backed away from the body.

"I don't like it," he said to Kate. "Better get a crime scene unit in here. There are some anomalies. He's been dead less than an hour, I'd say. The body's still warm. Probably not cooled by more than a degree or two. I'll know more when I get him on the table. Make sure they get plenty of photos, especially of the wound, the position of the body, and their relationships to the weapon." He looked again across the room at the body, dropped his chin to his chest, closed his eyes, breathed deeply, then looked up, first at Kate, then at me.

"They're already on their way, Doc, "Kate said. "I always bring them in when gunshots are involved."

He stripped off the gloves and the boot covers, put them into a plastic bag and sealed it, and then threw them into the open case.

"Yeah, well. I'm going home. See ya, guys. Nine in the morning. You'll be there?"

I shook my head.

"I'll be there," Kate said.

Sheddon nodded, picked up the case, and waddled out through the kitchen without a backward look.

"Now there's something to ponder, Harry," Kate said. "What did he mean 'anomalies?' Did you notice anything when you were checking the body?"

"Nope. Nothing." I shook my head. "But Doc Sheddon is rarely wrong. If he's thinking homicide, I wouldn't bet against it."

I heard a noise in the mudroom.

"We'd better move outside, Kate. It sounds like they're here."

The crime scene unit had arrived, four of them clothed from head to toe in white coveralls, overboots, hairnets, gloves, facemasks, the works; I couldn't tell if they were male or female.

"Kate, I need to go home, get some rest. Call me when you know something. Okay?"

"Yes, but I'll need to talk to you anyway. I need to know exactly what was said during that call. If it's homicide, it could be important. Your office, late morning, after Doc Sheddon gets done?"

I nodded, turned, and walked carefully out to where my car was parked. There was no sign of Lonnie Guest, so I got in and drove slowly home; my head was in a whirl.

Chapter Two

I hadn't been at work more than thirty minutes the following morning when my cell phone rang. I was in the outer office talking to Jacque.

"Hey, Kate. What's up?"

"I just wanted to pass along some information about last night. Is that okay?"

"Shoot."

"First, Tom Sattler. He was forty-two, wealthy, divorced ten years ago. The ex-wife is Gloria Sattler; she's forty-three. They have three children, all girls; Stephanie, twenty-one; Julie, twelve; Nicola, ten. He has a long-time girlfriend, a Wendy Brewer, twenty-six.... Are you taking notes, Harry?"

"Er... no. Some of it I already know. The rest I was

hoping you'd either fax or email. Either that or bring it with you when you finish with Doc Sheddon."

"Sheesh. Okay. I'm about to head over there now. It's almost nine, and he doesn't like to be kept waiting. When I leave the Forensic Center, I'll head on over to your office. Maybe we could talk over lunch."

Lunch? Wow! It's been a while. She's loosening up a little, or is she, I wonder?

"Sure. We can do that. Where would you like to go?"

"You pick it, and don't get any ideas. I still haven't forgotten your performance with Olivia Hansen and the senator. How is Ms. Michaels, by the way?"

Damn. I sometimes wonder if the woman isn't reading my mind.

"She's fine. She said she might come down for the weekend. Would you like to meet her?"

"Oh, I *don't* think so, and I'm sure as hell she doesn't want to meet me."

"You've got her all wrong, Kate. She's grateful; we saved her ass, and we managed to keep her name out of the media."

"Yeah, whatever. I'll pass, thank you."

"Suit yourself. See you for lunch."

"Bye, Harry."

Two minutes later, the office phone on my desk buzzed.

"Yes, Jacque."

"Amanda Cole from Channel 7 called a few minutes ago. She wants you to call her back. She says it's urgent."

Urgent, my ass. The bitch wants to do another hatchet job on me.

"I'll do it later." *Like hell I will.*

"I'll remind you." *I'm sure you will.*

"Fine. Now, if you don't mind, Jacque...."

"I know... hold all your calls."

A little after ten that morning, Kate called my cell phone for a second time.

"Kate? Is everything all right?"

"Harry, can you come down to the Forensic Center? I'd like you to hear what Doc Sheddon has to say, firsthand."

"I'll get there as quick as I can. The traffic... well, you know."

Doc Sheddon runs the Hamilton County Forensic Center. It's just a couple of blocks north of the PD on Amnicola. It's a small department, just himself and a forensic anthropologist. We are actually quite blessed to have it, as small as Chattanooga is. It means we don't have to rely on the State for what we need, autopsies and the like, thus we can get things done a whole lot quicker.

I pulled in at the back door of the facility and parked. I glanced at the road sign fastened next to the door and smiled, as I always did. It read *Dead End*. The good doctor was the king of gallows humor.

"Ah, Harry," Sheddon said. "Glad you could make it."

The doctor, Kate, and Lonnie Guest were seated at the table in the tiny conference room.

"Don't bother to sit," Sheddon said, rising to his feet. "Let's go in there. I'd like you to see the body."

It's funny how a dead body turns into something other than a person when you see it on the autopsy table, even when it's someone you once knew. I never did have much in the way of feelings for Tom Sattler; now I had none at all for the sad slab of meat he had become, a little over-weight, a little flabby, and a dirty, all-over gray color. The classic 'Y' incision to the chest had been stitched closed. *Damn, I've seen better work on a football.* The flap of hair and scalp that had been removed to give access to the skull had been pulled back over the top and stitched closed to hold the cap in place. The brain, sliced into several sections, lay in a stainless steel pan on a table just below the scales; the rest of the organs occupied several more pans on the stainless steel draining board at the sink.

"First," Sheddon said, "the cause of death was a single shot to the head. The .22 caliber bullet entered the skull just above and to the rear of the right ear. It disintegrated and scrambled a significant portion of the brain."

Thoughtfully, he looked down at the corpse and stroked the top of its head, almost as if he was petting a cat. "As soon as I saw the body, I was perturbed by the wound. It wasn't a contact wound, d'you see?" He pointed with a pencil. "There's stippling, tattooing, around it; more of it to the left than to the right, which means the gun was held at an angle. I estimated, even then, that the shot had been fired from at least two inches away from contact, possibly even as much as six inches. We'll have to wait for ballistics to confirm the exact distance. Then there was the position of the wound. It didn't look quite right."

He looked up at me and said, "Harry, would you do me a favor please? Would you pull your weapon and make as if to shoot yourself in the head?"

I did as the doctor asked, not a little curious.

"There, now. D'you see what I mean, Kate, Lonnie? Look where the muzzle of the gun is. The most natural place to put it is right there, where Harry has it, at the temple. Okay, you can lower the gun, but don't put it away, not just yet.

"The victim's wound, as you can see, is a little above and to the rear of the ear. That's not natural. Not only that, the trajectory of the bullet is angled slightly forward and downward, from here to here."

He inserted the pencil into the wound, and adjusted the angle slightly. "Like this. D'you see? That's not natural either."

He removed the pencil, wiped it on his lab coat, and paused for us to digest what he'd just said. It was simple enough.

"Okay," Sheddon continued. "Now picture this: he's standing with his back to the fireplace. He raises the gun to the side of his head, but instead of placing the muzzle against his temple, he holds it two inches away, maybe more, and slightly behind and above his ear, and he angles it slightly downward and forward. Does that make sense? Try it, Harry."

I did as he asked, and he was right. In fact, I didn't think it could be done.

"Not only that,' he continued, "if the gun *was* so positioned, the pressure needed to pull the trigger of that double-action Ruger, combined with the awkward angle of the wrist, almost certainly would have jerked the barrel upward. Hell, he could have missed himself, even from that close range. No! No, no, no. He was shot by a person unknown. Homicide. It was homicide."

The good doctor seemed to be very certain and well satisfied with his analysis, and who was I to argue with him? Kate, and even the erstwhile Lonnie Guest, must have felt the same, because they didn't say a word. I slipped the M&P9 back in its holster under my arm.

"So, here's how I think it happened." Sheddon looked first at Kate, then at me, and not at all at Lonnie.

"I think he was shot execution style. He could not have been seated; there were no chairs close to the body, and there would have been blood spatter on them if they'd been moved. So I think he probably was on his knees. That would account for the downward angle of the projectile, the placement of the wound, and possibly the gap between the wound and the muzzle of the gun. The impact of the shot would have thrown him forward, hence the position of the body."

I looked at Kate. She nodded. In spite of myself, I also raised my eyebrows at Lonnie. He shrugged; for once, he wasn't smiling.

"One more thing. I say it was homicide," Sheddon said, as he picked up Sattler's right hand, "but here's something else for you to think about. There's gunshot residue on his right hand, and only one empty casing in the cylinder of the weapon. That, I can't account for."

"So he *could* have shot himself, then?" Kate said.

"Nope. I don't think so, not from that angle, not unless he was a contortionist. I'm recording it as a homicide. Having said that, somebody went to a whole lot of trouble to make it look like suicide."

Kate dropped Lonnie and her car off at the PD and I picked her up from there. The drive to Henry's Cafe, just off Highway 58, took less than ten minutes. We talked as we traveled.

"Harry, why did Sattler call you instead of the police? If he was in trouble, surely that would be the natural thing to do, unless he had something to hide."

"I don't know. He said he didn't want to talk about it over the phone. Said it was important. He wasn't particularly excited, as I remember it, a little agitated maybe, but then I hadn't seen him in five years, so I wouldn't necessarily know what his state of mind was. There's something else: the timing. Whoever killed him must have gotten very lucky. I could only have missed him by a few minutes."

We pulled into the lot outside Henry's. The cafe was quiet, which is why I'd figured it was a good place to talk. We ordered coffee and sandwiches, and took a booth by the window.

"What do you remember about Sattler, Harry?" Kate asked, stirring sweetener into her coffee.

"Hmmm. Not a whole lot. It was a long time ago, back in '92 when we graduated. I remember him as being confident, enthusiastic, one of those people that no matter what you say, they've always done it better and more often. You know the type, right?"

She nodded.

"I think he tended to exaggerate, embellish, was not always truthful, but people grow up, they grow out of that sort of stuff. I lost track of him when he went off to college. Northeastern, I think it was. He studied finance. After that I saw very little of him. I'd bump into him every now and then, at the club, or a restaurant. He always went out of his way to say hello. You know how it is."

"And you don't know what he did for a living?"

"As far as I know, he was a banker or something like that. Where and for whom, I have no idea."

"Okay." Kate handed me several pieces of paper, clipped together. "Here's what I know. As I told you earlier, he was divorced about ten years ago. His ex-wife, Gloria Sattler, took him for a wild ride and ended up with a healthy settlement and substantial alimony. She just about cleaned him out."

"He must have recovered, though," I said, flipping through the papers. "That home must have cost close to a million."

She nodded. "Gloria is forty-three. The three children, all girls, live with her. He lived alone. He has a girlfriend, Wendy Brewer, twenty-six. We know nothing about her, yet, but we will. Gloria has a boyfriend, fiancé, whatever. His name is Richard Hollins. He's...twenty-five years old.

Nice one, Gloria. We don't know much about him either, yet."

I gave her the raised eyebrows look.

"The top page," she nodded at the papers on the table, "is a list of Sattler's known close contacts. The other two pages are just the little background we have so far. We have a lot of work to do. You in?"

I looked at the list; just six names, including Sattler's children.

"Oh yeah. I was in the moment I got the call from him. He wasn't a friend, but I still need to know what happened. If he killed himself, that's one thing; if he was murdered.... What about the scene? Did CSI. find anything?"

"Not much," Kate said. "There was a single hair under the body; fair, eight and a quarter inches long. Could have been there for a while, maybe not. Plenty of prints; at least ten individuals. The techs have only just gotten started, but they already know that most of them are his. Some will belong to his girlfriend and daughters, but there are at least a half-dozen others, all of which we have yet to identify. We should have something later this afternoon. Yours, just partials, were on the outer knob and two bell pushes." She paused and thought for a moment.

"There were two computers in his office: a desktop and a laptop," she continued. "There's nothing on them; fingerprints, yes, but no files, photos, nothing. All of the drives appear to have been wiped clean. He might have done that himself, but probably not. That sort of handiwork indicates a pro, or at least someone who knows what they're doing. There were no external drives, disks or flash drives present. That's also unusual. Most people do external backups these days. I do, and not to the Cloud either. I don't trust it. I back up to DVDs. I bet he did, too."

I nodded. "What about phones, iPads? He had to have at least a cell phone."

"Nope, nothing like that. There's a house phone. If he had them, they're gone. It looks like the house was searched, by a pro. Everything appears to be in its place. The clothes in the drawers and closets appear to be undisturbed; everything is neat and tidy, but here and there, especially in the unoccupied rooms, there are marks in the dust where something has been moved, but not quite replaced where it was. Sattler didn't clean much. There's no telling what the killer was searching for, but it wouldn't be too wild of a guess that it was the computer backups."

"Makes sense. Did any of the neighbors see or hear anything?"

"No one heard anything, and they wouldn't, unless they were inside the house; a .22 doesn't make a whole lot of noise. One of the neighbors thought she saw a dark-colored SUV, possibly black or blue, backed in the drive all the way to the garage doors, but couldn't remember what time. She thought it was around six o'clock, but it could have been later. We know he was still alive then, because he didn't call you until nine-thirty."

"If he was alone when he called me," I said, "someone must have been able to get in and out quickly. Either Sattler let him in, or he had a key. Either way, he knew his killer."

"Him?"

"Yeah, you're right. Could have been a woman. It could also have been more than one person. What do we know about the girlfriend?"

"Wendy Brewer? Not much. There's a photo; well, there was a photo of them together on the living room couch. It was on the piano. We took it to get copies made; I'll make sure you get one. She's somewhat plain, not much of an improvement on the wife, just younger. She looks nicely put together, in the photo. With his resources, he could probably have done better. We'll need to talk to her."

"How about the wife, Gloria? I met her a couple of times at the club, but I didn't *know* her. She seemed... okay, I guess. Not bad looking, but not carrying her age too well either; a bit too nouveau rich, acted like she was better than she was, but that's understandable. As I recall, she came from a working class background. Our boy Sattler married beneath himself."

"Christ, Harry. You're such a snob, sometimes."

I grinned at her. "You never complained."

"Yeah, those were the days," she said, dryly.

"Sarcasm, Kate. It doesn't become you."

"Hah. Okay, so she's as good a place as any to start, but... I wonder...."

"So, what's the plan?"

She looked at her watch. "It's after eleven. I need to get back to the PD, make some calls. I think we need to talk to Gloria Sattler, this afternoon, if possible. Why don't you go back to your office and see what you can dig up on the victim? I'll give you a call later on. If you find anything, you can call me."

"Sounds reasonable. Let's go."

Chapter Three

I dropped Kate off at the PD, and then drove downtown. I arrived back at my office at a little after noon. I have a small suite close to the courts and the law offices in Chattanooga. I own and operate a private detective agency, Harry Starke Investigations.

I started the agency some eight years ago, when I quit being a cop. I have a Master's degree in Forensic Psychology from Fairleigh Dickinson; I joined the CPD right after I graduated. I regarded my time there as a continuance of my education rather than a calling, but I did make a lot of friends while I was a sworn officer. Today, my client list includes just about every lawyer and judge in town, and even more in the big cities beyond – Atlanta, Nashville, Birmingham.

Because of where I was educated – I went to McCallie, one of the top private schools in the South – I enjoy a unique advantage over my competition. I know and have access to most of the movers and shakers in this fair city of ours, a fact that's resented by many of the folks in high places in the city government, and not just one or two of the lower ranks in the PD. Screw 'em. I'm good at what I do. I'm expensive, discreet, thorough, and I produce results. It's like that old saying, 'it's not always what you know; it's who you know,' and, among others, I know my father, August Starke, very well indeed.

My father? You have to know who he is. Hell, his ads run on most TV stations almost every day. Even I get fed up with that stupid jingle, so I know you do, too. Still, it works. August Starke is a lawyer, a very good one. He specializes in tort, which is a classy word for 'personal injury.' He is, perhaps, my greatest asset.

I parked the car, strode quickly around to the front of the building, hit the outer office door with the palm of my hand, sweeping it open before me. The bang of my hand on the steel doorframe startled everyone, causing them all to look up.

"Hey, Ronnie, Tim," I said, as I swept by. "My office, bring something to make notes. Mike, I need a coffee: Italian Dark, black. You can sit in, too."

Mike Rogers is my intern. He's a geeky kid with an ambition to become a PI. Right now, he's a criminology major at U.T. Chattanooga.

Ronnie Hall handles my white-collar investigations. He's been around since I opened the office. His background was in banking. He has an MSc Finance from the London School of Economics. Tim Clarke is my computer geek. He handles all things to do with the Internet, including operating and maintaining the company website, and he also handles background checks and skip searches. He can find people, addresses, phone numbers, you name it; no one can hide from Tim. He's a geek, and he looks like one. Tall, with long, straight hair he keeps tied in a ponytail, sometimes a man bun. He's skinny, and he wears glasses. He's twenty-five years old. His looks, however, belie his abilities. He is, perhaps the most useful and effective tool in my bag.

"Okay, guys. This is what I need." I filled them in on what had happened the previous evening, and then laid it out for them.

"Ronnie. I need you to dig into Tom Sattler. His background, as far as I can tell, is in economics, something financial. I need to know what it is. I also need a full financial breakdown on him, his wife Gloria, his eldest daughter, Stephanie, and his girlfriend, Wendy Brewer. I'll also want one on Gloria's boyfriend, Richard Hollins. Mike, you sit in with Ronnie, help where you can, learn how it's done. Yeah?"

They both nodded.

"Tim. The same. I want to know everything there is to know about Tom Sattler, and I want to know yesterday. You guys keep me up to speed. As soon as you know something, get it typed up and send it to me. We all on board? Any questions?"

There were none. They left. I grabbed my coffee, leaned back in my chair, put my feet up on the desk, and waited. What for, I had no earthly idea, but the coffee was good. It wasn't more than a minute later when the office phone buzzed. I picked it up and hit the button.

"Amanda Cole for you." Click! Jacque had put her through before I could say anything. *Dammit, Jacque.*

"Okay, Amanda. What is it you want?"

"I'd like to see you, Harry. I have something I want to run by you."

"I'm sure you do, but I seem to remember telling you not to bother me again. I don't want to talk to you...."

The door opened. I looked up. Amanda walked in, gifted me with a sweet smile, put her cell phone into her pocket, and closed the door behind her.

"What the hell...." Oh, I was pissed.

"Hello, Harry. I'm sorry I had to barge in on you like this, but it was the only way I could get to see you."

I shook my head, stunned at her temerity. Nevertheless, I pointed to a chair, thumbed the button on the phone, and asked Jacque to bring her a cup of coffee.

Amanda Cole is a strikingly beautiful woman: tall, strawberry blonde, built like a Greek goddess, with an attitude that shouts, 'don't screw around with me, by God.'

On that particular day she was wearing a navy blue two-piece business suit with the skirt cut four or five inches above the knee, and black shoes with five-inch heels. As far as I could tell, she was wearing nothing under the jacket, which was cut just low enough to show a little cleavage, but not so low as to attract undue attention. She was also carrying a slim, black leather satchel.

She wore her hair bobbed, cut three inches below the point of her chin. Her heart-shaped face was defined by her high cheekbones and wide-set, pale green eyes. She was thirty-two years old and single. As far as I knew, she'd never been married.

I wonder why not. No, I don't. I know damn well why not: she's a total bitch, that's why.

"So, Harry Starke, we meet again, at last."

"That we do, Amanda. That we do. Jacque, come on in and take a seat."

Jacque closed my office door, placed the cup of coffee on my desk in front of Amanda, and then sat down at the rear of the room. I glared across the room at her; she just looked at me and shrugged. *Yeah, I know. What could you do?*

"Harry," Cole said, with a sly smile as she looked at me

through her eyelashes. "Don't you trust yourself to be alone with me?"

"Amanda, you know what? I don't trust you at all," I said, getting up and walking around my desk. "Stand up, turn around, and lift up your arms."

She tilted her head to one side, still smiling. I could tell she was very much amused, but she did as I asked. She stood, her feet slightly apart, and raised her arms. I stepped forward, facing her. Jacque also stood, stepped forward, and stood just behind me, her arms folded across her chest.

I am almost six feet two inches tall. In those five-inch heels, Amanda was able to look me straight in the eye; she must have been at least five feet ten inches in her bare feet. I could smell her breath; a gentle breeze, sweet and fresh. *Mints.*

"Hold still, Amanda." She did, and I ran my hands up both sides of her upper body, all the way to her armpits. I didn't bother with her thighs and buttocks. The way her skirt was cut, it was easy to see she wasn't wearing a wire down there, or anything else by the look of it.

"Why, Harry. How nice. We must do that again some-time, when we're alone." She looked pointedly at Jacque.

Jacque smiled sweetly at her.

I picked up her satchel, opened it, and glanced inside: there were some papers, a laptop, an iPad, and a small digital recorder, nothing else. I grabbed the recorder, made sure it was turned off, then flipped open the battery door, and tipped the two double As out into the satchel, dropped the recorder in after them, and handed it to her.

"Sit down, Amanda. You, too, Jacque."

Jacque returned to the chair at the rear of the room. Amanda sat down again in front of my desk; her skirt had ridden up to show almost an acre of thigh. She set the satchel on the floor and folded her hands together in her lap.

"So, what is it you want?" I asked, as I sat down behind my desk.

She ignored her coffee, leaned back in the chair and crossed her legs. I was wrong. They were white, and she knew damned well she was showing them to me. I gave her a tight smile, but said nothing. I was waiting for her to start talking.

"Tom Sattler. I know you found the body."

"So?"

"Would you care to tell me about it?"

"Amanda, it's been almost eighteen months since you did that hatchet job on me. I told you then, and I'm telling you now. You'll never get the chance to do that to me again. No, I would not like to talk to you about it. Now, if you've nothing to tell me, I'm busy. Jacque will see you out."

She wasn't the slightest bit perturbed. "Harry, I was just doing my job. It wasn't personal. It's what I do. You know that. I'm not going to apologize. You may not have liked it, but what I said was true."

"You called me a bounty hunter and a predator with the conscience of a grizzly bear. None of that is true. I'm not a bounty hunter, I'm not a predator, and I have a very powerful conscience."

"Okay, so I embellished things... a little. You're a pro, Harry, and so am I. Let's put all that behind us and move on. There are bigger things to be concerned about than your ego, or mine for that matter. If it helps, I'll promise to treat you with... more respect... on air, that is." She finished the statement with a smile that was about as cheeky and alluring as I think I've ever seen.

I sighed, shook my head, and said, "Jacque. Would you mind? I'll buzz if I need you."

Jacque gave me one of those looks that said, 'watch your back.' Then she got up, left the room, and closed the door behind her.

"All right, Amanda. Talk to me."

"As I said, Harry, I know you found Tom Sattler's body, and I also know you attended the autopsy and spent some time with Gazzara.... Okay, look, I've been looking into his business for more than six months. I know... I *knew* Tom Sattler. He was dirty. I also know you were a friend of his. Whoa, Harry."

The look on my face when she said that must have frightened her.

"I'm not saying you're dirty. Goddamn it, Harry, take it easy."

I leaned back in my chair, somewhat mollified.

"All I'm saying is that I know you were a friend of his and, knowing you as I do, I'm sure you're going to get involved, find out what happened to him. I'm telling you that he was dirty and that he had a lot of enemies."

"So?"

"So I'd like for us to work together."

"Can you hear yourself, Amanda?"

She smiled at me.

"Of all the people in the world to choose from, you are the last one I would pick to work with. You called me a predator. That's a word that sums you up absolutely—"

"Not true, Harry," she interrupted. "I am not a predator. I'm damn good at what I do, and I have resources that you don't. I can go places you can't. Likewise, you can offer resources I don't have, namely your contacts, both inside the PD and out, and your investigative staff. Now, let's get out of here. I'll buy you lunch and we can talk about it. What do you say?"

I sat there for a long moment, staring at her. She was serious. I almost believed her... almost. She stared back at me, those pale green eyes unblinking. She wasn't smiling.

I nodded, stood, walked around my desk, and opened the door.

"Let's go."

She grinned, unlocked her legs, stood, picked up the satchel, and walked past me, through the outer office and out of the front door without a glance in the direction of any of my staff. I followed, shaking my head. I flapped my hand at Jacque as I walked past her desk. She smiled and rolled her eyes. Bob, my lead investigator, winked. I had an idea it was going to be a long afternoon.

We took her car to the Mt. Vernon restaurant on Broad Street, just below Lookout Mountain. It was after two o'clock when we arrived, so the place was fairly quiet, which suited me well. Have you ever been in a restaurant with one of the local TV celebrities? The attention can be a little unnerving.

Amanda ordered a Greek salad with a glass of Pinot Grigio; I had a club sandwich and a Heineken – they didn't have Blue Moon. We ate for a moment in silence, each of us trying to size up the other. Me? I'm an open book. Amanda? Not so much.

We finished the meal and relaxed; Amanda with her wine; me with a second beer.

"Nice job, Harry, the Congressman Harper thing. I

didn't think you could have become any more notorious than you already were. Now... you have national fame, and several new and important friends, including Senator Michaels. Well done."

"Is that what you wanted to talk to me about? If so, you can take me back to the office. I said no interview, and I meant it."

"No, not at all. I want to talk to you about Tom Sattler."

"Well? So tell me."

She took a deep breath, which was an attention-getter all by itself.

"Okay. So let me start by asking you a question. How well did you know him?"

"Not that well. We were at McCallie together. Haven't seen him in almost five years."

"Do you know what he was doing for a living?"

"Something in finance, I think. Wealth management, maybe?"

"Oh, he managed wealth all right. He managed his own very well. His clients he managed not so well. Most of them lost money. No one knows what's happened to it."

"Where are you going with this, Amanda?"

"Bear with me, Harry. You know our consumer advocate, Charles Grove, right?"

I nodded. Who didn't? Grove's a loudmouth, nosey son of a bitch, and about as popular as a wet dog at a wedding. He was, however, extremely good at what he did, which was to put the screws, on air, to any and all businesses, small or large, that he felt might have taken advantage of one of Channel 7's viewers. Just a hint that Pit-bull Charlie was sniffing around was usually all it took to bring justice to the masses. Love him or hate him, he got the job done, and he brought in the ratings.

"How is the Pit-bull of Channel 7 these days? I haven't seen him in a while."

She ignored the question, but continued, "Sattler was a hedge fund manager; an investment fund manager, along with three partners. It was a very big deal."

"*Was?*"

"I'm getting to that. Some months ago, back in June, I think it was, Charles began receiving complaints from investors. Their monthly checks were coming later and later. So he began to make visits, first to Sattler and then his partners, and he got absolutely nowhere; a first for him, I might add."

I nodded and waited for her to continue. She called the waiter and ordered another Pinot for her and a beer for me.

Three is way more than I need at lunchtime, but what the hell.

"Anyway," she continued, over the top of her glass. "Charles came to me. He gets results for the consumer, I do the investigative work at the station, you know...."

I nodded. I did know, much to my regret. I'd fallen foul of her in the past.

"Well, I did some digging and I found that it was true. I found a half-dozen investors that were becoming a little... well, 'antsy,' might be a bit of an understatement." She opened the satchel and removed a single sheet of paper. "Here's a list of their names, addresses and phone numbers. I've also included the names of his partners. The company is New Vision Strategic Investments, Inc."

I took it from her, glanced at it, and then looked at her.

"Sal De Luca? Come on, Amanda. I know damned well he didn't talk to the Pit-bull. What gives?"

"That name came up during my own investigation. I have a few CIs of my own. De Luca is another reason I wanted to talk to you. You know him, right?"

"CIs? Confidential informants? You've been watching too many of your own programs. They're called snitches, Amanda."

She gave me a dirty look.

"Unfortunately," she continued, "they, the contacts on the list, all knew who I was and wouldn't talk about it. De Luca wouldn't even say hello, much less talk to me. Public embarrassment is not something the movers and shakers in this city want, especially him. As to the other five on the list, the best I could do was get a few answers to a few off the record questions, and those only basic questions at that. What I did manage to find out was that the monthly dividend checks were consistently late and falling steadily behind. One elderly lady admitted that she hadn't had a check in three months. So, Harry... that's where you come in."

"Me? How? I don't think so."

"Come on, Harry. You can get to people like De Luca. Tom Sattler was your friend, and your firm handles white-collar cases. That's what this is, white-collar, prob-ably a Ponzi scheme. You're a licensed private investi-gator with a staff of... well, a staff, *and* your friend committed suicide. Why wouldn't you want to get to the bottom of it?"

So, Amanda, you don't know he was murdered.

"For a whole bunch of reasons, the first and most impor-tant of which is I don't do pro bono. I like to get paid, earn enough to pay my staff. Second, he wasn't my friend. I hadn't seen him in years. Third, and I hope I can make this abundantly clear: I. Don't. Want. To. Work. With. You! There's no win in that for me. I can only see the downside."

"What downside, Harry? This could be a huge story. That fund is, was, worth almost a half-billion dollars, and most of it came from right here in Hamilton County."

"You, Amanda. You're the downside. You know the old saying, don't you? Screw me once, shame on you. Screw me twice and I'm one stupid son of a bitch. Never again, Amanda."

Now that brought forth the sweetest smile I think I've ever seen on a guilty woman. She dropped her head, looked up at me through her eyelashes, and smiled. It was a masterpiece. *Oh, she's good, this one.*

"Harry.... Harry. Okay. You're right. Maybe I treated you a little harshly. I said I wouldn't apologize, but it's quite obvious that I hurt your feelings. So," she looked at me, reached across the table, put her hand on mine, her beautiful eyes wide, and whispered, "I'm sorry, Harry. It won't happen again. I promise."

Damn. Where do they learn how to do that?

I shook my head and rose to my feet. "You're something else, Amanda. No wonder the public loves you. I'll think about it. Take me back to the office, please."

The ride back to my office took about ten minutes. During that time, she opened her mouth four times as if she was about to speak, but changed her mind. Finally, when she pulled up outside the front door, she turned to me.

"I really am sorry, Harry. Please, let me make it up to you. Let me buy you dinner."

I couldn't help it. I laughed out loud. She recoiled, as if

she'd been slapped.

"No, no, don't take that the wrong way, Amanda. It was just so unexpected. Thank you for the apology. Tell you what. I'll buy *you* dinner, and we can talk about it. What do you say?"

She smiled. On anyone else, it would have been a grin. On her, it was something much more, a lovely... smile; but not just with her mouth. There was something else there that came deep from within those enormous, pale green eyes. *She's a goddam witch... Circe!*

"You're on," she said. "When?"

"No time like the present. How about tonight?"

"Sure. Why not? I have to do the news at six, and again at eleven. Let me call Bill and see if he'll do the late night set for me."

She did, and he would. I arranged to pick her up at eight.

Back in my office, I sat at my desk and added the six names from Amanda's list to those on Kate's. I now had fifteen names. I must have sat and stared at them for ten minutes, maybe more. *Was it one of you?*

1. Gloria Sattler: ex-wife
2. Richard Hollins: ex-wife's boyfriend
3. Wendy Brewer: Sattler's girlfriend

4. Stephanie Sattler - age 21; Sattler's eldest
5. Julie Sattler - age 12: Sattler's daughter
6. Nicola Sattler - age 10: Sattler's youngest
7. James Westwood - Partner
8. Marty Cassell - Partner
9. Jessica Steiner - Partner
10. Michael Scoggins - Retired
11. Salvatore De Luca - Slimy, crooked bastard
12. Dawson Conley - Plumber
13. Sandra Porter - Widow
14. Elsie Smith - Widow
15. Fred Jones - ? Unknown

Fifteen names, and I had no doubt the list would grow. It was too much, and too little. We needed to know a whole lot more about all of them, and before we talked to them. The only one I was remotely familiar with was Salvatore De Luca. Him, I knew a lot about. None of it good.

Salvatore 'Sal' De Luca also knew me quite well. Sal was a shady character, part of Chattanooga's burgeoning underworld, burgeoning since the arrival of big business — Volkswagen, Amazon, Etc. – and the unions. He had, so it was rumored, connections, both in New York and Miami. He operated out of a small, but exclusive, Italian restaurant just off MLK. Perhaps that would be as good a place to start as any.

I sat back in my chair and stared at the ceiling, my mind a whirlpool, a maelstrom of disjointed thoughts, fragments of ideas, and... not much else.

Maybe I need someone to bounce it all off. Kate? Nah. Once upon a time, perhaps, but not anymore. Linda? Yup!

I dialed the number. The phone at the other end rang interminably. I was just about to hang up when she answered.

"Hello, Harry. Is it urgent? I'm kind of tied up."

"No. Not at all. I just wanted to touch base; see if everything was all right."

"Of course it is…. Harry, is everything all right with you? You sound a little out of sorts."

"Yes, everything's fine… I just wanted to talk, that's all, but if you don't have time…."

"Not right now, Harry. I'm just on my way into committee. Um… by the way, I'm not going to be able to make it this weekend after all. It's gotten pretty hectic around here, and I have things I must do. Can I call you this evening? We can talk about it then, okay?"

"Yes, of course. Anytime."

"Wonderful. I'll talk to you then. Bye, Harry."

I lowered the phone, let my hand drop heavily on my desk.

Damn. That's what you get when you get yourself involved with a senator, I guess.

Chapter Four

I hadn't been back in the office more than fifteen minutes when Kate called.

"Hey. I have an interview with Gloria Sattler. You want to come?"

"Sure. Should be interesting. Pick me up?"

"Of course. You ready?" The door to my office opened and she walked in, grinning.

Geez, twice in one day. I'm going to have to have a word with Jacque.

Gloria Sattler lived in a home only slightly less grand than her dead ex-husband. In fact, it was in the same Mountain Shadows subdivision, and not more than a short walk away on Stony Mountain Drive.

Kate parked the car out front and we walked to the front

door; it opened before we reached the steps. Gloria Sattler was just as I remembered her, five-six, well put together but a little on the heavy side, dark roots showing through her dishwater blond hair. She was wearing sweat pants and a T-shirt, looked harassed, tired, and a little wary. She was not happy to see us.

"Good afternoon, Mrs. Sattler. My name is Lieutenant Catherine Gazzara, and this is my associate Mr. Starke. Thank you for agreeing to see us at such short notice."

"Yes, well. I didn't have much choice now, did I? You'd better come in."

She turned and walked away, leaving the door open and us standing in the porch. Kate looked at me, shrugged, and followed. I closed the door behind us.

Stephanie, the eldest daughter, and the two youngsters Julie and Nicola were in the kitchen. The two children were seated at the kitchen table eating cookies and doing homework.

"Let's go in there where we can talk," Gloria said, waving a hand at an open door that led into what obviously was the living room. She led the way. Stephanie followed her mother. Kate followed Stephanie, and I brought up the rear. I felt a little like an unwanted dog dragging along on the end of a leash.

Kate and I sat together on the sofa, facing the two women who were both seated on high-backed dining chairs. I was kind of surprised by the set up; there were at least ten feet separating the two of them. *Is that by design, or do they just not like each other?*

Gloria Sattler looked older than her forty-three years. The crow's feet were sharply defined, her eyes were tired, her neck sagging a little. She was not aging well, nor did she have the sophistication of her eldest daughter. Yes, Tom Sattler had definitely married beneath himself.

Stephanie Sattler I'd never met before. She obviously took after her father, five-nine, slim, large breasts that might or might not have been real, a heart-shaped face with enormous blue eyes and a smile that could light up a room. Her hair, a little lighter than her mother's, was neatly trimmed to just above her shoulders. Her clothes were expensive, a white silk blouse, black slacks, and black, high-heeled shoes. The girl was a class act. She sat erect, her back stiff, feet to one side, crossed at the ankles, her hands clasped together in her lap.

This girl is twenty-one going on thirty-five.

I looked from one to the other, not quite sure what to make of either of them. They were an incongruous pair, to be sure.

"Why are you here?" Stephanie said. "Dad committed suicide. That doesn't warrant a police presence, surely."

"Until we get the official results of the autopsy," Kate said, taking a small notebook and a pencil from her jacket pocket, "we have to treat his death as if it were a homicide."

Not quite a lie, Kate, but it should work.

"This is just a routine enquiry," Kate continued. "We won't take up too much of your time. Now, if–"

"I know you," Stephanie Sattler interrupted her, looking at me. "I've seen you on TV. You're not a police officer."

"You're not with the police?" Gloria Sattler looked at me, puzzled.

"No, Mrs. Sattler, I'm not. I'm a licensed private investigator and, yes, as your daughter said, once in a while I make the local news–"

"Local news, my ass," Stephanie interrupted. "You're Harry Starke. You brought down Congressman Harper."

"That's true, Miss Sattler," Kate said. "He did, and he solved three murders at the same time. He is here with me as a consultant. I pick his brains whenever I need an out-of-the-box analysis. So, as I don't want to intrude any longer than necessary, I'd like to ask you both some questions?"

Neither one of them answered, so she continued.

"How well did you all get along with your ex-husband, Mrs. Sattler?"

I watched with interest as mother and daughter exchanged glances.

"We didn't get along... well, Stephanie got along with him okay. Tom and me... well, we didn't see eye to eye on anything, especially money, or... Richard."

"Richard is...?"

I smiled inwardly at Kate's attempt to be diplomatic.

"Richard Hollins is, as the English would say, Mom's Toy Boy, her bit of rough."

"*Stephanie!* He's no such thing. He's... well, he's my friend."

"Yeah, a friend with benefits, and he's almost half your age. It's disgusting! Hell, Mother, he's only four years older than me."

Kate waited, but Gloria had no more to say on the subject, so she gave her a gentle push.

"So... Richard. Where is he?"

Gloria shrugged, looked away, and then said, "I sent him to the grocery store. We needed a few things."

So, you wanted him out of the way.

"I'd like to talk to him," Kate said, in a tone of voice that would brook no argument. "When would be a good time for me to do that?"

"I... I... don't know. You'll have to call him, set something up. I can give you his cell phone number."

Kate made a note of the number. "So, Stephanie. You saw quite a bit of your father?"

"Yes... I suppose so. I dropped by now and then. I had to pass the house going back and forth from here. Sometimes he was in, most times he wasn't. When he was, depending upon my mood, I might stop off and say hello, have a cup of coffee. I also helped him with his business, not often, but some." Her tone of voice was... a bit off; forced, maybe.

"And your relationship with him, it was close?"

"Not really. We had very little in common, and he was always wrapped up in his business. He never had much time for any of us."

An almost furtive glance passed between mother and daughter.

Something's going on between those two. I wonder what. Time I stuck my oar in the water.

"And the two youngsters," I asked Gloria, as I looked down at my notes, "Julie and Nicola. How did they get along with their dad?"

Gloria shot Stephanie a somewhat nervous glance, then looked down and was about to answer when Stephanie answered for her.

"Julie and Nicola *loved* our father." It wasn't what she said; it was how she said it. Her voice was cold, icy.

I looked at Gloria. Her face was... I don't know; expressionless would probably be the right word to describe it. She stared back at me, almost without blinking. Stephanie's face was unreadable.

The unasked question must have showed on my face, because Stephanie, with some feeling, said, "They *loved* their father. I loved him. He was a prick, but we, all three of us, *loved him.*"

"*Stephanie!*" Gloria did her best to sound outraged at her daughter's language, but it didn't quite come off. I had a feeling that Mrs. Sattler had called her ex-husband a whole lot worse.

"Well, it's true, Mother. We did love him. Much as you wished we didn't, we did, and he loved us. He *did not* love you, and he sure as hell hated Richard with a passion. There was no love lost on Richard's side either. They couldn't stand the sight of one another."

Gloria's reaction to the outburst was not what I expected. She didn't look at all upset, though she wouldn't meet my eye, or Kate's. It was beginning to cross my mind that the whole thing was being staged for us, had been rehearsed. Then again, maybe it was me; maybe I was looking for something that wasn't there.

Time to change the subject.

"Miss Sattler," I said. "Do you work?"

"I have a part-time job, but I'm still in school, at UTC. I

graduate in the spring with a Bachelor's degree in Psychology. Why do you ask?"

"Just background stuff. Where do you work?"

"I work three afternoons a week, Wednesday, Thursday and Friday, at Heather's Boutique, from two until six. I also work there all day Saturday."

I looked at Kate. She shrugged. I guess she'd never heard of it either.

Stephanie heaved a sigh and said, "It's a high-end lady's boutique. We sell beautiful clothing."

"How about you, Mrs. Sattler? Do you work?"

"No. I am financially independent, thanks to my divorce settlement."

"And your ex-husband," I said. "Was he wealthy?"

"You could say that." Stephanie answered the question. "I sometimes worked on his books. He earned two million a year in fees, sometimes more."

"Did he make a will? If so, who benefits?"

"I don't think he did," Gloria said. "There's an insurance policy, though; $300,000. It benefits all three children equally. They are listed as his next of kin. His estate is probably worth several million, so I suppose they'll get that, too."

"Hmmm, that's not a large amount of insurance, considering his income." Kate looked from one to the other. "Well, I think that about does it for now." She started to get up then changed her mind.

"There's just one more thing," she said. "Where were you both between 9:30 and 10:45 on Tuesday evening?"

Gloria was about to answer, but before she could speak, Stephanie said, "We were both here. We watched Megyn Kelly on Fox, then Hannity. We heard the sirens, but thought nothing of it. I went to bed at just after eleven. I think you went a few minutes after I did, Mom. Someone woke us up early this morning, to tell us about Dad. That was the first we knew." The answer came quickly, too quickly, as if she had been expecting the question.

"And Richard?"

"Richard came in just before one o'clock in the morning," Gloria said. "I know because he woke me up."

"I bet he did. Horny little bastard," Stephanie muttered to herself.

Gloria glared at her, but then continued, "He'd been out with his friends, bar hopping, I think."

Kate looked at me. I made a slight nod. She wrote something on the pad, snapped it closed and slipped it into her pocket.

"I also have a question," I said, looking at both of them. "Did either of you know he owned a gun?"

"Yes, of course. We both did," Stephanie said. "He kept it in the living room, in one of the desk drawers. I wondered why he bothered. It wasn't as if it was powerful enough to stop an intruder."

"It was powerful enough to kill him," I said.

There was no answer to that, just stony stares.

"Well, okay, thank you both for your time," Kate said, getting to her feet. "We may need to talk again. In fact, I'm sure we will. In the meantime, if you think of anything that might be helpful, anything at all, please give me a call." She handed each of them one of her cards, and we left.

"What's going on between Stephanie and her mother, do you think?" I asked, as she pushed the starter button.

"You caught it too, huh?"

"So it wasn't just me?" I said. "I had a distinct feeling that we were being led down the path."

She nodded, swung the car out of the driveway and headed back toward my office.

"Yes, that alibi was a little too glib and a little too quick off the tongue," she said. "I don't think either of them are capable of murder, but you never know. The family is always the prime suspect, at least until we can rule them out, right? What about Hollins?"

"I'd be inclined to believe that he *was* out with his

friends. There was a little too much acid in Stephanie's voice when she heard her mother say he woke her up. Yes?"

"Yep," she said, "but there's no way to confirm either of *their* alibis, unless.... Maybe we should talk to the youngsters."

"My thought, too, but we'd have to be damned careful how we did it. Mom's going to want to be present; you know that."

"Oh yeah," she agreed. "Let's give it some thought."

"Yeah, let's do that. Then there's the insurance policy; I don't think it's big enough to provide a motive. Sattler's estate, though?

"I agree," she said, nodding. "If he earned as much as the girl said he did, I'd say it's substantial. There's the house, which must be worth... what? At least seven or eight hundred thousand, do you think? And there's no telling what he has in the bank and investments. If there's no will, it will all go to the next of kin, right? And that would be the three daughters."

"Yes. I'll have Ronnie check into that," I said, as she stopped the car in the lot by my office. "Kate, I need you to give me a call in the morning. I met with Amanda Cole earlier this afternoon, and she gave me some names of interest. I would have brought it with me, but when you barged into my office, I lost track of what I was thinking."

She grinned. "Okay, but why not now?"

"Because I'm not going inside. I don't want to get caught up in there, and because we need to discuss it, and because it will keep overnight."

"Tomorrow then. Bye, Harry. Have a good night."

Chapter Five

I arrived at Amanda's home in Hixson a few minutes early. She opened the door but obviously was not quite ready. She was dressed, but had a slightly harassed look about her.

"Hello, Harry. I'm on the phone. I'll be just a minute. Pour yourself a drink; they are over there."

"Take your time. No hurry."

She smiled, nodded, and went into what I assumed must be the bedroom and shut the door. I poured myself a very small scotch and soda, carried it over to the window, and looked out. There wasn't much to see; the backyard was surrounded by shrubs and tall trees.

Methinks the lady likes her privacy.

"Well... don't you look nice?" I hadn't heard her come in.

"It does make a change to see you in something other than a Tee and leather jacket."

I turned and smiled at her. "Thank you."

I was wearing dark gray slacks, Gucci loafers, a pale blue shirt with a royal blue tie, and a navy blue blazer: my IBM look.

"You don't look so bad yourself." In fact, she looked gorgeous. It wasn't what she was wearing, it was how she filled it. A simple, sleeveless light gray woolen dress that came to just below her knees and black high heels. I say the dress was woolen, but don't get the wrong idea. It was delicate, almost transparent, chic, and it clung to her body like a skin. The clutch she held matched it perfectly.

"Why don't you pour one for me, Harry? I'll have a tiny vodka tonic, please."

I poured. She took it from me, turned, and walked to the sofa, sat down, and patted the cushion beside her. I looked at her, skeptically.

"Oh, come on, Harry. I won't bite."

"A bite, I could handle. It's the knife in the back I'm worried about."

She laughed. I hadn't meant it to be funny. I shrugged and sat down beside her anyway. She smelled intoxicating.

"So where are you taking me?" she asked.

"I always feel like a prize pony when I'm out in public with someone of your... shall we say, stature? So I thought we might go somewhere quiet. I made a reservation at the club for nine o'clock. It's quite near, the food is good, and we won't be bothered by gawkers. Is that okay? Oh, and it *will* be my treat." I was being sarcastic, but she didn't seem to notice.

She laughed, quietly. It sounded like a mountain creek in the early morning. I was all but hypnotized.

"Harry. You are, despite your sometimes weird appearance, a gentleman." Now it was my turn to laugh.

Over the next thirty minutes, I learned a great deal about the enigmatic Amanda Cole. Contrary to what I expected, she was quite engaging; disarming, might be a better word. I must admit I was a little perplexed. The hard-ass news reporter seemed to have disappeared, replaced by an attentive, witty, and often funny conversationalist. I had a feeling I was going to enjoy my evening. *Wow! Amazing!*

We finished our drinks and drove to the club. Fortunately, on Wednesdays it's very quiet. Of the half-dozen couples in the dining room, I recognized only two; all six of them recognized Amanda, but I'd known that was how it would be. With her celebrity in mind, when I made the reservation I had asked for us to be seated in the bay window overlooking the ninth green. Not that there was much to see, just a few lights of the homes along the ninth fairway. It was, however, quiet and out of sight of most of the rest of the dining room. Secluded? No, not quite.

"What would you like to drink, Amanda?" I asked, when the wine waiter arrived.

"I'll have a dry martini, please, Joe, two olives."

Joe?

"Gin and tonic for me, Bombay Sapphire. Amanda, do you have any wine preferences?"

"I'll leave that to you, Harry."

"Fine. We'll have a bottle of the Leonetti Cabernet Sauvignon 2012. Thank you, Joe."

"Thank *you*, Mr. Starke."

"So, you've been here before," I said, "and quite often, too, it would seem."

She nodded. "Actually, Harry, I'm a member."

"You are? How come I haven't seen you here before?"

"I don't come up here that often, and when I do it's usually during the day, most often for lunch, and I mostly play tennis, but I play a little golf, too; I'm not very good."

"Good evening, Mr. Starke, Madam."

I looked up. "Hello, George. What do you recommend tonight?"

"The swordfish with capers is excellent, Mr. Starke, and so is the lamb. Either one, you can't go wrong."

I nodded. "What do you think, Amanda?"

"George, I would like the filet, butterflied, but medium rare, with asparagus and a small portion of red potatoes, and I'll have a small Caesar salad to begin with. Thank you."

"Thank you, Madam. What about you, Mr. Starke?"

"The lamb sounds good, and whatever comes with it will suit me fine, and I'll have a Caesar salad, too."

The meal came and went and it was, as George had said, delicious. We ate, for the most part, in silence. Me? I was content just to sit and look at her, watch her eat. Her manners were impeccable. Having said that, however, she certainly wasn't afraid to enjoy her food. She ate with relish, seemingly with little regard for calories or carbs. What was going through her mind was anybody's guess.

The plates were duly cleared away and we both ordered coffee. To this point, it had been a decidedly pleasant evening. I hoped it would continue, at least until I got her home.

"So, Harry. What about it?"

"What about what?"

She sighed, looked down at her coffee, and then back up at me. The look was almost electric. I felt something stir deep inside me. Nope, it wasn't what you're thinking. It was like one of those sensations you get deep in the pit of your stomach when something unexpected happens. Inwardly, I shook it off. I looked her in the eyes and shrugged.

"About us working together, you mean?"

She nodded.

"I don't know. I have Bob and Heather, and the rest of the crew, and I don't know you–"

"Oh, come on, Harry," she interrupted. "I'm not asking for a job, dammit. I'm simply suggesting that we collaborate on the Sattler thing."

Shit. I just know I'm going to regret this.

"Okay, Amanda. We'll give it a shot, but there have to be some rules."

She smiled – it was devastating – and nodded. "That, Harry, goes both ways. What do you have in mind?"

I looked her right in the eye. "Everything, and I do mean *everything* we do and learn is off the record until I decide otherwise. You will *not* broadcast anything without my approval. If you don't agree to that, well, we can say goodbye right now."

She didn't like it, I could tell, but she also knew she had no option.

"I can go along with that, Harry, provided that it's understood that I get exclusive rights to everything. If something leaks out, and I get scooped by one of the other stations, the deal is off. Agreed?"

"Agreed, insofar that you understand I have no control over what the PD or the M.E. might deem to release. I will have a word with Kate, but I can't promise anything. I'm not the most popular person in her book these days."

She smiled at that and shook her head knowingly. "I wonder why?"

"Maybe I'll tell you one day."

"Oh, I can guess. I'm sure Senator Michaels has something to do with it. Just how did you pull that one off, Harry? I've always wondered."

She smiled as she said it, but I had a feeling it was a serious question, one I wasn't prepared to answer, ever.

"So, tell me," she said. "What do you have?"

"What do I... oh, you mean the case. Well, for starters, Tom Sattler was murdered–"

"Hah, I knew it," she interrupted. "He screwed one too many, and I don't mean between the sheets. Go on."

"His place had been searched, his computers wiped, his external hard drives, cell phones, tablets, are all missing. He called me last night, around nine-thirty. Said he needed to talk to me, needed help. He wouldn't say anything else, which is why I went over there. I arrived not much more than an hour after the call. I found him in the living room: one shot to the head. The murder weapon was on the floor next to his hand. I thought he'd shot himself, but Doc Sheddon says it would have been impossible, and no, you can't use any of that, not yet."

"Okay," she said, reluctantly. "So what's the next step?"

"I added those names you gave me to the list of his known contacts and family members. We now have a list of fifteen people to interview. I'm not sure how you can help with that, you being who you are, but it has to be done. Kate and I will have to do it, with a little help from Lonnie Guest, and maybe others. By the way, I know one of those people on your list quite well."

"Let me guess... Sal De Luca."

"Yep, small town mob boss, big time creep. That's one I'll do myself. Have you tried talking to any of the others?"

"Just one. Elsie Smith. She's a widow, retired. She has her life savings tied up in Sattler's fund, or whatever it is. Right now she's living on her dead husband's social security and his military service pension. It's not much, but at least she can pay her bills. I don't think there's anything there, but you might want to talk to her, get a feel for her dealings with Sattler."

"I'll do that, but it won't be a priority. Anything else?"

"Not that I can think of right now, but if I can help in any way.... Look, Harry, my job takes up most of my days, and nights, but I'll help where I can. I think I can be most useful doing what I do best. I'll dig into Sattler's fund. Can I use Ronnie, if I need to?"

I nodded. "I've already put him on it. I'll let him know that you're in the loop, that it's okay for him to work with you. Same with Tim. I'll also need to put Jacque in the picture and... Kate Gazzara. You ready to go?"

Somewhat reluctantly, I thought, she nodded, pushed what was left of her drink to one side, and then rose from the table. The drive home was short and, for the most part, silent. We arrived outside her house just a little after eleven-thirty.

"Turn off the engine and come on in for nightcap."

"Better not. It's late and I have a busy day tomorrow."

"Come on. Five minutes. One drink. Yes?"

"Okay, but one cup of coffee, and no more than five minutes."

We got out of the car, she opened her front door, and breezed in ahead of me.

Where does all that energy come from? I'm absolutely bushed.

We sat in the kitchen, at least I did. Amanda made coffee and I watched. As I did, I couldn't help thinking what an enigma the woman was. In less than eight hours, she had turned my utter dislike for her into something bordering on admiration.

Weird.

She set the two cups down on the breakfast bar and eased herself up onto the stool next to me. It was quite a performance, and she couldn't help but giggle as she wiggled. Finally, she made it, picked up her cup, raised it to her lips, blew gently into the steam, and stared at me through her eyelashes. The effect was, well, startling. Her eyes seemed to shimmer in the steam, and what she was doing with her lips defies description.

I drank my coffee, scalded my mouth, and then slid off the stool.

"Time for me to go, Amanda."

She nodded, set her cup down, raised both arms high above her head, and said, "Help me down. I'll see you out."

I smiled at her. It was after all, an alluring pose, and I thought I knew exactly what she was up to. I didn't want to play, but she sat there, with her wings spread wide, her chin lowered, and a mocking smile on her lips. So I did. I stepped forward, put my hands under her armpits, lifted her off the stool, and set her gently on the floor. She was a lot lighter than I had thought, or was that the adrenaline?

She stood in front of me, looked down at herself, adjusted her dress, stepped around me, and walked to the door.

Yep, I was surprised. I followed her, and I couldn't help but admire the way her hips rolled under the form-fitting dress as she walked.

Now that, my old son, could get you into serious trouble.

She reached the door, extended her hand toward the latch, and then hesitated. She turned, took a step forward, put both her arms around my neck and pulled me in close.

You would have to experience that kiss, to understand the effect it had on me. I was, but I shouldn't have been, taken totally by surprise. She put her heart and soul into it, full-bodied, lips parted, tongue probing; I couldn't help myself. I responded in kind.

Well, what the hell would you have done?

She broke contact, leaned back in my arms, and smiled at me. Those pale green eyes were less than a foot from my own. Slowly, deliberately, she leaned in again, her breasts pressed hard against my chest, and she put her lips to mine. I was screwed, done for, beaten, and it had taken her less than sixty seconds. Resistance was useless, not that I resisted. How could I? She gently ground her hips against mine, and for several minutes, we stood there by the door. My head was spinning. I thought for a moment that it might have been the effects of the two bottles of wine and three gins? But it wasn't.

Finally, she released me. Her arms slipped from around my neck and she took a small step back. The look on her face was... well, she was no longer smiling. Her eyes were narrowed; her lips parted. I could see the tip of her tongue between them. She was breathing deeply and steadily and, for Christ's sake, so was I.

She took my hand, walked around me, and pulled. I didn't move. She tugged a little harder. I stayed where I was.

"What's wrong, Harry?" I could barely hear it.

"It's not on, Amanda."

"Why not?'

"Well. I'm sort of otherwise involved, and I'd like to keep a clear conscience."

"Hmmm. That would be Senator Michaels, I presume. That's hard to compete with, Harry, even for me."

I smiled at her. She didn't smile back. She wasn't joking. For the first time in my life, I wondered if I was making a mistake. I hadn't seen Linda in weeks, and we'd made no obligations to one another, she'd cancelled her weekend visit, and Amanda was.... *Damn, she's... beautiful.*

I inwardly shook the thoughts out of my head, leaned in close, and kissed her. Her lips parted. She tasted like sweet white wine, and she was just as intoxicating.

"Goodnight, Amanda. I'll call you tomorrow." I turned the latch, opened the door, and walked out into the night.

You don't believe me? Neither do I, but that's what I did.

Chapter Six

※❀※

Early the next morning, Thursday, found me sitting alone at my desk gazing at the list of fifteen names, and I had no idea of where to begin. All I had was just the basic personal information, and that was precious little: name, date of birth, gender, address, phone number (several of those were missing), and occupation. I'd given copies to Ronnie and Tim, along with the name of Sattler's company, New Vision Strategic Investments, Inc. Now they had that to work with, Ronnie would probably have something for me by the end of the day.

Fifteen names, of which I was familiar with only one, and at this point, there was no indication that any of them were involved in Sattler's murder. It looked like I was in for a long haul.

At just after nine o'clock, my cell phone buzzed. I looked at the screen and flipped it with my thumb.

"Hey, Kate. What's up?"

"I've officially been assigned the Sattler case, and I have the go ahead from Chief Johnston for you to consult. He wasn't too happy about it, but I reminded him of your agency's white-collar resources and your success in bringing down Congressman Harper. For some reason, I'm not sure why, I don't think he likes you. Anyway, you're in, if you want."

"I'm in, Johnston's approval or not. That's why I left the PD. So I can do what the hell I like, remember?"

"Yes, I remember. Now, do you want to talk or not?"

"Sure. You want to come here, to my office?"

She did. In fact, she was already on the way, and she walked in less than five minutes later.

Summer is a good time for Kate. She always looks lovely, but somehow the warm weather turns her into a swan. She had her hair piled on top of her head, no makeup other than a pale pink lipstick, tight, black jeans, a white Tee, and thin, pale green blazer she wore only to cover the baby Glock on her right hip. She was also carrying a tan briefcase, which she dumped on the front edge of my desk, and then flopped down into one of the two armchairs and draped her right leg over the arm.

"So, Harry?"

"So, Kate?" I said with a grin. "Where do we begin? Here, I suppose." I picked up the list of names, waved it in the air, and then flipped it across the desk to her. She caught it just as it was about to slide off the edge.

"It's a copy," I said. "Keep it. I have another one right here."

"Where did the extra names come from?"

"Amanda Cole. Three of them are Sattler's partners; the other six are disgruntled investors. Five of them contacted Charles Grove at Channel 7, panicking about their monthly dividend checks. One came from what she called one of her CIs."

"Amanda Cole? I thought you and she didn't get along."

"We don't, didn't. But, well, she has some resources we don't, and she was... persuasive."

"Yeah, I bet she was," Kate said, as she scanned down the list of names.

"I said I'd keep her in the loop, all off the record, but she gets 'the exclusive.' Any objections?"

She nodded, slowly. I don't think she heard what I said, because then she slowly shook her head. She swung her leg off the arm of the chair, sat bolt upright, and looked up at me, her eyes wide.

"*De Luca?*"

"You noticed. Happy days are here again, at least for me, but maybe not so happy for him."

She nodded, excited. "De Luca. Geez. Now that's what I'm talking about. I've been after him for... forever. If we could–"

"Stop," I interrupted. "From what you've told me, he has the Department in a net. Didn't he go to the DA and complain that he was being harassed?"

"Yeppy. That he did, but that was vice. He doesn't know me. You're right, though. He has friends in high places, and we were all warned off, unless there's probable cause, which there never is. We have to get the DA's okay before anyone can go within a mile of him."

"Right. You can't touch him, or even go near him without probable cause, but I can." I grinned at her.

In return, she gifted me with a beautiful smile. "Now isn't that exactly why I keep you around? You don't *have* to follow all of those silly little rules that I do, now do you?"

I ignored that; but the smile....

"I don't, and maybe De Luca is as good a place as any to start. In fact, I was already planning a visit–"

"Awesome," she interrupted, and started to get to her feet. "Let's go."

"Whoa... not so fast. *You* can't go with me."

"The hell you say. If you're going, I'm going, DA be

damned. I'll stay back. Let you do the talking, but don't think for a minute you're going without me."

Sadly, I shook my head. I knew Kate too well to argue with her. If I wanted to continue working with her, it would have to be done her way.

"Okay, fine, but for God's sake *do not* even open your mouth. Sit down. We need to go over the rest of the list."

She smiled that smile again, nodded, and looked again at the list. For the next fifteen or twenty minutes we talked it over, but I could tell her attention was elsewhere. She has a one-track mind, does Kate.

Finally, she put the list away and said, "What are you doing over the weekend? Maybe we could go visit some of the others. What do you think?"

Oh hell, here we go!

"I can't. I have plans."

"Oh you do, do you? What plans?"

"Private plans. I'm taking the weekend off."

"Ms. Michaels, I presume."

I didn't answer. She didn't press it, but the atmosphere in my office had gone chilly; no, it had gone cold, damn cold. It was time to get out of there. I got up and walked around the desk.

"Let's go. Let's go see Sal."

She got up, grabbed her briefcase, and stalked out of my office and then the front door, with never a glance at my staff or at me. I sighed, shook my head, and followed her. The six faces in my outer office all were grinning at me.

Okay, so she's pissed again. What's new?

Chapter Seven

Il Sapore Roma is a grand name for a small but exclusive Italian restaurant just off MLK. A one-time small dry goods store, the dark, narrow interior had room enough only for two single rows of six booths with a central walkway from front to rear. At the far end, next to the kitchen and the restrooms, a small, semi-circular bar could seat six people, shoulder to shoulder, on tall stools.

Salvatore De Luca's the owner of record, but I often wondered if he was just the front man; this little shop of horrors might just as easily have been found in South Philly as downtown Chattanooga. Having said that, the food is authentic Italian cuisine, always good, and the place is almost always busy, but not so much at two-thirty on a weekday afternoon.

Sal was a mean-spirited bastard, greedy, sadistic, and

larger than life. He stood six feet three inches tall, and was as thin as a rake. He wore his lank, jet-black hair long, shoulder length, slicked back. Sallow skin, stretched tightly over a narrow face, was accented by a beak a vulture would have been proud of set above a pair of thin lips that reminded me of two tightly stretched red worms. Pendulous lobes dangled and swung like two cadaverous earrings from ears that were too large for his head, but it was the eyes that defined him: two cold slits of obsidian that glittered in the artificial light. It was a face that could, and did, strike fear into the hearts of many a strong man.

Perched on a stool, hunched over a plate of food, something with spaghetti, Sal was picking at it like some giant, predatory bird. Flanked by two lesser birds of prey, he seemed to care little for what was going on around him. Like two harpies, they sat one on either side. One was skinny like his boss; the other was the image of Tony Soprano. *How appropriate.*

"Afternoon, Sal," I said, cheerily. "Looks like you're enjoying that." Actually, it didn't look like that at all, but what the hell.

He looked at me sideways, still hunched over the plate, "Harry goddamn Starke! If that don't goddamn trash my already ruined goddamn day? Get the hell out of here before I set the goddamn dogs on ya."

"Now, Sal. Is that any way to talk to an old friend?"

"Old friend, my ass. With friends like you, I woulda bin makin' it with the worms years ago. Whadda ya want, and who's the bimbo?"

I put my hand on her arm. It was stiff, the muscles tensed, but she relaxed. I put my hand back in my jacket pocket.

"The *lady* is a friend of mine. Kate, say hi to Sal De Luca, Chattanooga's answer to John Gotti."

"Screw you, Starke. Say what you want, or get the hell out of my restaurant."

"*Restaurant,* you call it. Bit of a stretch, wouldn't you say, Kate?"

"Okay, you've had your fun. Now tell me what you want or get out of here."

"What do you know about Thomas Sattler?"

For a moment, I thought the world had stood still. You could have heard the proverbial pin drop. Even the two goons stopped chewing, which was nice. *Pigs, both of them.*

"Who?"

"Geez, Sal, you heard, Tom Sattler. I hear he's into you for more than a handful."

"Never heard of him."

"How did I know that? You're not so subtle, Sal. You

know who he is. You and your two gorillas just gave it away. Y'all need to watch that body language."

He said nothing

"Look, Sal. I know what I know, and I know you were somehow involved with him. So come on. Give!"

Sal stared at me, weighing his options. "Show him out, Tony." Then he turned away again and hunched over his plate.

Damn, the big guy's name is Tony. Don't that beat all?

I looked at them both, Tony and his partner. They were sure of themselves, smiled, like a couple of hyenas. They didn't know me. Sal did, and he smiled, too. They were pros, deadly, confident, maybe a little too confident. Soldiers like these two think they're invincible. They tend to forget the lessons of the past however: 'no matter how good you are, there's always someone better.'

Tony eased down off his stool, all 260 pounds of him; he was taller than I thought, maybe five eleven. As he began to turn toward me, his hand slid inside his jacket. I heard Kate's sharp intake of breath.

"It's okay, Kate. I'll handle it."

The forty-five came into view and as it did so, I brought my hand out of my own jacket pocket. With one easy flick of the wrist, the ASP Talon expandable baton opened to its full sixteen inches and I whipped it down hard across the back of his hand, WHAP.

Were those bones I heard cracking?

Tony howled like a beaten dog. The forty-five flew across the bar and landed with a crash and a splash among the glasses in the sink. Sal looked at me in blank astonishment.

"You wanna go next, sunshine?" I said as I took a step closer to Sal's other goon. He didn't answer, nor did he move, flinch, or even blink, and nor did Sal.

"Pick it up, you stupid prick," Sal said to Tony, "and get the hell outa here." I thought for a minute Sal was going to slap him.

Apparently, Tony did, too, because he flinched and raised his forearm. But Sal just shook his head, exasperated, and Tony... he did as he was told. He walked around the bar, retrieved the weapon from among the broken glass, and then he left through the kitchen door, nursing his hand.

"Who did you say?" Sal's voice had ice in it.

I grinned at him, closed the baton, slipped it back into my pocket, and took a step back.

"Sattler, Tom Sattler. He's some kind of financial genius. What's your connection to him? And don't deny you have one, because I already know that you do."

He looked rattled for a moment, then his eyes narrowed, and he nodded. "Yeah, I know him. What d'you want to know for?"

"I want to know because he's dead."

"Dead? Whadda ya mean he's dead?"

"Dead, as in no longer living, Sal."

"You know what I mean, Starke. How come he's dead?"

"It looked like suicide. Why would he want to take his own life, Sal?'

Okay, Kate. I'm just pulling his chain.

"How the hell would I know? You're the detective, so I've been told. What's it to me anyhow?"

It wasn't the question, it was how he asked it that made me wonder. He asked as if he didn't care whether I answered or not. The man had something else on his mind. Money perhaps?

"One more time. What's your connection to him, Sal?"

He was quiet for a long moment, then looked sideways at me, put down his fork, and sat upright on the stool.

"He handled some of my finances, well, his outfit did. He invested some of my money. No big deal. I didn't see much of him. Mostly I did business with one of his part-ners, Marty Cassell. Now, if you don't mind, I have stuff to do."

He slid off the stool and stood in front of me; his crony did the same. Whew, I never experienced so much bad breath all at once. I almost choked. I took a step backward, an instinctive reaction that brought forth two toothy grins. I soon wiped those off their faces.

"Where were you last Tuesday night, Sal, between 8:30 and 10:45?"

"Why? Whadda ya wanna know for?"

"Someone broke into Sattler's home right about then, that's why."

"I was here. Right here. We had a full house. Ask anyone. Why would I want to do that anyway?"

"You say you had money invested with him. How much?"

"Not with him, with his company, with Marty, and it's none of your goddamn business how much. What I do with my money is nobody's business but mine. Now get the hell outa here, Starke, and take the whore with ya. I got better things to do. Gino, walk 'em to the door." He smiled – it was a look that could have frozen water – and then he turned and walked out through the kitchen door, leaving me and Kate with Gino. For the first time, I got a good look at him, and I didn't like what I saw. He was almost as tall as Sal, and not as skinny as I'd first thought.

He stood in front of me, feet apart, thumbs hooked into his belt, his head tilted slightly to one side, his mouth twisted into a lopsided grin that exposed a row of crooked teeth that reminded me of a crocodile. The narrow, hawk-like face topped six feet of tightly strung sinew and muscle. The belt bore a knife with a blade that had to be at least eight inches long. It was sheathed, but his right hand was less than two inches from the haft. This was one to watch, carefully.

Gino took a step sideways to block my way to the kitchen door. He stared at me through slitted eyes. His body language, and the lopsided grin said it all: 'I'm better than you, Starke.'

Yeah, buddy. As if.

I started to move, but I felt Kate's hand on my arm. She was right. It was time to leave, and we did.

"Don't come back, Starke." The voice was soft, the words a low growl.

I winked at him, turned and, together, Kate and I left and walked out into the sunshine.

"What do you think?" I said, when we got back into the car.

"That was some performance, with the baton. I didn't know you had it with you. Nice move."

"That wasn't what I meant, but anyway.... If you hadn't been here, it could have been a whole lot worse. I might have shot the stupid bastard, but I couldn't do that in front of you, now could I? We couldn't let them know who and what you are, not yet anyway. So, how do you think it went?"

"I'm not sure," she said. "There's no doubt that Sal is into

New Vision, and I wonder for how much. No matter; even if it's only five bucks, if the dividends are late, his broker is in for some big trouble. De Luca does not take kindly to people who steal from him. Legs get broken, kneecaps get shattered, and thumbs become detached from hands."

"Yeah," I said. "They also have a nasty way of disappearing completely. They say that Sal has more than one friend propping up the Imax Theater downtown. I have a feeling I might be seeing more of Tony and Gino in the not too distant future, especially Gino. Where did he find those two, I wonder?"

"Imports, probably," Kate mused. "So, what's you next step?"

"That depends on you. What are your plans?"

"One of us needs to see Cassell. Why don't you do that? I'll go see his partner, James Westwood, but it will have to wait until later. I have things I need to see to."

"I can do that. You need to go back to the office now?"

"Yes, if you don't mind."

I was on my way to drop Kate at the PD, when my cell phone rang.

"This is Harry."

"Harry, it's Ronnie. Where are you?"

"On my way to take Kate back to her car. Why?"

"I think you'd better drop by here, both of you. I have something you're gonna be interested in."

"Give me a minute, Ronnie."

I looked at my watch. It was almost four o'clock.

"Kate, Ronnie has something for us. You up for it?"

She was. "Okay, Ronnie, we'll be there in five minutes."

Chapter Eight

✦❀✦

We gathered around the table in the conference room: me, Kate, Ronnie, Tim, Mike, and Jacque. Ronnie handed everyone a stack of eight or nine sheets of paper stapled together.

"Okay, if you'll follow along," Ronnie began, "I'll explain what's on the report you have in your hands. Harry, you asked me to look into the New Vision Strategic Investment Fund, and I did. What I came up with is... well... someone will be going to jail.

"The fund, as of Tuesday afternoon at 5:30, had 382 investors and was valued at $422 million. As of 2:30 this afternoon, it was valued at just over $68 million."

There was a collective gasp from everyone around the table.

"How in the hell could it drop that much in just two

days?" I asked. "Did something happen I didn't hear about? Did the markets collapse?"

"They didn't collapse, but there are going to be some very unhappy people when the crap hits the fan," Ronnie said. "First a little background: New Vision is an investment fund. It was initiated five years ago in January of 2010. Its 382 investors each receive a monthly dividend check, at least that's what's supposed to happen.

"New Vision is a legitimate deal, but it wasn't producing enough income to meet its obligations, namely the monthly dividend payments, the payments to the four partners for administrating the fund, and the everyday expenses.

"The investors were supposed to receive a guaranteed annual income of eight percent, paid monthly. The four partners take a two percent fee off the top for administering the fund; this involved investing the funds and bringing new investors on board. The two percent fee of roughly $8.5 million is split four ways, between the partners, about $2.1 million per year each. Nice job if you can get it. I have a feeling that all four were skimming a little more off the top besides. The daily operating costs were roughly another million. This was used to pay the everyday expenses, to pay the staff, rent, and so on. This brought the pre-distribution total to $9.5 million, or two and a quarter percent. Questions, anybody?"

There were none.

"Okay then. To make it work – to pay both the partners and the investors – the fund had to bring in a minimum of ten and a quarter percent profit/interest. Unfortunately, that wasn't happening. The fund was bringing in a little more than six percent. The partners felt they were entitled to their two percent, and they were unwilling to give up a dime. The commitment to the investors was eight percent. So there was a shortfall of four and a quarter percent. Doesn't sound like much, but that's almost $18 million. In order for them to pay the full eight percent to the investors, and their own fees and expenses, they would have to dip into the fund's principal; or they would have to use funds received from new investors. This would effectively turn New Vision into a Ponzi scheme."

Ronnie paused and looked around the room, but no one spoke. We all gazed at him, fascinated.

"My confidential source at New Vision told me that for more than three months the partners had been arguing about what to do to solve the problem. The situation, as far as my source could tell, was unacceptable to the four partners... well, only two of them made any real fuss about it: Tom Sattler and Jessica Steiner. In any event, they all agreed that something had to be done to increase the fund revenue. The answer, they decided, was to liquidate $350 million in fund assets and reinvest it in more productive offerings.

"This was done. The assets were sold, liquidated, and the

money was parked in an interest-bearing bank account with access restricted to the four partners."

Again he paused, and again no one had anything to say.

"Now for the good stuff," he continued. "On Tuesday afternoon, at precisely 5:29 in the afternoon, Sattler, or someone else using his access codes and password, wired all $350 million to a numbered account in Dubai–"

"$350 *million?*" I was dumbfounded. "You mean it was stolen?"

"Yup. Within minutes, the money had been split into fifty equal parcels and moved out of Dubai into fifty off-shore holding accounts spread all around the world. From there, the money moved onward, and simply disap-peared. It's untraceable, gone. Whoever set this deal up is now very wealthy."

"Okay," I said, "so what you're telling us is that Sattler ripped off the fund for 350 mil?"

"That is correct. He either did the deed himself, or someone went to a great deal of trouble to make it look like he did."

"But his computers are wiped clean," I said. "How do we prove he did or he didn't?"

"If they were professionally scrubbed, we can't."

"Kate. Your people have them. Any word from them yet?"

"No. Let me give them a call."

We waited, and listened while she talked.

"They've looked at them. They have been cleaned, but to what extent, they can't say. They want to send them off to the FBI for analysis."

"That's not good, dammit," I said. "It will be months before we get anything. The thief will be long gone. All hell will be let loose when word of the theft gets out. The fund will collapse and there'll be no containing the media, much less the SEC. How come they are not involved already?"

"Oh, I'd say they are," Kate said. "Right now they're just getting all their ducks in a row, and then... well."

How about if Tim takes a look at the computers?" I looked at Kate as I said it.

She looked at Tim, thoughtfully. Tim smiled at her, his geeky face was all enthusiasm. "Let's see. Maybe Chief Johnston can do something. I can use your office, right?"

I nodded.

"Back in a minute," she said, as she got up from the table and left the room.

"Tim," I said. "Is there any way we can trace the money, find out what happened to it?"

"Not without the data. If the hard drives are wiped...."

"What about backups?" I said.

"Maybe, but we don't have them, right?"

"No," I said. "The place had been searched, and I'd be willing to bet that whoever did the search was looking for them."

Ten minutes later, Kate came back into the conference room. Her face was red and she didn't look happy.

"Tim, you can have access to the computers, but only in the PD lab. It was the best I could do, and Johnston wasn't happy even about that. Will that work for you?"

"I suppose," he said. "I can cart my gear over there. I won't really know what I need until I open 'em up, but yes. I can do that." He looked at me. "Maybe I can find some answers."

"It needs to be done quickly, Tim. Can you go over there now?"

"Sure. I'll go pack a few things."

"Kate, can you give them the word that he's coming?"

"I'll do better than that. I'll go with him. Tim, you can follow me over there."

They both left, leaving me with Jacque and Ronnie.

"Jacque. You go on home. I'll see you here bright and early tomorrow morning."

I leaned back in my chair, hands clasped behind my neck,

and stared up at the ceiling. "Okay. How the hell do we figure this mess out?" It was a rhetorical question and required no answer, but Ronnie answered it anyway.

"You're the detective," he said with a grin. "That's your job, yours and Kate's."

"Smartass," I said. "What did you find out about Sattler and his partners?"

"For the most part, they're pretty clean; good credit all round, money in the bank. Sattler was a loan officer's dream. His credit score was 827. His house is paid for, and he has no credit card debt. He has three bank accounts, two checking and one savings, totaling $133,632. His investment portfolio is worth $9.7 million."

"Geeze, my old buddy has done well for himself."

"His ex, Gloria Sattler, is the exact opposite. Credit score 615, a judgement against her last year, and she's past due on three of her four credit cards. Her home, though, is also paid for.

"James Westwood, almost as good as Sattler. Jessica Steiner, the same. Both have homes that're paid for, and substantial bank balances and investment portfolios. Marty Cassell, however, is an enigma. His credit score is 783, but I could find only one checking account with less than ten grand in it. I guess his assets are all off-shore, but his home is paid for, too."

"So, getting back to the money transfer," I said. "What are your thoughts, Ronnie?"

"As I see it, we have only four prime suspects: Sattler himself, and the three partners. If it's one of the surviving partners, we'll need to figure out which one, and quickly, before he or she makes a run for it."

"I don't agree," I said. "If the perp was going to make a run for it, he would already have done so, and we'd know about it. Nope, whoever did it thinks they're safe. He set it up so we'd think Sattler made the transfer and then killed himself in a fit of remorse. It might not be a bad idea to let him go on thinking that Sattler killed himself."

"But there's more than just four suspects," I said. "What about the family members, girlfriend, Hollins? They could have had access to his computer, too."

"That's true," Ronnie agreed, "but it was Sattler's codes that were used to access the bank account. I think it had to be one of the four. That's where you need to start looking."

"Maybe you're right. I don't think Sattler did it, but I do think it's why he called me. I think he found out about the transfer that same evening and panicked."

"Maybe. You'd know that better than me. You were there. You knew him. You saw the scene. He must have figured he needed serious help. The kind only you could provide: discreet and quick. It has to be one of the three remaining partners.... I think it's highly unlikely to be anyone else."

I never argue with Ronnie. He has a brilliant mind and is very rarely wrong about anything. He was probably right this time, too, but I wasn't going to let Gloria Sattler off the hook that easy. There was also the boyfriend, Richard Hollins, and Sattler's girlfriend, not to mention Sal De Luca and whatever hold he might have over Marty Cassell. We had a lot of work to do.

"Okay," I said. "I'll go along with you to a point. We'll have to prioritize, put the family members to the back of the line. One of the partners needs immediate attention, Marty Cassell. He's in bed with Sal De Luca. That alone would be reason enough to pull a stunt like this, especially if Sal is squeezing him."

"Yeah, and he's the one we have the least information about. I'll do some more digging, but I think he may well have covered his tracks. He's a smart one."

"You're right. Methinks I'll pay him a visit, now, tonight."

I looked at my watch. It was after five-thirty. I needed some time alone, to think.

"See you tomorrow."

He took the hint and left me alone with my thoughts. I took a legal pad from my desk drawer, placed it on the desk in front of me, took up a pen, and leaned on my desk, elbows on either side of the pad.

Thursday, 6p.m.

So, where do I go from here? Basics! Motive, opportunity, means. Okay, good. What's the motive?

Motive:

1. *Financial - The money's gone, so yes.*
2. *Revenge - Possibly: Sal? Nope. That would lose him his money. Anybody else? Unknown at this point.*
3. *Greed - Again, the money. Oh yeah! Life Insurance $300k Sattler's estate $9 million plus.*

Opportunity:

Who could have had the opportunity? Hmmmm.

1. *The three partners for sure: Cassell, Westwood and Steiner*
2. *The wife, Gloria? Yes, and the boyfriend, Richard. Can't leave out the eldest daughter, either.*
3. *Sattler's girlfriend Wendy? Yes.*
4. *Sal? Nope. He wouldn't get his hands dirty. Gino or Tony? Yep.*
5. *The investors? Yes, but unlikely, except for Sal.*

Means?

1. *Who out of the above could have had access to Tom's gun? Geeze! Any one of them, or all of them, given the right circumstances.*

And those circumstances would be? Being alone with Tom between 9:30 and 10:30.

Hmmm. What about the computers? Who would have access to them? See above, but that would not be tied to the time and date. It could have been anytime up to and including the hour when he died.

Okay, so who would have had access to Tom's codes?

The partners, family, girlfriend. That could mean as many as seven, maybe more, could have wired the money, but how many of them would know how? Shit. All seven could, and all seven could have had opportunity, and all seven could have had the means. Damn. This is going nowhere

I don't think Sal would have risked losing his twelve mil.

Okay, that's enough of this. We need to know more. A lot more, and we won't until we've interviewed all the suspects, including the five disgruntled investors that we know of so far.

Let's go see Cassell.

I closed the pad, put it back in the desk drawer, and went out. I grabbed an Arby's Max Roast Beef sandwich and a coffee in the drive through, and then headed out across the river to see Marty Cassell.

Chapter Nine

Marty Cassell lived in a vast, six-bedroom home on Palisades Drive up on Signal Mountain overlooking the Tennessee River Valley and the city of Chattanooga.

I arrived, unannounced, at the front door a little before nine o'clock in the evening.

Cassell came to the door himself. He was not an imposing man, not a big man physically, but he had a certain presence about him. He was dressed in corded pants, a red and black flannel shirt, and house shoes that would have been more at home on my grandmother's feet than on his. I figured he was probably the same age as me, forty-two, but he could have been slightly older. His close-cropped hair was already showing a little gray. His face was lean, his eyes a piercing blue, and at some time in the past his nose had been broken.

"Who are you?" he asked. "What do you want?"

Abrupt, and definitely unfriendly.

"Mr. Cassell. My name is Starke. Harry Starke. I'm an investigator. I understand you're a partner in New Vision Strategic. I was hoping you might be able to spare a few minutes to talk to me."

"I know who you are, Starke. It was you who took down Congressman Harper. No, I don't want to talk to you, so piss off."

He backed into the foyer and started to close the door. I stuck my foot in the gap, denying him the satisfaction.

"Okay, Cassell, there are two ways we can do this. You can let me in and we'll talk like civilized human beings or, by God, we can do it the hard way, which means you'll probably get another busted nose and maybe lose a few teeth. Which way would you like to play it?"

He glared at me through the gap, then flung the door wide open, turned and walked off into the house. I followed him, closing the door behind me.

The living room was vast, a caricature of the one in Herman Goering's Carinhall, all-over wood paneling, antlers, and animal heads. A huge, two-story window provided a stunning, panoramic view over the river valley.

He threw himself down in an overstuffed leather chair that could only have been custom built to complement the room. It was one of four surrounding an ornate, carved coffee table; there were also two matching sofas. He waved me to one of the other chairs. I sat; no, I was engulfed by the chair. For a long moment, we stared at each other, each of us waiting for the other to speak.

"Well," he said, finally. "This is your party. Go ahead." *I win, asshole.*

"Fine," I said. "I'll not waste any time screwing around with you. What do you know about the theft of $350 million from New Vision?"

If I had expected a reaction, I was disappointed. He simply sat there, comfortable in his chair, legs crossed at the ankles, elbows on the overstuffed leather arms, hands clasped together in front of his face, and he smiled at me. Now when I say smiled, he tightened his lips and turned up the corners of his mouth. It was somewhere between a grin and a snarl.

"It's gone. That's about all I know."

"How do you know?"

"Christ, Starke. Do you think I'm stupid? Of course I knew. I knew less than two minutes after it disappeared. I happened to be in the account when the money left it. One minute it was there. The next I was staring at a zero balance, and there was not a damn thing I could do about it. I haven't set foot out of this house since. You, I assume, are only the first in a long line of visitors I can expect, right?"

"I would say so. Have you talked to your partners?"

"Oh yes. We've talked."

"And?"

"And nothing. They know no more than I do... I think."

"Did you call Sattler when you discovered the money was missing?"

"Yes. I called him, but I haven't talked to him since. I also called the others. I have no idea if they've talked to each other. I do know this: everyone, including me, was pissed off and scared shitless. God only knows what's about to happen. I've already heard from the SEC, and they ain't to be fooled with. They've already frozen the fund, what's left of it, and changed all the access codes. I'm locked out, and so are the others."

"How does the loss of the money effect you, Mr. Cassell?"

"Me? Financially? Not at all. I keep my personal and business life separate. My peace of mind is another matter; my business and public persona have all gone, down the shitter. I'll probably not get a minute's peace until the money is recovered, and I have my doubts that it ever will be. I lost track of it when it left Dubai. So tell me, Starke. Who do you think did it? Who stole the damned money? Sattler?"

"I have no idea, not yet, but I'll find out. Sattler's dead. Looks like suicide."

That got his attention. He leaned forward, his elbows still on the arms of the chair, his hands were now clasped together under his chin.

"Suicide... goddamn... goddamn... Jesus. I talked to him right after. I called him just after the money disappeared, around seven o'clock that evening. I told him, but his reaction wasn't quite what I expected; I think he already knew."

Cassell seemed to be genuinely surprised to hear of Sattler's death, or did he? He seemed unable to maintain eye contact with me. *This guy's sharp. I wonder....*

"His reaction?" I said. "How do you mean?"

"I've known Tom a long time. I know how he thinks... thought. He sounded surprised, but I thought at the time that he might have been putting it on, acting. I dunno, maybe he was, maybe he wasn't. Perhaps he already knew, about the money being gone, I mean."

"So you have no idea of how it happened, how the money disappeared?" I asked him.

"Hell no. I don't, and if you're thinking I stole it, you're goddamn crazy. If I had done it, do you think I'd be sitting here shootin' the shit with you? Hell no. I'd be on a beach somewhere, screwing the ass off some lucky, good lookin' bitch. As it is, *I'll* probably be lucky to see daylight for the next foreseeable future, and I'm not talking about jail either, although that's a distinct possibility."

I couldn't help but smile. He seemed more than a little perturbed at his gloomy prospects.

"Do you know what his access codes to the bank accounts are?"

He hesitated, and his eyeballs flicked to one side. "No. I don't know his codes." There was a slight tremor in his voice. *Liar!*

"Okay," I said. "Let's try this: tell me about Salvatore De Luca.

His eyes bulged, his face tightened, and his lips parted to reveal a set of yellowed teeth. *The man's a damned chimney. Either that, or he chews.* It was a question he hadn't been expecting. He was no fool though. In only microseconds, he recovered his composure.

"Who did you say?"

I had to laugh. "Nice one, Marty." He didn't appreciate it. "If I had a dollar for every time I was asked that question, I could be relaxing on that beach alongside you. You know exactly who. Now tell me, what's your connection to Sal De Luca?"

"I don't have to tell you anything, Starke, especially confidential client information. You, Starke, have no standing. You're not a cop, nor do you work for the SEC. So screw you. You've got all you're going to get out of me."

I sighed and shook my head. "Marty. A man is dead; $350 million are missing. I am officially involved in the police investigation. Sal De Luca is a piece of shit; he has connections in New York and Miami; and somehow he's involved. I need to know why and how you are involved with him. I already know he has money invested in the fund. I'm not going to leave until you tell me the rest of it."

He said nothing. He stretched out so that he could get into his pants pocket and fished out an iPhone.

"Oh dear, Marty. That's not a good choice."

I got up out of my seat, walked around the coffee table until I was in front of him, took the cell phone out of his hand and placed it gently on the coffee table. Then I sat down on the edge of the table, pulled the Smith and Wesson M&P9 from the rig inside my jacket, leaned forward, and put my elbows on my knees. The nine was level with my face and pointed upward.

"Christ, you crazy son of a bitch. You wouldn't goddamn dare." His face had gone pale.

"A long time ago, Marty," I said, quietly. "I learned a little trick. I also learned, back when I was five or six years old, that most people can't stand pain. Are you one of those people that can't stand pain, Marty?"

He didn't answer.

I leaned in closer. He cowered back in the chair until he could go no further. I leaned forward, he threw his hands in the air, and I tapped him gently on the bridge of his nose with the barrel of the gun, right where I figured the old break must have been. Well, I thought it was gently. Marty didn't seem to think so. It works every time. He howled.

"Ow, ow. Oh Jesus, ow. You goddamn idiot, Starke. That hurt, you crazy bastard."

"Tut, tut, tut, what kind of language is that? And from such an upstanding and respected member of the financial community."

His eyes were watering, and he was clasping his nose as if it was about to escape.

This time I tapped his kneecap, only a lot harder.

"Ow, oh shit. Stop it, you crazy son of a bitch."

He grabbed his knee in both hands and I went straight back to his nose and whacked it again.

"Ahhhgh. You bastard, Starke. You've busted my nose again. I'll sue you, you crazy son of a bitch."

"Nope. I don't think you will, because then Sweet Swingin' Sal De Luca would know you've been talking to me, and he wouldn't like that at all, now would he? And it's not busted; not yet."

Marty didn't answer. He looked at me through watery eyes, rubbing his nose with one hand and clasping his knee with the other.

"You ready to talk, Marty, or do you need a little more pain? I can go on all night. How about you?"

"All right, you piece of shit." He was gasping for breath, like he'd run a mile flat out. "Look, Starke, De Luca can't know I talked to you. He'll, he'll, huh, kill me. What do you want to know?"

"He's invested in New Vision, right?"

He nodded, still nursing his nose.

"How much?"

He hesitated. I raised the nine. "*Okay*, okay. He has a little over $12 million in the fund."

I stared at him, astonished, dumbfounded.

"Where in God's name did he get that kind of money?"

"I dunno. He has it invested under a dozen different names. Most of it came in from off-shore accounts, untraceable."

I continued to stare at him.

Organized crime! It's Mob money. Oh, Marty. You silly son of a bitch.

"I get it, Marty. You are going to be in serious trouble, and not just with Sal De Luca. It's Mob money you're playing with, and you're laundering it for him. Money in, money out, right?"

He didn't answer, just stared defiantly up at me.

"Did he know New Vision was in trouble?"

He nodded.

"Tell me about it."

"We hadn't paid the last two dividends. He wants those plus vig, ten percent per day, plus he wanted to get the whole twelve mil out. We couldn't do it. The dividends totaled almost $100,000 a month each. The vig was/is climbing exponentially; right now it's almost $1 million. If I'd stolen the money, don't you think I'd have paid him off?"

"You, my friend," I said, shaking my head, "are in a world of shit. Does Sal know the money is missing?"

"Yeah. He does, and he wants it back, all of it. I have a week to come up with it, plus the interest... or else."

"Yeah, I can believe 'or else.' Sal and his boys are famous for 'or else.'"

"What am I gonna do, Starke? The bastard will shoot out my kneecaps if I don't come up with the twelve mil. I don't have that kind of money. Best I could do, if I sold everything, is maybe five."

"If I were you, I'd call the FBI and throw myself on their mercy. They might find you a spot in WITSEC if you come clean and give them what they need."

"Yeah, right! I'd never make it down the goddamn mountain. I'm being watched night and day, and don't think they don't know you're here. They do, and when you're gone, I'm gonna call him. I'm gonna tell him you were asking about him and the money. I'm gonna cover my ass, so you'd better be on the lookout. If he thinks you know anything, he'll want to shut you up, too."

I nodded, tilted my head and looked at him sideways. *Yeah, I bet he will.*

"Can't say that I blame you," I said. "That Sal De Luca is one nasty son of a bitch, especially if you steal his money."

"I didn't steal it, goddamn it. Tom Sattler did."

"Well, unfortunately, Sattler's not with us anymore; he took the easy way out.... That's always an option, I guess," I said, looking pointedly at him.

"You mean... you mean I.... Screw you, you crazy bastard. I ain't toppin' myself."

"Just a thought, Marty, just a thought."

"Yeah, well, you can keep stupid thoughts like that to yourself."

"When did you last see Sattler, Marty?"

Again, he gave me a wary kind of look, hesitated, then said, "I dunno; Tuesday lunchtime, I think. One o'clockish?"

"Are you asking me, Marty? Think, friend. When was it?"

"It was Tuesday. He asked me and Jessica to drop by for a drink; James, too, but he couldn't make it. Tom wanted to talk about the fund; strategy; stuff like that."

"And?"

"And what? We had a couple of drinks, for Christ's sake. We talked, about the fund, and... what else I can't remember. Just... stuff. Hell, Starke, he was worried about the state of the fund. We all were, but we'd already taken the necessary steps to put things right. It was no big deal, at least not then, when we still had the 350 million."

I could tell I wasn't going to get anything else out of him. It was time to go. I had what I needed, well most of it. If I needed more, I could always come back. If Marty lived that long.

I went out to my car. Cassell didn't bother to see me out. I didn't blame him. I did, however, take heed of his warning. I was willing to bet that even then he was on the phone to De Luca. *So be it!*

I pulled out of the driveway and had started along Palisades Drive toward Signal Mountain Road when I noticed a black SUV sitting off the road in what once must have been an access road to one of the demi-mansions on that side of the mountain. It was overgrown, long grass, maybe three feet tall; it was no place to park a late model expensive ride. As I drove past, I could see two shadowy figures in the front seats. I rounded the bend, turned off the lights, and slowed. *Here they come.*

I hit the gas, slung the Maxima round one tight bend after another, and then slowed a little at the junction to let them see me turn left toward the town of Signal Mountain. My lights still off, I hit the gas hard, drifted round the tight bend, then slewed right onto Balmoral, hit the brakes, and made a tight left turn into a driveway twenty yards, or so, from the highway. I watched through my driver's side window as they hurtled on by, heading north on Signal Mountain Boulevard. I made a quick reverse out of the driveway, turned left, and drove on down the mountain toward Chattanooga.

Chapter Ten

I t was already raining when I left Cassell's house on Palisades. By the time I'd turned onto Balmoral, it was bucketing down. On Signal Mountain, that's not a good thing. There are only two ways down from the top: Signal Mountain Road, and the 'W.' Knowing I was being followed, I considered taking the 'W.' In dry weather, I would have, but in those conditions, if you don't know that road, it could kill you. For me, at that time of night, and in the rain and darkness, it wasn't an option. The highway wasn't a whole lot better. The rain had turned the twisting ribbon of black asphalt into a mountain river that threatened to wash the unwary driver off the road into God only knows what. The drop off in places was more than a hundred feet. Overhead, the clouds boiled and split, visible only when they were pierced by colossal spears of forked lightning. Thunder crackled, rumbled, and reverberated along the river gorge. It was not a night to be abroad.

As I drove down the mountain, doing my best to make what speed I could, I kept my eyes on the rearview mirror. My mind was in a whirl, but I didn't see the SUV again. I guess I must have lost them on the mountain.

I made it off the final slope and swung right, heading west toward Highway 27. As I passed the Komatsu plant, I had a thought. Well, I had several – dozens, in fact – but there was something bugging me, had been all day. Something about the living room where I'd found Tom. I'd known it then, but couldn't figure it out, and it was still bothering me. I needed another look at that living room. *What the hell. Let's go take a look.*

I didn't have a key, but I did have my set of picks in the glove compartment. That would work. By the time I arrived at Tom Sattler's house, at just after 10:30 that evening, the rain had dwindled almost to nothing. As I drove up Royal Mountain Drive, I saw a car parked some 100 yards or so before I reached his drive. I took no notice of it. In fact, it didn't really register, except that it was a dark color, possibly black.

There was a light on in what I figured was the kitchen. I parked beside the garage and, for some reason, I have no idea what, I walked back almost to the road, turned and surveyed the house. Except for the light in the kitchen, it was in blackness. I was just about to walk back to the garage door when I saw a flash of light in one of the rooms on the upper floor.

The yellow crime scene tape was hanging loose; the

garage door was unlocked. I have one of those little flash-lights on my key ring. I turned it on and crept slowly through the house to the stairs.

Carefully, trying not to make a sound, I stepped my way upward to the landing. At the far end, behind a closed door, I could see the beam of a flashlight flickering in the gap under the door. I put my ear to the door and listened; all was quiet. The light was gone. I didn't like it. I didn't like it worth a damn.

I took a step backward, took a deep breath, pulled the M&P9, worked the action, leaped at the door and hit it with my left shoulder. The frame splintered. The door flew open, and I landed on the floor, rolling, twisting, trying to see in the darkness.

The ear-bursting explosion, the blistering flash of white fire, and the wind of the slug on my face, almost took me by surprise, almost. Before the light from the flash had subsided, I swung the nine and jerked the trigger, BAM! The gun bucked hard against the heel of my hand, and a voice across the room yelled. Something heavy hit the floor with a thud, followed immediately by a horrendous crash of broken glass. I rolled sideways, twice, and then brought the gun up, ready for another shot, but all was quiet. Nothing was moving.

I lay there, great spots of white light rotating slowly in the blackness before my eyes, the result of the muzzle flashes, mine and his. I was bathed in sweat, the grip of the nine was slippery in my palm. I licked my lips, rolled slowly over onto my back.

"Give it up, buddy," I said. "I already hit you once. Don't try me again. This is not a good time to die." Nothing. All of a sudden, I had the idea I was alone in the room, but I wasn't taking any chances.

"Give it up. Drop it and stand up." Nothing. Now I was faced with two options. I could lie there and wait until daylight, or I could make a dash for it. I chose to dash.

Head down, on hands and knees, I crept through the blackness toward where I thought was the door, listening intently for the slightest sound. Nothing.

Okay then. He's either dead or gone, or he's waiting for me to give him a shot at me. Awe, what the hell.

I felt for the doorframe, jumped to my feet, flipped the switch and turned on the lights. He was gone. On the floor by the open window was a broken vase and a scattering of wilted flowers. There were drops of blood on the carpet, and smears on the window ledge. I shined my tiny flashlight down onto the roof of the front porch; more drops of blood. In the distance, I heard the sounds of a car starting and then being driven away.

I went back down to my car and called Kate Gazzara.

It was twenty minutes before she arrived. When she did, she had Lonnie Guest with her.

Well, if that doesn't just make my friggin' day.

"Hello, Kate, Lonnie."

"What now, Harry?" Kate said. She was angry. "Why are you here?"

Lonnie had that stupid, halfwit grin on his face again.

"Kate, I've been up to see Cassell. I was followed, probably by De Luca's two goons. I managed to lose them, but something was bugging me. I needed another look at the room where I found Tom's body. I didn't think there was any point in dragging you out in this weather. I just wanted a quick look, okay?"

"Why didn't you call me first? You know better. The house was supposed to be locked down. How did you think you were going to get in?"

I didn't answer. She would have been even less pleased if I told her, so I changed the subject. I told her about my visit to Cassell.

"I didn't tell him he was murdered, but he seemed genuinely surprised to learn that Tom was dead, that he committed suicide, but that's not all. He's into De Luca for more than twelve million, and he's scared out of his mind."

"You serious? Twelve million?"

I nodded. "Yep, and Sal has given him a week to pay it back to him, or else."

"Not nice, that 'or else.' What's he going to do? More to the point, where did De Luca get twelve mil?"

"It has to be Mob money, Kate. Cassell must have been laundering it for him."

"Yeah, now it's all been washed away, ha, ha."

I had to grin at her. Maybe now was a good time....

"Kate, I think maybe whoever it was that broke in here, was looking for information about the transfer."

She rolled her eyes. "No shit, Sherlock. The bigger question is... what were *you* looking for?"

"I don't know. I hope I'll know it if I see it. I had a feeling I was missing something the other night, when I was calling you. Maybe I was, maybe I wasn't. Let's take a look, yes?"

We stood in the foyer, the three of us, looking into the room. The carpet over the bloodstain in front of the fireplace had been cut out, removed. The blood had spread, soaked into the particle board subfloor, dried, and turned into a dirty brown, crusty patch that was already beginning to smell. I closed my eyes, concentrated, and it all came flooding back.... I don't have an eidetic memory, but what I do have is pretty damn good. I could see Tom lying in front of the fireplace; the room was tidy, undisturbed, nothing.... Ashes. There were ashes in the fireplace.

It's the middle of August, for God's sake. It's in the nineties out there. Why would there be ashes?

I opened my eyes and walked to the fireplace. Nothing!

"What?" Kate said.

"Nothing. I thought there were ashes in here."

"There were. Someone had burned some papers. CSI took them away, what was left of them. They didn't get anything, though. They were too far gone."

"Dammit, Kate. Why didn't you tell me?"

"I didn't think it was important. There was virtually nothing left."

She could tell I wasn't happy, but she just shrugged. "Get over it, Harry. It's done and gone. Move on."

We went back outside. The CSI team was pulling into the driveway. Both sides of the street from one end to the other had lights on. Kate leaned against her car door and stuck out her hand.

"Hand it over, Harry."

"Hand what over?"

"Your weapon, of course. Shots fired. Someone was wounded. You know the drill. Hand it over."

Reluctantly, I did as she asked. She took it in her gloved hand, bagged it, wrote the label, and dropped it on the passenger seat of her car.

"When do I get it back?"

"You don't, at least not for a while, a long while if the guy you shot dies, then maybe not at all. Now get out of here. Let me and CSI do our jobs. Lonnie, I'll also need a statement from Harry before he leaves. Harry, I'll call you if I need you. Lonnie, when you have his statement, you hang around out here. When the techs get done, get those tapes back up."

Lonnie didn't look any happier than I was. Kate was turning into a hard ass.

Chapter Eleven

A s always on Friday morning, I called the staff together for a breakdown of the progress of the week so far.

Aside from the Sattler case, it was all routine, quickly dealt with and put aside. I went into the front office, poured myself a fresh cup of coffee, and settled back down at the conference table.

"So, Tim," I said. "What did you get from Sattler's computers? Anything?"

"Not much. I'd barely gotten started when the FBI charged in and snatched everything out from under my nose, including my personal thumb drives, and some of my own proprietary software. The SEC has frozen the fund, what's left of it."

"Well, we should have known. The theft of $350 million from an investment fund was bound to get a quick response from the Feds. Were you able to get anything at all?"

"Not really. Nothing I can show you, just what I can remember. The drives on both computers had been wiped, but they hadn't been overwritten, so the information on them is recoverable, and there was a lot of it. I only got a peek at some of it before they swooped. I can tell you this, though. The wire transfer *was* made from Sattler's laptop."

"His laptop, huh? Now that opens up a whole new set of possibilities. That laptop could have been anywhere when the transfer was made. Hell, Sattler could have disturbed the perp returning it. That is, if it ever left his home. What do you think, Tim?"

"There's no telling. It was wired at exactly 5:29. That gave the perp just about fifteen hours free from attention by the authorities. Only those people with direct access to the account, namely the partners, would know that the money was gone, and there's absolutely no way of tracking it once it was streamed out of Dubai. It's gone, Harry. Someone is suddenly very rich. It should be easy enough to find out who it was, though."

"Oh, and how do we do that?"

"So, all we have to do is wait and see which one of them does a runner, right."

"Geez, Tim. Do you really think it will be that easy? Come on. What would *you* do?"

"Me? I'd be long gone by now. I'd have made the transfer and headed straight on out. By now, I'd be on a tropical beach somewhere, surrounded by beautiful women."

Tim, old son, I don't think even 350 mil could do that for you. You, my friend, are the epitome of the word Geek.

"Well, that hasn't happened, at least not yet. If it had, we'd have known it by now. Whoever it was is sitting tight. As far as I know, all the partners, and anyone else who might have had access, is still present.... Tim, could the account have been hacked by some outside entity?"

"Nope. I don't think so. I saw no sign of hacking on either of the two machines and, as I said, the laptop is the one in question."

"Well, it was just a thought. Anybody else have any thoughts?" I looked around the table. No one had, so I closed the meeting, grabbed another cup of coffee, and went to my office. It was time to make some more visits.

Chapter Twelve

I called James Westwood at his office at a little after nine o'clock that Friday morning. It came as no surprise that he didn't answer. I called Kate.

"Hey, it's me. I just called Westwood. He's not answering his phone. Can't say I blame him. I'm going to head down to his office. You want to come? Your badge might get us inside."

"How about I meet you there, in say, thirty minutes?"

I was there in twenty. The outer doors to the building were open. The door to Westwood's office was locked, but the lights were on inside and a harassed-looking young woman was seated at a desk facing the door. Several people were seated in the lobby talking together. They didn't look happy.

The vultures are gathering.

Kate walked in a couple of minutes later. As soon as I saw her, I could tell she was in one of her moods. I sometimes wonder if Kate has dual personalities. I know of at least two. One is the nice girl with the bright smile and easy-going attitude everyone loves; the other is the tough, intimidating no nonsense cop that nobody dares to fool with. Today, it was the latter. Even so, she looked stunning. Her hair was tied back in a ponytail and she had on a sleeveless white top, a dark red skirt cut just above the knee, and black shoes with three-inch heels.

She nodded to me as she walked to the office door, banged on it, and flashed her badge through the glass. The woman jumped to her feet, came to the door, flipped the lock, and opened it a crack. Behind us, I heard the seated folk all get to their feet.

"Police," Kate said, pushing the door open and walking through. I closed the door behind us and locked it. The folks outside sat down again.

"Who are you?" Kate said, looking at the closed inner door. "We need to see James Westwood. Please tell him we're here."

"I'm Jenna Forbes, Mr. Westwood's PA. He's not here. He didn't come in this morning, and I haven't heard from him. He's not answering his cell phone."

Kate opened the inner door and looked inside, and then closed it again.

"I'll need his home address and his cell phone number."

"Well... I'm not supposed to...." Forbes looked at Kate's face and knew there was no point arguing. "Oh well." She sighed and shrugged. "I was looking for a job when I found this one. I can find another, I hope." She turned to her desk, wrote a few lines on a notepad, tore off the page, and handed it to Kate.

Kate punched the number into her iPhone and listened. After four rings, the call went to voicemail, and Kate cut it off.

"He lives on Lookout Mountain, on West Brow. Let's go. Oh, by the way," she said, turning again to Forbes. "Where is Thomas Sattler's office?"

"It's on East Brainerd Road. I have the address. He's not there much, and he doesn't have any staff." She wrote it down and handed the paper to Kate, who thanked her, folded the paper, and put it in her jacket pocket.

"Your car or mine?" she said as we walked out of the office building.

I shrugged. "Mine, if you like. It's just over there, and... you need to relax. Take a deep breath. Let's enjoy the ride up the mountain."

She stopped at the edge of the sidewalk, looked at me, took a deep breath that seemed to come all the way up from her feet, then she grinned.

"You're right, Harry. Sorry. I just had a run in with the chief. He's not happy. The Feds are all over the department, them and the SEC. If this wasn't a homicide, the case would already have been taken away from me. As it is, it's still CPD jurisdiction. I was warned, however, to keep both our noses out of the New Vision affair."

I held the car door open for her to get in, and then got in myself.

"Kate, that's not going to be easy," I said, as I pushed the starter. "Everyone at New Vision, and their clients, are suspects in Sattler's death."

"Yeppy! That's true, but I have to do as I'm told. It is what it is."

"*You* have to do as you're told, but I don't, which is why I'm no longer a cop."

"Oh how true, Sherlock, which is why I love working with you. Just try to keep your nose clean, okay. I have no pull with the Feds, and if you screw up too badly, I may not have any with Chief Johnston either. I did get the vibe that he was kinda pissed the Feds were all over him. Still...."

"Gotcha," I said, as I negotiated the turn off Cumming's Highway onto Scenic. A few minutes later, we were on West Brow Road, high above the Lookout Valley. The view was stunning.

"How about this?" I said. "We'll do this one together, and then I'll handle Steiner by myself."

"Sounds good to me, but be sure to keep me in the loop. I

do not want to get blindsided. Turn left here. It should be just down the road, on the right."

It was, and as I expected, it was another of those expensive mansions, a rambling, single-story structure set back some fifty yards from the main road behind a six-foot high iron fence and an electronic gate. Kate hit the button on the electronic keypad and we waited, but not for long.

"Yes. Who eeze it?" The voice was female, made tinny by the speaker inside the metal box.

"Police. Lieutenant Gazzara. I need to see James Westwood."

"One moment, please?"

The one moment turned into two, then three, and then the gate began to slowly open. We drove through the trees to the house, a dark, brooding structure perched on a natural stone ledge high above the Tennessee River Gorge. The house was dismal in its outlook. It reminded me of something from a 60s horror movie.

James Westwood was waiting for us on the front porch. He looked to be in his mid-sixties, fit, muscular. Most men who lived to be his age should be so lucky. He had matured well, better than most. He was tall, lean, tanned, and had a smile that must have cost almost as much as the Porsche Carrera parked in the driveway. His blue eyes were set deep under a shock of pure white hair that made his tan look even darker than it was, as did the pale blue golf shirt and white pants. He was one of those men that carried himself with confidence and looked good no matter what he was wearing.

He came down the steps to greet us, first Kate, and then he offered me his hand. His grip was strong and sure.

"And you are?" He looked me in the eye as he shook my hand.

"My name's Harry Starke, Mr. Westwood. I'm a private investigator."

"A PI? That's a bit unusual, isn't it, Lieutenant?"

"Not so much. Mr. Starke was a sworn officer for many years. Now he works with me as a consultant. Will that be a problem, sir?"

"Oh... no, not at all. Call me James, and please, come on in. Can I get you anything? A soda, tea, or would you prefer something stronger?"

"Nothing for me, thank you," Kate said.

I shook my head and followed the two of them through the door into the house.

Geez, I thought the outside was gloomy. This is damned depressing.

The foyer, if you could call it that, was a long, musty, narrow passageway that stretched from the front of the house all the way to the back. The walls were covered with dark, almost black wood paneling; even the ceiling was paneled. Heavy antique furniture was crammed in everywhere. The floor was inlaid with brownstone tiles. It was like walking into a cave. In the distance, I could see an open door and beyond that what must have been a vast bay window overlooking the valley.

"Let's go into the lounge, shall we?" Westwood said, pushing open a door and standing to one side to allow us to enter. "Please, sit down."

The room appeared to be an extension of the foyer – the paneling and decor were much the same – but it was much brighter, lit by three large windows that stretched the width of the room and provided a view of the driveway.

We sat together around a circular dining table that was probably older than the house. Kate and I together on one side, Westwood sat on the other. He had his hands clasped together on top of the table, staring at us intently.

"This must be about the fund, I presume?" His attitude was upbeat, but I had the impression he was forcing it.

Hell, who wouldn't have to force it after losing such a truck load of cash?

"That, and the demise of Thomas Sattler," Kate said, watching for a reaction. She got one.

"T... Tom's dead," he spluttered. "How? What happened? When?"

"Tuesday evening, late," Kate said. "It looked like he shot himself."

"Looked? You said it *looked* like suicide. Does that mean... he didn't?"

Hah. He's quick, this one. Good try, Kate, but now you have to tell him.

"I don't have the final results of the autopsy yet, but the gun was next to his hand and there was a single wound to the head."

Nicely played, Kate.

"But you do think he might have been murdered?"

Kate sighed and nodded. "Yes, Mr. Westwood. I think perhaps he was. Now, can we get on? I have a few questions, and if you don't mind, Mr. Starke may have some, too. Is that all right with you?"

"Yes, yes, of course... but who...? Whew. Never mind." He shook his head and leaned back in his chair. "How can I help?"

"When did you first learn that the $350 million was missing? I assume you do know that, right?"

"Yes, of course. I found out from Tom. He called me on Tuesday evening. It must have been around eight o'clock. He'd talked to Marty – Marty Cassell, that is. He's one of our partners. Tom was panicking. I pulled up the account and sure enough, the money had gone. I was... was... I don't know what I was. I called Marty myself; waste of time that was. He was in a blue funk. I also called Jessica. She also knew the money was gone, but that was all. She said she'd call me back, but she hasn't. I haven't been out of this house since I heard. I tried to trace it, but... well; I'm not a computer expert."

"How many people had access to the account, Mr. Westwood?" I asked.

There's something about this guy that I'm not getting. I don't like him.

"Just the four of us. Tom, Marty, Jessica, and me."

"And exactly how were you able to access the account, all of you?"

"It's simple enough. We each have our own set of secret codes: user name, password, and several security questions. None of us knows the others' set of codes. At least we shouldn't." There was something about the way he said that bothered me.

"Shouldn't?" I said. "Does that mean some of you do know them?"

"Maybe. I knew Tom's. I also know Jessica's. That is, if she hasn't changed them, and Tom knew mine. I wouldn't be surprised if Marty knows them all, too, although I've never given him mine. It was one of those things. We all trust each other."

"So what you're saying is that anyone of the four of you could have made that money transfer using one of the other partner's access codes?"

"Well... I suppose... but...."

"Would it surprise you to know," Kate said, "that the transfer was made from Mr. Sattler's laptop computer, and that his own access codes were used to do it?"

He shrugged. "Not really. So it was Tom, then?"

"We don't know that," Kate said. "Why would it not surprise you?"

"Er... well, I'm not sure. Tom was... he was not really too concerned about security. Took it for granted, even at the office he'd leave his machine unattended. Who could have done it, then, if Tom didn't?"

"We *don't* know that he didn't. All we know is that that the wire transfer was made from his computer using his codes. Anyone with access to them could have done it, and then killed him to cover it up. When did you last see Tom Sattler, Mr. Westwood?"

"Hmmm, it would have been Saturday evening. He asked me to drop by for a drink. I was in town so I did. I often did. Tom was a bit of a loner, but he was always pleased to see me. So, yes. About seven o'clock. We had a couple of drinks, chatted some, then I went home."

"How long were you there?" She said

"Until a little after ten-thirty."

"What sort of mood was he in?"

"Pensive, thoughtful, but that was not unlike him. He

always was quiet, but he could be excitable, when the mood took him."

I nodded. That's how I remembered Tom.

"Did you have access to his computers?" I said.

He nodded. "Yes. In fact I used the laptop to check my email while I was there."

"Who do you think it was, Mr. Westwood? Who stole the money?" I asked, looking him squarely in the eye.

He blanched and looked away, hesitated, then looked back at me. There was the light of defiance in his look.

"I don't know, Mr. Starke. It wasn't me. I can assure you of that, and if Tom was murdered.... Well, I suppose it could have been him, but I can't, won't believe it. I'm also certain it wasn't one of my other two partners. You have a puzzle on your hands, I think."

"Surely," I said, "something like this could not have been done on the spur of the moment. It would have taken a great deal of planning. From what I've been told, there are perhaps hundreds of offshore bank accounts involved. Just setting them up would have taken months."

"That's what you'd think, but it's not entirely true. There probably are a hundred or more accounts involved, but they wouldn't have been difficult to set up. It's all done by computer these days. Still, it would have involved some in-depth knowledge of the world banking system and, as you say, no little planning."

"Could you have done it, Mr. Westwood?"

"I, I, I, could," he stuttered, "but I didn't."

"Okay," I said. "If you were a betting man, which I know you are, who would you put your money on?"

"Betting man? What the hell do you mean by that? I've never laid a bet in my life."

I grinned at him, a nasty, toothy grin, my best impression of a barracuda.

"And what you do for a living, Mr. Westwood; what would you call that? I'd say it was gambling, the smart way, using other people's money, or would I be wrong, Mr. Westwood?"

"Yes, you would be wrong. I don't gamble. What we do is scientific, a detailed and informed analysis of the markets and then a balanced and structured set of purchases made using that information. It's virtually foolproof."

"If that's true, sir, how come the fund was making a loss and was unable to meet its commitments to its investors?"

"Uh... I... that is we..." he spluttered, "suffered a series of downturns in the market facilitating a reexamination of the fund's direction. This, after much discussion between the partners, resulted in an agreement to partially liqui-date the fund and reinvest the proceeds into higher yield equities."

"And those higher yield equities," I said, "would also present a much higher risk. Is that not correct?"

"Well... yes... but...."

"They would, in fact be something of a gamble. Correct?"

"Well, yes, but...."

"There you go. You make my case. You are, in fact, a gambler, and you gamble with other people's money. No, no, no," I said as he was about to interrupt. "Let me finish my point. Here's my question, and I bet I already have the answer. How much of your own money do you have invested in New Vision?"

He closed his mouth, his lips tight together, bloodless, and he stared at me across the table.

They say if looks could kill....

"Precisely!" I said. Now, I decided, was the time to give him a push, put on a little pressure.

"I understand the four partners take a fee for administering the fund," I said, "and that fee is two percent of the value of the fund, and it comes right off the top, yes?"

He nodded, slowly.

"So, by my calculation, that comes to roughly $8.5 million split four ways. That would be $2.1 million per year each. No gamble there. Again, that means the only gamble is the investors'."

"But, but...."

"Hear me out, please, sir. On top of the fee, you folks take another mil, for office expenses. Not bad, considering I have yet to see a bona fide office–"

"It's on Brainerd," he interrupted. "We employ four secretaries, and we have to pay the rent–"

"Oh that's funny. Rent. What? Say $2,000 a month. That's twenty-five K. Pay for the secretaries, another $200,000, and then the utilities. You four sharks are making at least another $150,000 a year each on top of more than a couple of mil. That's not gambling, but it's damned greedy, I would say."

"Whatever it is," *oh, he was upset*, "it's none of your damned business. What we do is absorb the risk for our investors. What we get paid for doing so is industry standard."

"Risk," I said. "There's that word again. Isn't it just another word for gambling? You know what I think, Mr. Westwood? I think you and your partners have had a nice long and lucrative ride on the coattails of New Vision's investors, but the wheels were loose, and about to come off. Some of them, the investors, had not been paid their dividends for three or more months. Those that have, had been paid either out of the principal, or out of funds provided by new clients, and that, as we all know, is illegal. A Ponzi scheme is the technical term, I think. Isn't that right?"

I didn't give him a chance to answer.

"But that's enough of that," I said. "I'm sure the Feds will sort all that out, so let's move on. Tell me about Marty Cassell."

He was breathing heavily, obviously offended, but then he seemed to gather himself together and calm down.

"Marty has been my partner for more than ten years. I trust him completely."

"What do you know about his clients?"

"His clients? What have they got to do with Tom, or the fund?"

"Would it surprise you if I told you he was in bed with the mob, and that he was laundering money for them through the fund, and that they are looking for the return of their $12 million?"

"Whaaat? What Mob? What the hell are you talking about?" His face had turned a dirty gray color.

"Your friend Marty Cassell has a very influential client of Sicilian descent. Salvatore De Luca has been investing his company's money with him for the past several years, and when I say company, I don't mean his Italian restaurant. Marty told me that Sweet Sal has more than twelve million invested in New Vision. That means not only Marty, but the other surviving partners, too, owe Sal the money, all of it. Marty has just one week to come up with it, or else. You see, unlike you, Sweet Sal doesn't gamble, not with other people's money, and especially not with his own. If he can't get his money from Marty, he will come after the rest of you for it."

James Westwood was looking decidedly sick.

"Okay. Here's my theory," I said. "I think that when things at the fund started going downhill, you guys panicked, decided to liquidate some of the funds and reinvest them, as you said. I also think that one of you had a bright idea: why not just steal the $350 million and be done with it. Now that may or may not have been Sattler – and frankly, I don't think it was – because as soon as the money disappeared he got on the phone to the rest of you vultures and he said something that got him killed, and James...." I looked him right in the eye. "I'm going to get whoever that was, you can bet on that; you can take it to the bank."

"You need to leave," he whispered. "I need some time. Please, Lieutenant, leave now and take this... this *person* with you."

He got up from the table and left the room, leaving us sitting there. Kate looked at me, shrugged, and then she, too, rose to her feet. Together, we walked out of that dismal mausoleum and into the late morning mountain sunshine. It was so bright it hurt my eyes, but oh what a relief it was.

"So what do you think?" I said, as we drove on down the mountain toward the city.

"I have the distinct impression that you don't like Mr. Westwood," she said. "You pushed him a bit hard toward the end."

"No, I didn't. I just stated the truth, and no, I don't like him. My first impression was that he's slick, superficial. Now I think he's just plain dirty, a crook. I think all four of them are crooks, to one degree or another. I wouldn't trust Westwood or Cassell with two cents of my money, but the investing public must have been okay with him. I wonder how they'll feel when it gets out that their money has gone."

I looked sideways at her, but she just stared stoically out across the valley, seemingly lost in thought.

"You know, Kate, there has to be some serious information knocking around somewhere. There has to be a list of all of those bank accounts, the access codes to them, and the final destination of the cash. If it's not on Sattler's computers, and Tim would have said something if it was, then where the hell is it? It must be either in the Cloud, or on thumb or flash drives, or disks. I have to believe that's what whoever it was I shot last night was looking for."

"As best I can figure it," Kate said. "There's only one person who could tell us where the information is and that's the person who made the transfer and then wiped the hard drives. If that was Sattler, we're out of luck, and even if it was someone else...."

"Yeah," I agreed, "we have a problem, a big one."

"Harry, I have to ask you. Do you think Sattler transferred that money?"

"Right now, I have an open mind. It makes sense that he did, and then was killed for it, but I keep coming back to the question, 'If he stole the money, why did he call me?'"

Chapter Thirteen

We stopped for an early lunch at the Boathouse on Riverfront Parkway. I dropped Kate off at her car and was on my way back to the office, when I had a thought. I pulled over and parked in front of a Food City supermarket, hit the Bluetooth and called Kate.

"Hey, it's me," I said. "Look, we need to get a handle on the rest of the prime suspects so I'm going to go see Wendy Brewer and then head on over to see Jessica Steiner. Do you want to come with me?"

"Can't. I have to go back to Amnicola. I just had a call from the chief. He want's to see me. It's something I can't get out of. Yes, you go. That will get the three main suspects out of the way, or not. Let me know what happens."

I wonder what the hell the chief wants with her. Nothing good, that's for sure.

"You got it." I flipped the button and disconnected. Then I called the only number I had for Wendy Brewer. She answered on the first ring.

"Hello." The voice was subdued, tentative.

"Is this Wendy, Wendy Brewer?"

"Yes, who *is* this?" I wondered about the emphasis.

"My name is Harry Starke, Miss Brewer. I'm an investigator. I'd like to talk to you about New Vision and Tom Sattler. Can I drop by for a few minutes?"

"Are you with the police?"

"I'm working with the police, yes."

Not exactly a lie, but what the hell. You have to do what it takes, right?

"Well... I suppose...."

"Great. I have the address. I'll see you in about ten minutes."

I didn't give her a chance to think about it, or even answer. I hung up and swung left out of the parking lot, heading north. Brewer lived in a small rancher on Hickory Valley Road, just off Shallowford Road. When I pulled up outside her house, behind a silver BMW Z4, she was waiting for me.

I wasn't exactly expecting a swimsuit model, but this young woman was more Plain Jane than Heidi Klum. Maybe I was being a little hard on her. After all, she *had* suffered a major loss in her life. Even so, she could not have looked less like the girlfriend of a millionaire if she'd tried. Average size, maybe five feet six tall, she looked like she could do with losing fifteen pounds or so. Her hair was a wild halo of blonde ringlets and in desperate need of a stylist. She was dressed in jeans and a tank top. The jeans had at least a dozen large holes in them, by design, so I'm told. Her eyes were red; she'd been crying. Understandable, but I could tell she'd made an effort to tidy her makeup. The lipstick was horrible, a gaudy shade of crimson and the huge gray eyes were heavily outlined in black. The whole appearance was a little, shall we say, startling.

Whew. Sattler swapped one mediocre ride for another. The only thing she has over his ex-wife is that she's seventeen years younger. This is one miserable-looking woman.

"Ms. Brewer, first let me say how sorry I am for your loss, and that I wouldn't be here unless it was absolutely necessary."

"It's okay," she said, sniffling and wiping her nose on what could only have been a piece off a roll of paper towels. "Please, come on in. Can I get you some coffee, or something?"

"No. No thank you. I just have a few questions, if you don't mind."

She nodded and waved a limp hand at the chairs around the kitchen table. "Please, sit down."

"Ms. Brewer—"

"Please, call me Wendy," she interrupted.

"Okay. Wendy, then. When did you last see Mr. Sattler?"

"That would have been just after one o'clock on Tuesday. He was expecting Marty Cassell and Jessica Steiner for lunch. I made sandwiches for them and then I had to go. I had a doctor's appointment. I have this thing, you see. It's kind of—"

"*Yes*, yes," I interrupted, not wanting to know the ins and outs of her feminine problems. "I understand, and that was the last time you saw him, correct?"

She nodded, slowly, sobbing.

"Did you see anyone else while you were there?"

"Yes. As I said, Jessica and Marty came for lunch."

"What time would that have been?"

"Marty arrived first at around twelve-thirty. Jessica a little later, around one o'clock, maybe a little earlier."

"How well did you know his partners?"

"I knew them all quite well. We were all great friends."

Really? Wow, that's a first, and not the impression I got

from Cassell and Westwood, especially Marty. Who are
you trying to kid, girl?

"Tell me about that," I said.

"Well, they were always like dropping round for drinks,
and to talk, mostly about business, you know. It wasn't all
like, about business. Sometimes we'd cook out, swim,
catch a few rays, you know. They are all nice people."

"Did you help him with his work in any way?"

"Oh yes. I did like typing for him. Sent emails. Worked
with the investors. Anything he needed, really."

"And you would have had access to his computers, and
his codes, then?"

She nodded. "Yes, of course. I worked on them every day.
It was part of my job, to like keep track of new clients,
investments, distributions. I handled a lot of that stuff
for him."

"Wendy, when did you find out that he'd shot himself?"

Shit, Harry. Lighten up a bit. That was brutal.

She had tears in her eyes. "Stephanie called me that
night. It was about one o'clock in the morning. She'd just
found out herself. I rushed right over. The police were
still there, but they'd taken Tom away.... I never saw him
agaaain," she wailed, and burst into tears.

I waited, uncomfortable, until she calmed down, wiped

her eyes, and gazed at me, her mascara black rivers that undulated down her cheeks.

"Well," I said. "Thank you for talking to me. I'll take up no more of your time. Again, I'm sorry...."

I left Wendy Brewer with the distinct feeling that she was a wretched, inadequate individual. Without Tom Sattler in her future, she was in for a very rough time.

Chapter Fourteen

I sat in the car for a moment, thinking. I really didn't know what to make of Wendy Brewer. She was in a sad state, that was for sure, and that made the woman hard to read. I was worried about her... but there was not much I could do. *Check on her, from time to time, maybe? Hmmm.*

I shook myself out of my reverie and called Jessica Steiner. She didn't answer.

Damn. I hope this isn't going to be a waste of time.

I pulled out of the parking lot and headed for the interstate. Steiner lived on Fairy Trail high on top of Lookout Mountain.

Why is it that all the wealthy folk live way up there?

I arrived outside her home at a little before two-thirty that afternoon. She lived in a single-story rancher that stretched for at least a half a block. It was surrounded by a six-foot high brick wall. The iron gates were locked and the place looked deserted: the lawns needed mowing and the bushes trimming. I pressed the buzzer on the electronic keypad but no one answered.

Okay. I didn't come all this way for nothing. Let's go see what we can find.

I backed the car out of the entrance to the gate, and then drove it back in again, this time close to the right-hand wall. I got out of the car, locked it, adjusted the rig under my lightweight golf jacket, and stepped up onto the rear bumper. There wasn't a whole lot of room, but fortunately I was wearing loafers with soft leather soles. From there I was able to boost myself up to the top of the wall. I dropped down the other side and walked confidently to the front door and rang the bell. It was working. I could hear it chiming far off somewhere in the bowels of the home.

I waited, rang the bell again. Nothing.

Hmmm! Okay, so let's go take a look around the back.

She was by the pool, lying on a lounger, reading a book.

"*Ms. Steiner,*" I shouted, not wanting to frighten her. Well, I frightened her anyway, and oh boy, was she angry!

"*Goddamn it!*" she yelled, jumping to her feet. "You almost gave me a heart attack. Who the hell are you, and how did you get in here?" She walked toward me, sure of herself, her hips swaying, rolling.

My mouth went dry, I swallowed; no, I gulped. The woman was all but naked. The scarlet bikini she was wearing would easily have fit inside my wallet. The top, just two tiny triangles of iridescent material and a couple of feet of ribbon, barely covered her nipples. The bottom, a similar triangle, had to be the front of a thong. Her figure was amazing, a rare symphony of soft curves and mounds that was designed to drive even a strong man wild with desire.

"Um... um...."

"Oh for God's sake, man. Stop looking so stupid. Why are you trespassing on my property?" She had an iPhone in her hand and was already punching in a number.

"Wait!" I said, as I held out my badge and ID for her to see. "I'm Harry Starke, a licensed private investigator working with the Chattanooga Police Department. If you'd like to call this number." I handed one of Kate's business cards to her. "Lieutenant Gazzara will confirm."

"Well, I was wondering when someone would show up." She handed the card back, turned and walked back to the lounger. I was right. It was a thong.

She was barefoot, and bare assed, maybe five feet eight tall, blonde hair tied back in a ponytail that hung at least two feet down her back. Her heart-shaped face was accentuated by high, prominent cheekbones and a pair of startling blue eyes. She was about thirty-five, maybe as much as thirty-eight. As far as I could tell, she was a true blonde.

"Mr... Starke, was it? Yes, I've heard of you. Who around here hasn't? Pour yourself a glass of tea and sit down. Pour one for me, too, if you don't mind. Oh, and please try to keep your eye balls in their sockets."

"You're asking for a whole lot more than I can manage," I said, with a smile, as I poured. "The tea is easy, the eyes... I'm sorry, they're out of my control. Why don't you just put something on? Don't you have a robe or something?"

At that, she smiled, looked up at me, and breathed deeply. It was devastating.

How the hell is she keeping that thing on, and why bother anyway?

"I wear it out of a false sense of modesty," she said.

Damn. She's a mind reader.

"Oh, don't look so startled. The way you were staring at me, it was obvious what was going through your mind. Look, this is my home. I can wear what I like, or nothing at all, if I so desire. It's supposed to be private. You're the intruder. If you don't like what you see... well, you know what you can do. Tell me: *do* you like what you see, Mr. Starke? I think maybe you do."

I shook my head, took a long drink from the glass of iced tea, and then said, "Look, Ms. Steiner–"

"It's Mrs.," she interrupted, "but you can call me Jess, that's short for Jessica."

"Okay... Jessica," I said. "I'd like to ask you some questions, if you don't mind. You say you're married. Where is your husband?"

"Widowed. My husband, John, died in a car accident two years ago."

I was already sweating from the heat of the early afternoon sun, and she could see that I was uncomfortable.

"There are some swimsuits in the pool house. Why don't you go and find one that will fit you... or... maybe you'd like to go *au naturale*? It's too hot for clothing, don't you think? Maybe you'd like to swim."

Geez, I would love to. Au naturale? I could do that, but this is not the time.

I stood, took off my jacket and the rig that held my M&P9, and dropped them onto a vacant lounger. Now I felt a little better. I was wearing a golf shirt and a pair of lightweight pants. I could almost feel her eyes on my back as I laid the jacket and gun down.

"Disappointing," she said, looking at me through her eyelashes. "I'm sure you look wonderful wearing nothing... but a swimsuit."

I had to smile. Under any other circumstances I'd have been glad to join her in her little game.

"Okay, Jessica. You've had your fun. Now let's be serious for a moment. You don't look at all bothered about what's happened to the fund or, and I'm sure one of the other partners has told you about it, Tom Sattler's death. Why not?"

She shrugged. "It is what it is. I learned from my father, many years ago, that it's pointless worrying about things you can't change. The money has gone. I didn't steal it. Tom is dead. I didn't kill him. I've done nothing wrong. What's to worry about?"

"What was your relationship to Tom Sattler?"

"Other than as a business partner, I didn't have one."

"When did you last speak to him?"

"We had lunch together, me, Marty and Tom, on Tuesday, but I last spoke to him on Tuesday evening, at a little after seven-thirty. He was in a bit of a state. He told me what had happened, that the money was gone, then he hung up, and I haven't heard from him since."

"You had lunch with him. What time was that?"

"It was around one o'clock. After I left, I did some errands and arrived back here a little after six, I think it was."

"And James Westwood? When did you last talk to him?"

"Right after I talked to Tom. It would have been around 7:45."

"That's what he told me. He said you were going to call him back. Why didn't you?"

She shrugged, dropped her eyes, turned her head, and looked off into the distance

"I'm not sure," she said. "There really was no reason why I should. The money was gone and, knowing what I know about such things, I was sure it was gone for good. So why bother... and I don't like James Westwood anyway."

"Why don't you like him?"

"He's a phony; full of shit. Likes to play the game, but doesn't have the balls for it."

"Game? What game?"

"High finance. He looks and acts the part, but it was Tom and I who made it all happen. The other two were just along for the ride."

"I take it you didn't like, Marty Cassell either."

"Oh he's not so bad. He has a good nose for investments, and he made a few good trades. He also brought some heavy investors into the fund. It was his friends I didn't care for.

"Sal De Luca?"

She smiled. "Yeah, that one. He's a crook. Not only that, for the past year he's been trying his damndest to get into my pants. He seems to think that because he has a little money invested with the company it gives him the right to screw the management, literally. It will never happen... You... on the other hand...."

I had my glass of tea up to my mouth. I almost choked. It went up my nose and down into my lungs. I thought I would drown. I coughed and spluttered, all to the inimitable Jessica Steiner's delight. She lay back on the lounger and laughed, her body undulating and shaking. That on its own was unnerving; the idea of what she seemed to be suggesting was something else again. I tried to ignore it.

"Jessica, did you know how to get into Sattler's...."

At that she went into another peal of laughter.

"Dammit, Jessica, I'm talking about his computers. Did you know his access codes?"

"All right... all right. Just give me a minute.... Yes, I did. We all did. Whew. That was fun." She took another minute, calmed down, drank some more tea, looked at me, and began to giggle again. I glared at her, but it was infectious, and then both of us were laughing. Finally, she got ahold of herself, shook her head, and continued.

"We all knew each other's codes.... Whew. It was a precaution; in case something happened to one of us."

"When I talked to James Westwood, he said the individual codes were secret. You're telling me different?"

"Harry. I can call you Harry, can't I?" I nodded. "Harry,

the codes *were, are,* secret, to outsiders, but we all know each other's. It made good sense. I don't know why he would tell you different."

"When you were at his home, was anyone else there other than you and Cassell?"

"That silly little girlfriend of his had prepared lunch. Wendy, I think her name is. She left just after we arrived. It was awful; she was awful, but then, Tom always did like his women a little toward the low end of the social ladder. Silly man."

"Did you have access to his computers?"

"No of course not, at least not then. I could have, had there been a need. I have in the past. Why do you ask?"

"We know that the wire transfer was made from his laptop computer late that afternoon. From what you're telling me, any one of the four of you could have done it."

She nodded, thoughtfully. "That's true, I suppose, but there are several people beside us who had easier access than we did. The family, for instance. The girlfriend and dear Gloria's toy boy."

"So you're telling me that he let anyone use his computers, even though they contained sensitive financial information?"

"Tom was like that. He was a dear in some respects, a complete dolt in others."

"Oh. Why do you say that?"

"For one thing, he had a total lack of any sense of security. I don't think Tom stole the money; not for a minute, but I'm not surprised it was his laptop that was used to make the transfer. Then there's the way he was with his kids, and his stupid girlfriend. He let them get away with murder, especially the little one, Nicola...." She paused, took a sip from her glass, stared absently at the pool.

"Go on," I said.

"Well, he never would make them mind, do as they were told, any of them, including Wendy, or whatever her name is. Money? He handed it out like candy. Have you seen the car that eldest girl of his is driving? It's an SL550 convertible for God's sake, red. They start at around $110,000, and the girlfriend drives a Beemer. He was pathetic where women and money was concerned."

"Tell me about New Vision, Jessica."

"Tell you what? It's a private equity fund. There's nothing complicated about it. People invest in the fund and in return are paid a dividend. In this case at an annual rate of eight percent."

"And that was the problem, wasn't it, Jessica? The fund was not generating enough to make the monthly payouts. It was about to turn into a Ponzi, right?"

"Absolutely not. The markets had collapsed, and we were behind on the dividends, which is why we decided to liquidate the bulk of the equity and reinvest it. Up until that point, we had not used a dime of old or new principal to pay dividends, which is why we were behind. We, none of us, broke the law. Nor did we ever have any intention of doing so."

"Talking of money," I said. "How about you? How did the loss of the $350 million effect you?"

"It didn't. I am independently wealthy. My husband, John, left me quite well off. He was one of *the* Steiners, you know."

I didn't, but what the hell. It sounded impressive.

"This house is paid for," she continued, "and apart from taxes, I've never spent a penny I earned from administrating the fund for the five years I was a partner. I'm a wealthy woman, Harry." The way she said that last part could easily have been taken as another invitation, but to what?

"Who do you think stole the money, Jessica?"

She shook her head. "I have no idea, but if I had to guess, it would be Marty, or James, or both."

"Did you steal it?"

She laughed, quietly, a delightful, teasing chuckle. "Now why would I do that? I just told you, I'm a very wealthy woman."

"Wealthy or not," I said. "For some people, more is better;

much more is ideal. Where were you on Tuesday night, between nine-thirty and eleven?"

"Let me see... oh yes. I was here. All by myself. I told you Tom called me. I was here from then until I went to bed, at around eleven o'clock."

She lay back on the lounger, shielded her eyes with her hands, and breathed slowly. Her chest rose and fell with a rhythm I would have been happy to sit and watch for the rest of the day, but it lasted only for a moment.

"I'm hot," she said, getting to her feet. "I'm going to swim. Are you sure you won't join me?"

As I watched her walk to the poolside, I have to admit it; I hesitated. From the back, she looked naked, and it was a beautiful sight. Her body shape was close to perfection, right up there with Kate, Linda and poor, dead Charlie Maxwell.

I sat on the edge of the lounger and watched. She dived cleanly into the water, swam swiftly to the far end and back again and surged up and out of the water like a seal. She stood glistening in the sunlight, hands above her head, wringing the water from her hair, looking at me, smiling. Fat droplets of water coursed down her body, hundreds of tiny diamonds glittering against her bronze skin. She was breathing deeply, her chest rising and falling.

Dammit. This is just too much. I gotta get outa here before I do something I'll regret.

I rose from the lounger, slipped into my rig, draped my jacket over my shoulder, placed one of my cards on the table, waved her goodbye, and then turned and walked away.

"Harry, wait."

She trotted toward me. It was an exhibition of the very finest in human engineering.

"You can't get out, unless you climb the wall again. Here, give me your phone." I gave it to her and watched as she punched in a number. "There, that's my private cell number. Please, give me a call... anytime. Now. I'll open the gate and let you out."

It was just after four o'clock when I got back to the office. To be honest, I'd had enough for the day, let alone the week. My time with Jessica Steiner had taken every bit of what little energy I had left. I waved at my staff, gave orders not to be disturbed, went into my office and poured myself a stiff shot of Laphroaig Quarter Cask Scotch Whisky.

I sat down at my desk, leaned back in the chair, closed my eyes, and let the world go away, at least for the moment. Then I leaned forward again, took out the pad with my notes in it, and flipped it open. I could now update it some. First though, I read it through, refresh my memory.

Thursday, 6p.m.

So, where do I go from here? Basics! Motive, opportunity, means. Okay, good. What's the motive?

Motive:

1. 1Financial - The money's gone, so yes.
2. 2Revenge - Possibly: Sal? Nope. That would lose him his money. Anybody else? Unknown at this point.
3. 3Greed - Again, the money

Opportunity:

Who could have had the opportunity? Hmmmm.

1. The three partners for sure: Cassell, Westwood and Steiner.
2. The wife, Gloria? Yes, and the boyfriend, Richard. Can't leave out the eldest daughter, either.
3. Sattler's girlfriend Wendy? Eeeee... don't know, but doesn't seem likely.
4. Sal? Nope. He wouldn't get his hands dirty. Gino or Tony? Yep.
5. The investors? Yes, but unlikely, except for Sal.

Means?

Who out of the above could have had access to Tom's gun? Geeze! Any one of them, or all of them, given the right circumstances.

And those circumstances would be? Being alone with Tom between 9:30 and 10:30.

Hmmmm. What about the computers? Who would have access to them? See all of the above, but that would not be tied to the time and date. It could have been anytime up to and including the hour when he died.

Okay, so who would have had access to Tom's access codes?

The partners, family, girlfriend. That could mean as many as seven, maybe more, could have wired the money, but how many of them would know how? Shit. All seven could, and all seven could have had opportunity, and all seven could have had the means. Damn. This is going nowhere

I don't think Sal would have risked losing his twelve mil.

Okay. We need to know more. A lot more, and we won't until we've interviewed all the suspects, including the five disgruntled investors that we know of so far.

I stared at the pages, flipped back and forth a couple of times, and stared some more; it made no more sense that it did when I wrote it. Okay, so now what?

I began to write.

Friday 5:30p.m.

What's new? I tapped my teeth with the pen, and then began.

Marty Cassell

Sneaky piece of work. A liar. Knew Sattler's codes. Had access to Sattler, gun, computers. Has the technical knowledge to make the transfer. Is deep in debt to Sal De Luca. Motive? Yes. He needed cash to pay De Luca. De Luca knew the fund was in trouble because dividends were late, and his request for liquidity had been ignored. He couldn't get it without stealing it because the other partners would not authorize such a large payout. Right now, he's our best bet for the wire transfer, and for killing Tom. It makes sense.

James Westwood

Slick, superficial, evasive, dirty, a liar, a crook. Knew Sattler's codes, and he, too, had access to Sattler, gun, computers. Also has the technical knowledge to make the transfer. Motive? Unknown at this point.

Jessica Steiner

A rare one. Confident, smart, evasive, extremely wealthy. Is she a liar? I don't know. Maybe. She's hard to read. She doesn't like Westwood. She doesn't like Cassell either, but to a lesser degree. She thinks Wendy Brewer is a bimbo, and that Stephanie Sattler and the other two kids are spoiled rotten.

She also knew Sattler's codes, and she, too, had access to Sattler's gun, computers. She, also, has the technical knowledge to make the transfer. Motive? Possibly, but what it would be, I have no idea. Greed? Power?

Revenge? I don't know. Opportunity? Yes. She has no alibi.

Wendy Brewer

A sad piece of work. Can't see her killing her bankroll. Devastated. Know how? Yes. Opportunity? Possibly. Means? Yes, she had access to gun, laptop.

Gloria Sattler.

Know how? I don't know. Means? Probably. Motive? Yes, revenge. Hatred.

Is there a will? The estate? Who benefits. Just the children - Stephanie Sattler.

Stephanie Sattler? Wow, I have no idea. ????

It looks like that, with the possible exception of Cassell, the partners are innocent of wrongdoing, at least as far as New Vision is concerned, but any one of them could have stolen the cash, and any one of them could have killed Sattler.

Conclusions: None. I don't know not nothin', dammit.

Whew, it's time I was out of here.

I closed the legal pad, turned off my iPad, shoved back my chair, hesitated, then rolled the chair back up to the desk.

I looked at the pad again, opened it, glanced at what I'd written, shook my head, closed it again, and slipped it into my briefcase. I was almost ready to leave, but first I had a call to make. I needed to go over it all with Kate, and we still had one more priority interview to complete.

"Kate?"

"Hi, Harry. I thought you would be headed home by now."

"No. Not just yet. Listen, I have a few things we need to go over. I went to see Jessica Steiner today–"

"Harry, no," she interrupted. "Not tonight, *pleeease*. I need some time off. I was just about to leave the office and go home. Can we do it tomorrow morning? I'll meet you somewhere. Will that work?"

"Damn it, Kate. This is important, and we still have Hollins to see. I was planning on doing that tonight, and I was also hoping that you could come with me."

"Harry. I need some damned rest. I feel like I haven't slept for days. Give me a break, will you, please? I'll meet you tomorrow morning."

"Okay. How about this. Why don't I drop by the Pizza Hut then come over to your place? We can eat and run through my notes."

There was a moment of silence, and then, quietly, "No, Harry. I don't think that would be a good idea. I know you: pizza first, and then...."

"Oh, for God's sake, Kate...."

"Tomorrow, Harry. Tomorrow!"

"Okay. I guess that will have to do. What time? Where?"

"Well, I don't want to drag you *too* far away from home. Any ideas?"

"Kate, cut the sarcasm. It doesn't become you. Panera at Northgate. Ten o'clock. In the meantime, I'll see if I can figure something out."

"Fine. I'll see you at ten. Bye. Have a won...derful evening."

Sheesh. She can be a.... Can't say I blame her.

There was a time when... I thought I was in love with Kate, and she with me. We had been an item for as long as I could remember, until senator Linda Michaels came along that is. She'd forgiven me a lot of sins and transgressions over the years, but not that one.

Oh well, maybe it's for the best.

Suddenly, my get up and go got up and went. I looked at my watch. It was well after six. *Screw it. I'll get me a pizza and go home. She ain't the only one who needs some rest. Pizza, Blue Moon, sofa, quiet music... sounds like a plan.*

Chapter Fifteen

❧

On the way home, I stopped by Food City, grabbed a six-pack of Blue Moon beer, then hit the drive through at the Pizza Hut. Ten minutes later, I was back on the road and heading home, a steaming hot Large Supreme on the passenger seat.

I have a condo on the north side of the river, on Lakeshore Lane. I bought it five years ago. It cost me a small fortune, and another one to decorate and furnish. It truly was my home: comfortable, elegant, with a stunning view of the mighty Tennessee and, in the distance, the Thrasher Bridge. At night, the view from the great picture window was stunning, and to me worth every penny the condo had cost.

It was just after seven o'clock when I arrived home, still light, and almost unbearably hot. I hit the garage door button and drove inside. I gathered up the pizza and the beer, struggled a little to get the door open, then backed inside and headed up the stairs to the kitchen.

I dropped the pizza on the breakfast bar, slipped the beer into the refrigerator, then went into the bedroom, stripped and hopped into the shower.

Ten minutes later, wearing only a pair of boxers and a T-shirt, I poured myself a beer and opened the pizza box... and then my iPhone rang.

I flipped the lockscreen, looked at the name, and sighed.

"Hello, Amanda."

"Harry. We need to talk. Where are you?"

"I'm at home, done for the day, finished, it's over until tomorrow, no more work until after eight in the morning. Got it? Sorry, Amanda."

"Don't be silly. Where's home? I'm already on the road."

"Amanda, I'm dressed ready for bed...." *Ouch, wrong thing to say.* "I'm about to eat. Can't it wait?"

Did she just chuckle?

"No, Harry. Give me your address, please."

Whew, no peace for.... Well, I could make the best of it, I suppose.

I gave her the address.

"Wonderful. I know where that is. See you in a few minutes. Save some food for me." She disconnected.

I just had time to change into something a little more fitting, lightweight tan slacks, a black golf shirt, and loafers. I'd barely finished when she knocked at the door. When I saw her, I didn't regret giving her my address one bit.

"That was quick. You must have been quite close."

She grinned. "I cheated. I rang your office, but got the answering machine, so I figured you might be here. I already knew where you lived. I was on 153 when I called you. I have the night off."

Damn. Wow, look at her.

The pale blue, soft leather clutch she carried perfectly matched the skimpy, strapless cotton sundress. Other than a pair of matching sandals, as far as I could tell, she wore little else. Amanda Cole is one of those rare women who looks good no matter what they wear.

"So, what are we eating?" she said, as she sent the clutch spinning into one of the easy chairs in the living room and hoisted herself up onto one of the stools at the breakfast bar.

"Er... not much. I grabbed a pizza and beer on the way home. You're welcome–"

"Perfect," she interrupted. "I haven't had pizza in years...

well, weeks. Not so keen on beer, though. Do you have wine?"

"Of course," I said, as I laid two plates and a small pile of paper napkins on the bar top. "I have a nice Riesling, Pinot Noir, or Cabernet. Which do you prefer?"

"Hmmm, why don't you surprise me?"

"My pleasure, ma'am."

I'd had a half-dozen bottles of Niersteiner Spiegelberg Riesling in the cooler for a couple of months. It was about time I opened one of them, or maybe two. Okay, I admit it. I'd had that kiss I gave her on Wednesday evening on my mind almost ever since. I'd almost called her a couple of times, but then thought better of it. Now here she was, and the evening was, without doubt, full of promise.

I poured a glass of the wine and set it in front of her, pushed the pizza box toward her, and then opened a bottle of beer for me. Then I sat down on the stool in front of her, on the same side of the breakfast bar. She had her feet on the crossbar of her stool, crossed at the ankles. The hem of her dress had ridden up and she was showing a generous expanse of what was perhaps the loveliest pair of thighs I'd seen since Linda left for Washington more than two months ago.

She sipped her wine, lowered the glass, looked at the liquid, tilted her head, nodded, and said, "Nice."

"Yes, nice." I wasn't talking about the wine.

She set the glass down, pushed her plate away, slid off the stool, stepped forward, slid her arms around my neck, leaned in close, and kissed me. It was a long, lingering kiss, lips slightly parted, her tongue timidly probing mine. She tasted of sweet white wine, her lips were cold, inviting.

She held the kiss for what seemed to me like minutes. I was totally lost in the moment, and totally involved in it.

She leaned back, her hands still clasped behind my neck, and looked into my eyes.

Dammit, she's laughing at me.

"Harry. I've been wanting to do that for almost a year, since long before you busted Congressman Harper."

"Wow," I said, somewhat breathlessly, "I hope it was worth the wait."

"Oh, sweetie. It was, and then some. I hope it was as good for you as it was for me."

I nodded, groped for my bottle of beer, hooked it up under her arm, and took a huge mouthful. She laughed. Her breath washed over my face like a fresh, fragrant cloud, and then she broke her hold, stepped back, and remounted the stool. The remount was a stunning piece of performance art.

How the hell do they do that?

"Suddenly, Harry, I'm not very hungry. Can we go and sit on the sofa and look at the river?"

We could, and we did. I tossed my empty bottle into the garbage can, poured two glasses of wine, grabbed them both, and the bottle and we headed for the sofa. She kicked off the sandals and sat down, drew her legs up underneath her, and settled back into the cushions like a great, tawny cat. She stared up at me, her pale green eyes half closed, and patted the spot beside her. I nodded, picked up the remote, and dimmed the lights.

We sat, we talked, we enjoyed the view, she laid her head on my shoulder, and we drank what was left of the wine. I opened another bottle, and we drank that, too. I don't know about her, but I was intoxicated, and not because of the wine. This woman was very special. I couldn't believe that I'd been avoiding her for all these years.

Yes, you can. Remember the hatchet job she did on you?

And that thought brought me back to my senses, temporarily, at least.

"Amanda." I sat up and looked at her. She had what I could only assume was a contented smile on her face. "You didn't come here because you needed to talk to me, did you?"

"Harry... you men are so gullible. Of course I wanted to talk to you, but, well, the moment just seemed to take over. Suddenly what I had in mind didn't seem so important anymore. Now, go get us some more wine and then come sit beside me."

Okay, so what the hell would you have done?

I went and fetched the wine, poured two more glasses, and sat down beside her.

"Harry."

"Mmmm?"

"Talk dirty to me."

"*Aagh!*" She shrieked as I choked and sprayed wine out of my mouth all over her.

"Oh my God," she laughed. She wiped her cheek with her hand, tried to flip the wine off her dress.

"Here, let me do that," I said, taking a gentle swipe at her left breast.

"Get away from me, you brute," she giggled. "Oh my God. I'm soaked. Harry, I need to use the bathroom."

"It's through there."

I heard the toilet flush, and then the water running.

"Harry, I need a hand, please."

Oh I just bet you do.

I took my time, rose from the sofa, walked to the open bedroom door, my glass dangling from my hand. I leaned against the doorjamb and looked at her.

She was on the bed; her head on the pillows, her hair a golden halo. She was naked, and she was exquisitely beautiful.

"Dress too wet?" I said.

She nodded, slowly, and smirked.

"I thought you said you needed a hand," I said, innocently.

"I need more than a hand, you ass, and you'd better be damned quick about providing it. Now for God's sake get out of those clothes before you burst out of them."

Well, I didn't want to do that, now did I?

Neither of us got much sleep. It was, as they say, a night to remember, and I will.

The next morning, we woke in a tangle of legs, arms and bedsheets to bright sunshine blazing in through the bedroom window. She lay there, on her back, her arms over her head, eyes, closed, breathing slowly, like a contented kitten. I got out of bed. She opened one eye and looked sleepily up at me.

"Coffee, please, and don't be too long. I'm not done with you yet."

I gave her a grin of which the Big Bad Wolf would have been proud.

I went into the bathroom, did the necessary, swilled cold water on my face, brushed my teeth, wrapped a towel around my waist, and went to the kitchen. When I returned with the coffee, she was already back in bed, the sheet pulled up to her neck.

I placed one of the cups on the table on her side of the bed. I was putting mine down when I noticed the time on the bedside clock. It was 9:15. *Dammit. I'm supposed to meet Kate at ten.*

"Amanda, I need to call Kate Gazzara. I'm supposed to meet her at ten. I need to call her and cancel. I'll be just a minute."

I went back out into the kitchen and made the call.

"Kate," I said. "Something's come up. I can't make it this morning... no... no, I don't want to talk about it over the phone. I'll call you on Monday. Gotta go, bye."

You're right. I didn't give her any chance at all to question me.

"Wow, you canceled the lovely lieutenant for me. I'm honored."

"My pleasure, ma'am. Now tell me, what do you plan to do with the rest of the weekend? Don't you have to work?"

"Oh, I'm all yours, Harry. Last night was... wonderful, and I want it to go on and on. No, I don't have to work. The station has a weekend crew. So we can spend it together, if that's what you want."

Silly question. Of course I do.

"Okay," I said. "So I have an idea. I have a cabin up in the mountains near Blue Ridge. How about we go up there and spend the weekend together?"

She stuck out her lower lip and frowned. "But I don't have any clothes, other than my dress and panties."

"Hell, who needs clothes? You're right though. Maybe we'll go out to eat.... Nah. How about we stop off at your place? You can grab a pair of jeans and whatever. You don't need toiletries. I have plenty, and steaks and wine. No phones, no TV, just you and me and the wild, wild, woods."

"Okay, we'll do it, but first...." She threw off the sheet and opened her arms.

We arrived at the cabin at a little after one o'clock in the afternoon. We spent the rest of the day hiking the woodland trails, watching the deer, and breathing the fresh mountain air. That evening I cooked steaks outdoors on the grill. By ten o'clock, we were in the hot tub under a full moon. At eleven, we flopped into bed and made love.

It was an idyllic weekend. I didn't realize just how much I'd needed a break, or the company of a wonderful woman. Unfortunately, as all good things do, it had to come to an end. Amanda had to be at the station by seven on Monday morning; I had to be in the office by eight.

Chapter Sixteen

That Monday morning, I hadn't been in the office more than ten minutes when my cell phone rang.

"Harry. It's Amanda. It's hit the fan. It's on the national news. Fox has it. I can't keep it under wraps any longer. I need to give the public something, and I need to do it in the next few minutes; they are holding me over."

"I understand. Give me a minute or two and I'll call you right back."

"Don't be long, Harry. I'm under pressure here."

I called Kate. She was as mad as hell.

"Where the hell have you been? I've been trying to reach you all weekend."

"Calm down, Kate. I decided I needed a rest, too, so I decided to follow your lead and take the weekend off."

"Oh yeah? And who was the lucky woman? Not Jessica Steiner, I hope."

"Are you nuts, Kate? That would not be ethical. I went up to the cabin. Look, I have Amanda Cole holding on the other line. She's gnashing her teeth. The shit has hit the fan. The news of the theft of the money has gone national and she needs something to give the public. This is what I'm thinking."

I outlined what I thought needed to be said, and what I thought should be kept back, namely the fact that Sattler was murdered.

Reluctantly, Kate agreed. I also suggested she come on over to my office, and that I would have Amanda join us after her broadcast. That done, I called Amanda and gave her a few suggestions, knowing that she was the ultimate pro and would be able to flesh it out and fill in the gaps.

That done, I turned on the TV in my cave and flipped to Channel 7, just in time to see the local morning anchor announce breaking news. I hit the record button on the cable box,

"Good Morning. This is Michael Webb with Channel 7 News A.M. Please standby for breaking news. Let's go straight to Amanda Cole. Amanda, what do you have for us?"

"Thank you, Michael. According to reliable sources, Channel 7 News has confirmed that there are major problems with the locally managed equity fund, New

Vision Strategic Investments. Sources close to the investigation have informed me that more than $350 million in liquid capital has disappeared, stolen, and that the managing partner of New Vision, Thomas Sattler, is dead as the result of a self-inflicted gunshot wound. It is not yet known what effect the loss will have on the fund's shareholders, but I have been assured that it will be significant. Many local investors, some of them retired, rely on their monthly dividend checks from New Vision to supplement their retirement income. Some have their life savings invested in the fund.

"We have also learned that local police are convinced that the apparent suicide of New Vision's senior fund manager is somehow linked to the money's disappearance. The New Vision offices are now locked. The FBI is involved and the SEC has frozen the fund and will not comment, but it's clear that the consequences of this enormous theft will be far reaching and will impact many local investors, such as Betsy Calder, whom I have here with me now."

The lady standing beside her had been chosen with care. She could not have been more than five feet two inches tall. She was overweight, gray-haired, and obviously very distraught.

Damn, Amanda. What you people won't do for ratings.

"Mrs. Calder, could you please tell us how this awful thing that has happened will affect you and your future?"

The poor woman's face was wet from crying. "I don't know how I'll manage," she blubbered. "I'm a widow. I'm sixty-six years old. The only other income I have is my social security. Without my monthly check from Mr. Sattler, I won't be able to pay my bills. I'll lose my home."

"How much do you have invested in the fund?"

"Everything. All of our savings. Mr. Sattler was a friend of my son. I trusted him. I don't know what I'll do now. I... I... I'm sorry." She turned and walked away.

"I'll be sure to keep you updated as the situation unfolds. For now, back to you, Michael. This is Amanda Cole outside the New Vision office."

Thirty minutes later, the three of us were seated together in my office. Kate was in a filthy mood. Amanda was flushed, fidgety. If I didn't know better, I would have thought she was on something.

I hit the play button on the remote, and Amanda's broadcast came up on the flat screen. We watched in silence. I hit the button and turned the unit off.

"Any comments, anyone?" I said.

"That was the worst piece of so-called journalism I've seen in a long time," Kate said, shaking her head.

"I hate to say it, but I agree with you," Amanda said, and it was easy to see now what was wrong with her.

"I had no advance notice, and the whole thing was engineered by my producer and that dick-head Michael Webb. All I did was add what little content you guys supplied. I apologize for the crappy job I did with it, but I was up against the clock and had no time to do anything else."

"Wow," Kate said, "There's one for the books, an apology from the media. Must make a note of it for future reference."

Whoa. That's bitchy. She knows I spent the weekend with her.

"So what now?" Amanda said.

For more than an hour, we discussed the situation, then Kate had to leave. We arranged to meet later, after lunch, in the conference room. I was hoping there might be some news from Tim.

"I don't think she likes me," Amanda said, as Kate closed the door behind her.

"Hell," I said. "She doesn't seem to like anybody these days."

"She knows, about us. You do know that, right?"

"Yeah, I figured as much. Can't be helped."

"You two were together a long time?"

"More than ten years."

"What happened?"

"Senator Michaels happened.... No, that's not entirely true. She was a big part of it, but it was something else that finally pushed her over the edge, Kate, I mean. I don't want to talk about it. It was stupid, and I regret it."

"You regret having an affair with Senator Michaels?"

"It's not an affair. Neither one of us is married, and she's a friend, a good friend."

"Yes, but–"

"No buts, Amanda," I interrupted. "My dealings with Linda are personal and no one's business but our own. So let's leave it, shall we?"

"Er... no."

"What do you mean no?"

"Harry, you and I just spent a wonderful weekend together. If you're still involved with Michaels, what was that all about?"

I heaved a huge sigh. "The truth is, I have no friggin' idea. I'm not in love with the woman, nor she with me, and I haven't seen her in more than two months. She was supposed to have been here this last weekend, but she cancelled. We talk on the phone, a lot, but she's very busy, and so am I for that matter. Our schedules just don't seem to gel." I shrugged, tried to look helpless, but I'm not sure how it came off.

"I see...." She stared at me. "So where do I fit into this... this.... I dunno what to call it."

I grimaced, stared back at her. "Amanda. A week ago, if anyone would have told me that I would be even the tiniest bit involved with you, I would have laughed in their face.... The truth is, now it's happened, I kinda like it." I shrugged again. "I'd like to continue seeing you. I won't make any promises, but...." I let it trail off, watching her.

She sat there for a moment, seemingly lost in thought, then grinned. "Sure. Why not? That was one hell of a weekend."

She got up out of her chair, walked around my desk, hitched up her skirt, straddled me, put her arms around my neck, and kissed me. It was a long, lingering, utterly erotic kiss that, had we not been in my office with a full staff in the next room, would certainly have led to an afternoon of wild sex and absolute abandon.

It lasted all of two minutes, and when she finally lifted her lips from mine, we were both breathing hard. She had a strange look on her face. It reminded me of a great jungle cat that had just finished a meal of raw meat. She unhooked herself, stood up, straightened her skirt and blouse, then leaned in close again, kissed me gently on the lips, and said, "Later?"

"Yes, please, ma'am."

"I'll call you."

She picked up her iPad and cell phone from my desk, took another deep breath. Then, with hips swinging, she strode purposefully out of my office, through the bullpen, and out through the front door; all without a backward look.

I went into the outer office, ignored the stares, grabbed a cup of Dark Italian Roast from the Keurig, went back into my office, flopped into my chair, put my feet up on the desk, cradled the cup in both hands, closed my eyes, and... smiled. Oh boy, did I ever smile.

It was the middle of the afternoon when she called.

"I have the evening off," Amanda said. "How about you?"

Just like that. No, hello. No, it's Amanda.

"Yeah, I can take the rest of the day off. Dinner at my place? I'll cook something?"

"Oh yeah. I am so damned hungry...." She burst out laughing. "I'll be there at seven. Make sure it's ready for me to eat." She hung up.

Damn. I hope she meant what I think she meant.

She did. Did she ever? It was another night to remember.

Chapter Seventeen

The following morning, Tuesday, we were all in the conference room, including Amanda Cole, when Kate walked through the door and dumped herself down in a chair at the table next to Ronnie. Amanda had arrived just a few minutes earlier. Tim was in his usual seat next to mine. Jacque was at the far end of the table, and Mike, my serious-minded young intern, was seated next to her.

"Good afternoon, Lieutenant," I said dryly. "Why don't you come on in and take a seat?"

She grinned at me, leaned back in her chair, put her hands together behind her neck, and looked around the table.

"Hey, everybody," she said. "The bear's in a good mood this morning, I see. Have I missed anything?"

They all smiled and looked away, in any direction but at me; even I had to smile.

"Okay," I said. "I invited Amanda to be here to keep her in the loop. Amanda. It goes without saying that everything said or discussed here is off the record, right?"

She nodded.

"Okay. Good. Let's get started," I said. "Anyone have anything to say before we do? No? Good. Well, here it is. We're eight days into this thing and we have nothing, just a half-dozen suspects, a few prints, a hair that might or might not have belonged to the killer, and a bunch of prints, all identified, and all with a reason to be where they were, and that's it."

I looked around the table. All was quiet.

"We have no idea who stole the money. It's reasonable to assume, however, that whoever did it, also killed Tom Sattler, right?"

They all nodded.

"You think so?" I asked. "Why? Why would we assume that? Tom was killed between nine-thirty and ten-thirty that evening. The money disappeared at five-thirty. There's a four-hour gap between the two incidents. Is it reasonable to suppose that whoever wired the money got out of there and then came back four hours later to kill him? I don't think so. I think it's entirely possible we're dealing with two perps."

Again, I looked at their faces. Mike's was screwed up in concentration.

"No!" Mike said, excitedly. "Maybe the killer had taken the computer earlier, maybe even one or two days earlier, and transferred the money from another location. Then he sneaked back into the house to return it, the computer, and Tom caught him, and he had to kill him."

I pointed a finger at him. "Good thinking, Mike. We've assumed all along that just because it was Tom's computer, that the wire transfer had to have been made at his home. Not necessarily."

"Yeah, but even if that's true," Kate said, "'it doesn't help any. In fact, it makes the situation even worse. It screws up the timeline completely."

"True," I said, "but it also narrows the field, a little. We know from what Westwood told us, that the laptop was there on Saturday night, as late as ten-thirty, because he used it to check his email. I had Tim check some cell phone records earlier. Only six of our persons of interest were in the Mountain Shadows area between ten-thirty on Saturday and eleven on Tuesday evening: Wendy Brewer, Marty Cassell, Gloria Sattler, Richard Hollins, Stephanie Sattler, and... Jessica Steiner. Any one of them could have taken the laptop. Three of them at least, and possibly all of them, had the technical expertise to make the transfer. So let's take a look at them. Tim, go ahead."

"Okay," Tim said, flipping the screen on his iPad. "I

couldn't pinpoint the locations exactly, just to within a block or two. Gloria Sattler was there the whole three days; so was Richard Hollins, except for a few short occasions, and that's because they live only a few hundred yards away. Stephanie, the same. Wendy was there most of the day on Sunday, and at odd intervals on Monday and Tuesday. Cassell was there on Tuesday around midday. Steiner must have been with him, because she was there at the same time."

"We know they were both there for lunch that day," I said. "They both admitted as much during their interviews, but what about between nine-thirty and ten-thirty on Tuesday night?"

"Only Gloria and Stephanie, again, probably because they were at home. Hollins and Brewer were not in the area during that time frame."

"So, neither Cassell, Wendy Brewer, Richard Hollins, nor Jessica Steiner could have killed him," Mike said. "They weren't there."

I smiled at him. "Nope. We can't say that, Mike. All we can say is that their *cell phones* weren't there. This little exercise just tells us when they *were* there; not when they weren't."

"Oh." He sounded disappointed.

"Amanda," I looked at her, "do you have anything to add?"

"I do, Harry," Amanda said. "I did a little digging into Sattler's divorce."

"Oh yeah? Did you find anything?"

"I did, and it may be significant. They cited irreconcilable differences, but the settlement split was something like eighty/twenty in Gloria's favor, by mutual consent. I wondered why that was, so I nosed through all the old files I could find. Harry, there were hints of child abuse, although it was never proved, and it wasn't brought up during the divorce proceedings."

"Child abuse? You mean he was mistreating the children, physical violence?"

"No. Molestation. Sexual abuse. There are rumors that Sattler was a pedophile."

"Sexual abuse? Pedophile?" I was dumbfounded. "The Tom Sattler I knew never gave any hint that he was into children. Was it outside the family? Boys? Girls? What?"

"I don't know. It was kept very quiet. I will say this though. I'd be surprised if it was outside the family. That would have been very difficult to hush up. His own daughters though. Gloria would not have wanted that to get out."

"Stephanie Sattler? She would have been what, ten or twelve at the time of the divorce?"

"She would have been eleven. The other two, I don't

think so. Nicola would have been a baby and Julie only two. It had to be Stephanie, if at all."

"Geez, that opens up a whole new bag of worms. I had a feeling there was something going on between mother and daughter. It gives the entire family and Hollins motive. Any one of them, Gloria, Stephanie, or Hollins could have killed him. If so, who the hell stole the money?"

"Then there's his girlfriend," Amanda said. "Wendy Brewer. She could only have been fifteen or sixteen when he started his affair with her."

"Shit, I never thought of her, but why? She was besotted with him. She also had the most to lose when he died. I need to get more on her. Tim, you need to take a look at her credit."

"I already did. She's good. No debt, no judgments, she owns her own home, a small one worth maybe $165,000, but it's paid for. She owns her car, a BMW Z4, a gift from Sattler; she has $28,761 in checking. She also has some investments Sattler must have made and managed for her totaling almost $430,000, and her credit score is 810. Not bad for a young single woman."

"Okay, so right now we have to talk to the Sattlers again, both of them, and separately, Cassell, Steiner, and maybe even Brewer. Richard Hollins was supposed to have been out somewhere at the time Sattler was killed, so he may be worth another shot. Kate, you've not yet met Cassell. I think it's time you did, so maybe you should come with me on that one. Can you do that?"

She nodded. "I can, but it needs to be done soon. Chief Johnston is pushing for a solution, and we're not supposed to be working on the theft of the money, just Sattler's murder."

"Okay," I said, "but we know the murder and the loss of the money are somehow linked, at least we think we do."

Hell, no, we don't. Tom could have been killed for any number of reasons.

"Jacque, please call Cassell and make us an appointment, not for me, for Kate. He's more likely to comply with a request from her than me. Tell him you're calling on her behalf, and that it has to be this afternoon. Don't take no for an answer."

Jacque gathered up her notebook and iPad and left the room.

"Okay," I said. "Depending upon whether or not Jacque can set something up with Cassell, we'll need to talk to Steiner and the Sattlers. Kate, you with me?"

"I can do that."

The door opened, and Jacque returned. "Two o'clock this afternoon. He wasn't happy, but he'll be there."

"All right then. Let's go to it. Kate, you want to join me and Amanda for lunch?"

She looked... pissed. She shook her head.

"No? Okay." I looked at my watch. It was almost noon. "How about you pick me up here at one 'o'clock, then? That gives us an hour before we're due. It shouldn't take more than thirty minutes to get up onto Palisades. We'll have a little time to discuss strategy."

"Fine. Later everyone." She leaped up from the table and stalked out of the room.

An hour later, I dropped Amanda off in the lot next to her car. Kate was already waiting, her engine running. The first thing out of her mouth was, "Don't you *ever* do that to me again."

"Don't do what?"

"Ask me to go to lunch with one of your girlfriends."

I grinned at her and was about to make a snide comment about her being jealous, then I saw the look on her face and decided against it.

"Okay." I nodded. "Let's go."

Chapter Eighteen

We arrived at the Cassell residence on Palisades right at two o'clock. We parked out front, walked together up the four steps to the front door, and I thumbed the bell push. We could hear the bell chiming somewhere away in the depths of the house, and we waited. Nothing. I looked at Kate. She shrugged, reached out, and rang the bell again, and we waited. Nothing.

Something's not right. I can feel it.

I tried the doorknob. The door was locked. I hit the bell push again, then again. Still nothing.

"Let's take a look around," I said, opening my jacket to allow access to the M&P9. "You go that way, I'll go this. Yell out, loud, if you find anything."

She nodded.

We met at the rear of the home, in front of the great picture window. I put a finger to my lips and pointed. One of the glass panels was shattered, and the door next to it was wide open.

Kate drew her weapon; so did I. I jacked a shell into the chamber and we stepped through the door into the living room. Cassell was sitting in one of the big leather easy chairs, his head in his hands. He was sobbing quietly, and bleeding; there was blood everywhere.

"Kate. Check the house. Mr. Cassell, can you hear me?" I said, sliding the nine back into the rig.

He took his hands away from his face and looked up at me. I winced. His hands were covered with blood. His face was a mass of bruises; his lips were bloody and the size of sausages. Someone had taken a knife to his ears, both lobes were missing.

"Marty. What the hell happened? Who did this to you?"

He mumbled something I couldn't understand, his swollen lips barely moving.

"*Clear!*" Kate shouted, holstering her Glock as she joined me at Cassell's side.

"What the hell?" she said, when she saw his face.

"Marty, this is Lieutenant Catherine Gazzara, Chattanooga PD. Can you tell us what happened?"

The look he gave me as he shook his head was pitiful to

behold. His eyes, bloodshot and bruised, were mere slits in a face that reminded me of a slab of raw meat.

"You don't know, or you won't say?" Kate said.

He simply shrugged and leaned back in the chair, blood dripping from his damaged ears onto his shoulders, the red and black checkered shirt now more red than black.

"Can you speak?" she asked.

He shook his head.

"We need to get him to a hospital," I said.

"I'll make the call." She walked out of the room, punching 911 into her phone as she went.

"Listen. Marty. I need to know who did this to you. Nod or shake your head, okay?"

He nodded.

"Was it Sal De Luca?"

He shook his head and looked away.

"Okay. Was it Gino or Tony?"

He didn't answer. He pointed to his desk. I walked over to it and looked down, then back at him. He mumbled something that sounded vaguely like 'paper.'

I nodded, searched, found a small note pad and a Sharpie pen. I handed them to him. He wrote something on the pad and handed it back to me; his fingers were stuck to the paper.

They will kill me if I talk to you. It was Gino. Tony held me. Don't say anything. PLEASE. NO POLICE!

"It's okay, Marty. Kate will understand. Was it about the money, Marty?"

He nodded. I handed the pad back to him and touched him lightly on the shoulder. "I got it, Marty. I'll tell De Luca that when I arrived, the ambulance was already here, taking you away, and that you were unconscious. Okay?"

He nodded.

"Can you answer me one question?"

He nodded.

Kate came back. "The paramedics are on the way. How is he?"

"He'll be okay. Messed up a little, but okay. So, Marty, when you had lunch with Sattler; what time did you leave?"

He scribbled on the pad and held it up for me to see. '2 - 2:15.'

"Did Jessica Steiner leave when you did?"

He shrugged his shoulders, and wrote, 'NO.'

"What time did she leave, do you know?"

He shook his head.

"Did you see anyone else while you were there?"

'WENDY.'

"She made lunch, right?"

He nodded.

"When did she leave?"

'1 O'CLOCK.' He shrugged again, dropped the pad onto his lap, leaned back in the chair, and closed his eyes. In the distance, we could hear the sound of sirens approaching fast.

We watched as they loaded him onto the gurney. I squeezed his shoulder. "It will be all right, Marty. I promise."

He just lay there, limp, like a bloody rag and shook his head. Pathetic.

"I promise, Marty."

They loaded him into the ambulance and drove away, lights flashing, sirens howling.

"Son of a bitch," I said, more to myself than to Kate. I'm not going to let them get away with this."

"Who. Who get away with it?"

"De Luca. Who else? You can't do anything. Cassell's scared shitless. He won't talk to you."

"Did he say who did it?"

"He did. It was Gino, ably assisted by the ape, Tony."

"Okay. Let's go talk to them."

"We can't. I promised Marty no police. And, anyway, I can do this better than you. I'll take Bob with me."

"The hell you will. I'm going with you. I can't let De Luca get away with something like this."

"You can, and you will. If De Luca thinks Cassell talked, he'll have him killed. This was just a warning about the money. Besides, Sal doesn't know you're a cop, and I'd like to keep it that way, at least for now. Let me do it my way, okay?"

She stood and thought for a moment, hands on her hips, feet widespread, head down, ponytail hanging down over her left shoulder. Then she looked up at me, twitched her head, and threw her hair back over her shoulder.

"Okay, but for God's sake be careful. Don't kill anyone. If this gets out of hand, I'll be in more shit than a herd of cows at milking time. Don't throw me under the bus, Harry."

"You got it, but De Luca will have to wait, at least for now. We need to get over to Lookout and see Steiner. They may have visited her as well. Do you want to come with me?"

"You'd better believe it. Let's go."

I called both of Steiner's numbers, but she didn't pick up. I didn't like it.

"She's not answering, Kate. I'd better give Westwood a call, make sure he's okay."

I did, and he was. I didn't tell him what had happened to Cassell, but I did tell him to be careful to whom he opened the door, and that I'd call him later, that I needed to see him. He started to question me about what I meant, but I didn't want to frighten him, so I told him it was probably nothing but he should keep his door locked.

Chapter Nineteen

We drove back down Signal Mountain in silence, hit Highway 27, then I-24 to Broad, and from there to the Scenic Highway. We arrived outside the front gate of Steiner's home at three-fifteen that afternoon. Again, the gate was locked and I had to climb over the wall. Kate followed me over. I thumbed the bell push, but no one came to the door. After the last experience, I wasn't inclined to waste time. We drew our weapons and circled the house, together. As before, Jessica Steiner was stretched on a lounger, a pair of headphones over her ears, and... she was naked. Her body jiggled in time with whatever music she was listening to.

We walked around the lounger, guns drawn, and stood in front of her. Her eyes were closed; she didn't know we were there.

Geez. It's at times like these I wish I'd left Kate somewhere else.

"Easy, big boy," Kate said, reading my mind. "That one is way too much for you. She would hurt you."

"Nah. I don't think so."

She opened her eyes. *"What the hell?"* she yelled, startled. She sat up, snatched the headphones from her head and leaped to her feet.

"You son of a bitch, Starke," she shouted. "That's twice you've crept up on me like some goddamn pervert. Who the hell is she?"

I have to tell you: she was quite a sight, a magnificent creature, a stunning vision of angry womanhood. I so wished I was there alone.

"I'm sorry, Ms. Steiner. I wouldn't be here if it wasn't an emergency. Marty Cassell is in hospital. Someone has done a job on him, taken him apart. You didn't answer your phone and we wanted to... well, we wanted to make sure you were okay, which I see you certainly are," I finished, with a smile.

She wasn't the slightest bit abashed, or embarrassed, nor did she make any attempt to cover herself up.

"Marty? Is he okay?" She sounded worried, but....

"No, he's hurt pretty bad, but he'll live. This, by the way, is Lieutenant Catherine Gazzara, Chattanooga PD."

The two women nodded to each other. Kate didn't seem to be able to take her eyes off the woman. Her mouth was open, and, if she'd been a man, I'd have sworn she was drooling, but I knew better. Kate isn't gay; that I know for sure.

"You two need a drink? There's iced tea in the pool house."

Neither of us did.

"Okay, let's go sit in the shade, over there." She nodded to a table with four chairs and an umbrella. She picked up a towel from the lounger, draped it over her arm, and led the way, still 'buck nekid,' as they say.

Wow. Thank you, Jessica.

Now, I've always had a thing for the way women walk, especially when viewed from the rear. I love it. They somehow have a way of turning the human body into an undulating, rolling thing of beauty. What this woman did with her body was way out of the box. At thirty-eight years old, she was fit, trim, had a six-pack of muscles any bodybuilder would have been proud of, and her breasts needed no help from anyone, Mother Nature included. Viewed from the rear, however, she was a goddess, with a walk that would have rivaled Naomi Campbell's.

She draped the towel over the seat and sat down. We followed suit. It was the first time I ever interviewed a woman dressed only in her skin; it was more than a little unnerving.

"So, who beat the hell out of Marty?" she asked.

"We don't know," I said before Kate could answer, "but it's a sure bet it had something to do with the money."

"Sal De Luca, probably," she said, not the least perturbed by the idea.

"Aren't you bothered he might come after you?" Kate said.

"Why should I be? I didn't handle that account. Looks like he has the man he wants."

"For now he does," I said, "but when he gets it into his head that Marty is not going to be able to produce, he'll go after the next in line, which is either you or Westwood."

"Right," Kate said, "and I would not want to be you if it's you they choose. You greet them looking like that, and well... you'll get more than a beating. You get the idea, I'm sure."

"Hmmm. Might not be so bad. I could do with a good man. Yours doesn't seem to be interested."

That took my breath away, and I could feel myself coloring up. Kate grinned.

Oh yeah, Kate. That's funny. Real funny.

"Oh, I don't know," Kate said. "He was always ready, willing and *more than able* when I wanted him."

Geez, Kate. That's way over the line.

"Okay, both of you," I said. "That's enough. Ms. Steiner, I was coming to see you anyway. Tom Sattler did not commit suicide. He was murdered, and I have some questions I need to ask."

"*Murdered?* Murdered?"

"Yes. He was shot in the head at close range. The scene was arranged to make it look like suicide."

"Shit," she said quietly, and leaned back in her chair. Her breasts rose and fell as she breathed. It was getting difficult to concentrate.

"When I was here last time, I asked you when you last saw Tom Sattler. You said you spoke to him on the phone that Tuesday evening. I know from your cell phone records that you were there, in his house that day, from noon until at least five o'clock that afternoon. Why didn't you tell me that?"

"You tracked my cell phone? What the hell is that all about? *He was murdered?*"

She didn't seem to be able to grasp the idea, much less believe it.

"We tracked the phones of all persons of interest," Kate said, still staring at her. "It's routine; nothing personal."

"It's damned intrusive, is what it is," Steiner said. "Anyway, Mr. Starke, you didn't ask me when I last saw him.

You asked when I last *spoke* to him, and I told you the truth. Look, I learned a long time ago, from a very smart man, always to answer questions as they are asked, and never to volunteer extraneous information; it can get you into trouble. Anyway, to answer your question, Tom asked us all to drop by for lunch and to discuss the fund shortfalls. I arrived just before one o'clock. Marty was already there. James had called earlier and said he couldn't make it. We talked for almost an hour, and then Marty left. I left a little later. I don't know what time."

"I need you to tell me exactly what time you left Tom Sattler that afternoon?" I said.

"I told you before, I can't remember, and please stop goddamn staring at me, both of you."

"Then cover yourself up," Kate said, without taking her eyes off her.

Steiner rose to her feet, grabbed the towel from the chair, wrapped it around her, covering her chest and upper thighs, and sat down again. Unfortunately, in the process, the towel hiked up and she presented me with an unrestricted view of... well, you know.

That's even more damned distracting than it was before.

"You'll have to do better than that, Jessica," I said, trying hard not to look down. "Your cell phone put you there until a little after five. What were you two doing?"

"Dammit, Starke," she said angrily, "it's none of your

damn business. I didn't kill him. I wasn't there that night. If you check my goddamn cell records, as you seem so fond of doing, you'll see I was here, at home."

"I did check them, and you're right. Your phone *was* here, but I'm not so sure you were here with it. Now, maybe you didn't kill him, but I need to know what you were doing there all afternoon. It's important. For all we know, you and he were stealing that 350 mil."

She took a huge breath, and her chest rose like an inflated balloon. She looked down at the tabletop, crossed her legs, and thus removed the distraction.

"Oh what the hell," she said. "What can it matter now?" She sighed, looked me in the eye, and said. "Okay." She took another deep breath. "No, we weren't stealing the money. I was screwing him. We spent the afternoon in bed. It wasn't something we did often, just once in a while, when... well, you know... when there was a need. I left just after five o'clock. I was home by six. I *was* here that night, all night. I can't prove it, but I was. Look, I wouldn't have hurt Tom for the world. He was, in some ways, a baby, a bit naive, but he was a nice guy, not much of a lover, but I liked him, a lot."

"So," Kate said. "You left at five o'clock? Who else was in the house?"

"No one. We were alone all afternoon. I showered, dressed, and left. There was no one else there."

"Okay," I said. "You say you were here, but you can't

prove it. We'll let it go at that, for now. Kate? Anything you want to add?"

Kate stood up, pushed back her chair, and looked down at Steiner. "No, but you have no alibi, Ms. Steiner. I'm not sure about motive... yet, but if you had one, we'll figure it out. In the meantime, do you own a gun?"

"Yes, but—"

"Oh, it's okay. I'm not about to accuse you of anything. I was just going to suggest you keep it handy, and keep your doors locked. The gate is great for stopping a vehicle, but it won't stop an intruder. Someone made a real mess of Marty Cassell. I wouldn't want the same thing to happen to you." She turned to me. "Let's go, Harry. I think Ms. Steiner has some thinking to do."

She dropped one of her cards on the table in front of Steiner. "If you do manage to remember anything, please give me or Harry a call." Then she walked away, skirting the pool, and the house, leaving me alone with her.

"Come alone next time, Harry. I didn't like the way she kept staring at me. You, however.... Go. She'll be wondering what you're doing."

"Next time," I said. "Answer your damned phone."

She was right. Kate was in the car, angrily gripping the wheel, tapping her fingers impatiently on the rim.

Damn, she's in a rare mood. What now?

"What was that all about, Harry?" she demanded when I closed the car door.

"What was what all about?"

"All that naked shit? What was she trying to prove, flaunting herself like that?"

"Well, yes. I understand what you mean. The first time I was up here, she was by the pool, and she wasn't wearing a whole lot more than she was today. I suggested she put something on then, but she as good as told me to go to hell, that I was the trespasser and if I didn't like what I saw I could leave. I guess it's just the way she thinks, feels. Anyway, what the hell were you doing, staring at her like that?"

For a moment, she didn't answer, concentrated on the road down the mountain, then said, "I have to admit, she is one very beautiful woman."

"Kate... you're not...."

"No, *goddamnit*, I'm not. I just appreciate beauty when I see it. Now drop it. When are you going to see De Luca?"

I looked at my watch. It was almost four o'clock.

Were we there only forty-five minutes? Hell, it seemed like hours. Must have been distracted, or something. I grinned at the thought. *Hahaha. I wonder what?*

"Well?" Kate said.

"Take me back to the office. I'll grab Bob and a couple of items, then I'll go see him, today, now."

I punched the speed dial number for my office. "Is Bob in, Jack? Okay, good. Make sure he doesn't go anywhere. I need him. I should be there in twenty minutes, or so."

Chapter Twenty

K ate parked her car in the lot outside my office, and I could tell she intended to accompany me inside. That would never do.

"Kate," I said, as I closed the door. "I don't think you need to come inside. I need to explain things to Bob, and you don't need to know what I'm planning to do."

She stared hard at me for what seemed like several minutes, but it could only have been a few seconds, then she nodded.

"Okay, but be careful, and don't kill anyone. *Please?*"

I smiled at her. The way she said 'please' brought so many fond memories flooding back.

"You got it, Kate. I.... Oh, never mind."

"What, Harry? *What?*"

"Nothing. I need to go. I'll call you when I get finished. Say, would you like to come over tonight? I could cook?"

"Are you kidding me? I thought we'd been over all that." She looked me in the eye and smiled. "I'll think about it. I *will* need a statement about what happens at Sal's."

"No statement, Kate, but I will tell you all about it. So you'll come?"

"I said I'll think about it. Now go do your thing, and for God's sake don't get hurt."

For some reason, when I entered the office, I felt like I was walking on air.

"Hey, Bob. Grab a coffee, and one for me, too. I'll be in my office."

Two minutes later, we were seated together, on either side of my desk, sipping coffee.

Bob Ryan is my lead investigator. He's a year older than me and has been with me almost since the day I first opened the agency. He, too, is an ex-cop – Chicago PD. He's also an ex-marine. He stands six feet two and weighs in at 240 pounds – all of it solid muscle – and he has a fondness for ball bats. He's quiet, dedicated, and not someone you want to screw around with.

"Bob," I began. "I'm going to ask you to do something you may not want to do. If that's the case, fine; no hard feelings. I'll do it by myself."

"What do you need? You know I'm in, whatever it is."

I nodded. Bob's voice is deep, almost a growl, menacing even when he's being nice, which he rarely ever is.

"I knew that." I grinned at him. "You still keep that short bat handy?"

He smiled and nodded.

"Okay, you're going to need it. This is what we're going to do...."

When we were done talking, Bob went out to his desk and then to his car, to 'get a few things together,' so he said. While he was gone, I changed clothes. It had been a warm day, and I'd dressed lightly that morning: light-weight tan slacks and a white polo shirt. When I'd finished dressing, I had on a pair of black jeans, a black tee, and black Bruno Magli Infano shoes. I love those thick, soft soles; they're quiet, too.

I slipped my arms through the straps of the DeSantis shoulder rig, nestled the nine securely inside the worn leather holster, climbed into my black leather jacket, and slipped my Talon expandable baton into the left-hand pocket. I was dressed and ready for action. Bob walked back into my office a couple of moments later. He was similarly dressed. We must have looked like a couple of bikers.

We ignored the questioning looks from the rest of the staff and walked out of the side door into the parking lot, climbed into my Maxima. We headed for MLK, Il Sapore Roma and, hopefully, a few quiet words with Sal De Luca.

Ten minutes later, at five o'clock, I pulled the car to a stop on the street outside the restaurant. I reached into the glove box, took out a pair of black leather gloves and pulled them on. I pulled the nine, jacked a shell into the chamber, replaced it in its holster, and we got out of the car. I locked the doors, looked at Bob over the roof, and nodded. He also nodded, and walked around the front of the car to join me. He was holding a shortened baseball bat in his gloved right hand. I grinned at him and we walked to the front door of the restaurant. There was a closed sign on the door, but it wasn't locked, so we walked right on in. Bob closed the door behind him and slipped the latch, locking the door.

The place was all but in darkness. Only the lights above the bar at the far end were on. The place didn't open until seven o'clock. We had plenty of time for what we needed to do.

As always, Sal De Luca was seated at the bar, drink in hand, his back to the room.

That's kinda foolish of him. Never know who might walk up behind you.

"Hello, Sal," I said. "How's it hangin'?"

"Starke," he said. He sat upright, turned and looked at us. "What the hell are you doin' here? Who's the gorilla? Where's your lady friend? You know the one. The cop."

"Sal, meet Bob Ryan. He works for me. Bob, meet Sal De Luca, all around no good sack o' shit. How did you know Kate was a cop, Sal?"

"Gimme a break, dumbass. You think I'm stupid? You think I didn't know she was a cop? Phuurrt." That last was a sound he made with his lips. It sounded like something between a raspberry and a pig breaking wind.

I nodded. "She took the night off, Sal. She doesn't have the stomach for blood and violence that I do."

By now, Bob was slapping the palm of his hand with the bat. Even I was unnerved.

"Violence? Blood? What you talking about, Starke? Ain't no one here gonna hurt you," he said, with a grin a barracuda would have been proud of.

"Not me, Sal. You, and your two boys. Where are Beavis and Butt-Head by the way? It's not like you to be sitting here all alone."

"Oh, I ain't alone, Starke. I have Mr. Colt here with me." He laid his left hand on the bar top. Grasped in his fist was a Colt 1911 .45 semi-automatic, and the hammer was cocked.

"Now, shithead," he said, amiably. "Tell me what the hell you want and get outa here before I blow your goddamn balls off. You, Daisy," he said to Bob. "You stay goddamn still. You move so much as your little finger and I'll deprive you of your *cojones*, too."

That was his big mistake, calling Bob, Daisy. With a flip of the wrist, Bob sent the bat spinning the ten feet across the top of the bar. De Luca didn't see it coming. The rounded, heavy end hit Sal in the center of his forehead, just above the bridge of his nose. His head snapped back, his eyes slammed shut, and he fell backward off the stool and landed in a heap on the floor. I looked down at him shaking my head; he was out like a light.

"Dammit, Bob. I wanted to talk to him," I said, picking up the huge Colt and tossing it to him.

"No problem," Bob said. He took a couple of steps forward, lifted a large jug of water from the bar, and poured its contents over the seemingly sleeping Sal De Luca. Then he picked up the bat and resumed slapping his gloved palm.

Sal came round slowly. Not like you see it in the movies, spluttering and gasping. He just came slowly to, and sat up, shaking his head.

"You crazy bastard son of a bitch," he said. "You'll pay for that."

"Hmmm, maybe," I said, "but before I do, I'd like answers to a few questions. *Capiche*?"

I think he did, because he clawed at the stool he'd so recently vacated and hauled himself up and leaned over the bar. A huge knot was rising on his forehead. Sal would have a nasty headache for the next several days.

"I asked you where Gino and Tony are," I said.

"They ain't here."

"I can see that, Sal. Where are they?"

"They've gone on a job, for me."

"Oh dear. If they've gone where I think they've gone, not only are they in deep, *deep* shit, so are you. If they've gone looking for either Jessica Steiner or James Westwood, you'd better grab a phone and call it off... *NOW!*"

He was so startled, he jumped almost a foot in the air. He did, however, pull a cell phone out of his pocket and hit the speed dial.

"It's off," he said into the instrument. "Come on back." He cut the connection and slipped the phone back in his pocket.

"Now, let's talk about Marty Cassell," I said.

"Cassell? Why him?" He asked the question, but his heart wasn't in it. He already knew the answer.

"You know why. He's in the hospital, Sal. Your boys almost killed him."

"What are you talking about, Starke?" he said, as he gently touched the knot on his head. "I haven't seen that piece of garbage since my money went missing last week."

"Not you, Sal; those two psychos of yours. They busted his nose, lips, and cut his goddamn ears off. *Hey! Wake up!* Are you still with me?"

Sal nodded, but I wasn't sure he was hearing me. His eyes were kinda glazed.

"Here's how it's going to go. *Hey! Are you listening to me?*" I shouted in his ear.

He just sat there and stared at me, the fingers of his right hand gently massaging his forehead.

"No more, Sal. You're going to leave Steiner and Westwood alone. If you don't, I'll be back, and it won't be pretty."

Again, nothing. He simply sat there staring at me, his eyes watering, filled with hate.

"Okay, I'll make it plain for you."

My right hand was already in my jacket pocket. With my left hand, I grabbed his right hand and slammed it down on the countertop, his fingers spread wide. I whipped the Talon out of my pocket, twitched my wrist, flipped it open, and then pounded it down hard on his outstretched fingers. It wasn't a particularly good shot; he resisted, tried to pull back. I was a little off target. I intended to hit the back of his hand, but the steel baton caught only his little finger and the two middle ones next to it. I could tell by the 'crack' that the little one had snapped.

He screamed, came up off the stool as if his ass had caught fire, and backhanded me a good one with the injured hand. The heel of his palm hammered into my jaw, knocking me sideways; the Talon spun out of my hand. Bob took a step forward, but it was too late. De Luca, howling at the top of his voice, was already staggering toward the kitchen door. He burst through it, slammed it shut behind him, and we heard the bar drop into place on the far side, effectively locking us out.

I shook my head, somewhat stunned. The blow to my jaw had been a hard one, and had taken me by surprise.

Damn. I must be getting old.

"You all right, Harry?" Bob said, placing his hand on my shoulder.

"Yeah. He's a big fella, is Sal. That was a good one. Rattled my damned teeth." I worked my jaw, massaging it with my hand. "No harm done. Wow. Shit. Whew!"

"Let's get out of here, Harry. He may just call the cops."

"Nah, I don't think so. He doesn't want cops anywhere near him. Do you think he got the message?"

"Oh yeah. He got the message all right. That hand will be in splints for months."

"I dunno. He's a tough son of a bitch. Maybe we should go round the back and make sure."

"No, Harry. He got it. We need to get out of here. If his buddies get back before we do, there could be a real ruckus; someone could get killed."

Reluctantly, I nodded. "Maybe you're right, but I dunno. Sal won't forget either of us in a hurry, and he's likely to come after us, or send his two goons. Hey, nice shot with the bat, by the way."

He grinned as he unlocked the restaurant door and we walked out into what was going to be a lovely evening. The sun was already low over the brow of Lookout Mountain, turning what few clouds there were into golden pillows against a deep blue sky.

A beautiful evening, a nice dinner, a bottle of wine, and Kate. Oh yeah!

I dropped Bob off at his car and made the call.

"Kate. It's Harry. We're out of there. No... no... no harm done. Well, not much. I took a bit of a shot to the chin, but you should see the other guy." I was smiling as I said it, even though I knew she couldn't see me. "Look, I'm on my way home. You're coming over tonight, right?"

"Harry, I'm sorry. I can't. Lieutenant Conway is off sick. I have to fill in for him. Raincheck?"

"Sure," I said. I shook my head. I should have known better.

"So tell me," she said. "What happened? Am I likely to hear about it through official channels?"

"I doubt it. Only Sal was there. I warned him off the two partners, and we got out of there."

"That's it? That's all you're going to tell me?"

"What's to tell? I warned him to leave Steiner and Westwood alone. Bob whacked him with his bat. I whacked him with the baton. He locked himself in the kitchen, and we left. No big deal."

"Did he take it seriously, the warning?"

I laughed at that. "He'll remember it. That's for sure. Whether he took it seriously or not, only time will tell."

"Okay, Harry. Good job, but I gotta go. I'm on 'till midnight. See you tomorrow?"

"Sure. Call me first thing... you sure...."

"Yes. I'm sure. See you tomorrow." She hung up.

Well... damn. What the hell am I going to do now? I sure as hell don't want to spend the night home alone.

Chapter Twenty-One

It was a little after ten o'clock when I arrived at the Sorbonne, part of Chattanooga's 'night life.' It's one of the city's sleaziest bars, not a nightclub. Back in the day, when I was a cop, I spent many a long night there, watching, listening. Even these days, I frequent the place more often than I probably should, mostly to keep an eye on the lowlifes that inhabit the sleazy dump, but more than that. Every now and then I like to have a chat with the bar's owner, Benny Hinkle. Benny... he likes it not so much.

Now Benny is a weird little creep. I say little, but the fat bastard is almost as wide as he is tall, a greasy, unshaven slob, who inhabits the nether regions of the Sorbonne like some great nocturnal sloth, coming out only at night to short his customers on watered liquor and deafen them with brain-numbing noise the younger generation seem happy to call music.

Benny is aided in his endeavors by his trusty sidekick and barmaid, Laura something or other. She's a busty, blowsy bottle blonde usually attired in a tank top that barely covers her nipples, and Daisy Dukes that don't quite cover the cheeks of her backside. The two of them are a match made in hell, but it works. After ten o'clock, no matter what day of the week it might be, the joint is always jumping. Benny, despite his looks and demeanor, is one wealthy son of a bitch.

"Benny, you fat little stud," I said loudly in order to be heard over the cacophony. "What's the good news?"

He looked at me as if I'd just crawled out of the urinal. We don't get along, Benny and me. I can't think why.

"I thought I told you to stay outa here, Starke. Piss off before you scare my patrons away."

"*Patrons? Hah.*" I couldn't help it. I laughed out loud. "This scruffy bunch of skanks and degenerates? No wonder this place stinks. How the hell you hang onto your license beats me."

"Hey. Who you callin' a skank?" a woman asked.

I turned and looked at her. She was the closest to me of a group of three females, all of whom looked as if they'd escaped from the primate house at the zoo. She had purple hair that hung like a curtain almost to her waist, a huge brass ring through her nose, tattoo sleeves that completely covered both arms. She wore a skirt that didn't quite cover her ass, and a tank top that made Laura's look like an overcoat.

"Have you ever taken a look at yourself in a mirror, sweetie?" I asked pleasantly. "If you had, you'd know it was you I was calling a skank. Now, unless you want me to toss you and these two harpies you have with you out on your asses, I suggest you move away to the end of the bar, because you stink like a rancid hot dog. Now go."

And they did, right out of the door, muttering and casting furtive glances at me as they went.

"Well now, Starke," Benny said, scrubbing his hands with a wet, filthy-looking rag that once might have been called a dishcloth. "You did it again. You cost me money. They was spendin' big. What the hell did I do to deserve you, an' what the hell do you want anyway?"

"What's the word on the street about Sal De Luca?"

He looked at me sideways, his eyes narrowed almost to slits. He frowned so hard it looked like his forehead had been ploughed.

"You're kiddin', right? You outa your mind? What d'you want with De Luca? He's bad news; real bad news."

"Yeah, I know that, Benny, but what's the word on the street? What's he up to?"

"I ain't heard much, an' he don't come down 'ere, ever."

"What about his people? Any of them been in here lately?"

His eyes shifted, he hesitated, then looked at me again.

"Gino and Tony come in now and again. They was in 'ere earlier tonight. They didn't speak to me." Again his eyes shifted. "They ordered two beers from Laura, drank 'em, an' then they left."

Oh, Benny. You can't lie worth a damn.

"What time was that?"

He screwed up his eyes and concentrated. "'Bout nine... nine-thirty. I dunno. I don't keep time when I'm in here; you know that."

"They didn't ask questions?"

"Nope, not of me. Laura, maybe, but they wasn't in here more'n five minutes."

I stared hard at him. He flinched; his face turned red. "What?"

"You know what, Benny. Now give. Tell me what they were after. If not...."

"Oh shit, Starke. First Shady Tree an' now De Luca. You're gonna get me chopped. Gino, the tall skinny one, likes to use a knife, an' he's good."

"What did they want, Benny? I won't ask again."

"Oh shit.... You; they wanted you. They asked if you'd

been in lately. I said no. They asked how often you came in. I told 'em once in a while. That's it, Harry. I swear. They drank up an' left... hold on." He turned to the register, opened it and took out a slip of paper and handed it to me. "The big one, Tony, gave me that. Said if you was to come in, I was to call that number."

I looked at it. It was a piece of paper torn out of a small spiral notebook. It had a phone number written on it in pencil. Nothing more. I looked at Benny. He almost cringed.

"You going to call this number when I leave?"

He shook his head. I laughed. "You think I don't know you, Benny? You won't even give the goddamn door time to hit me in the ass before you start punching in the numbers, but that's okay. Might even be a good thing."

He nodded. "Gino Polti and Tony Carpeta; they are two bad dudes, Harry; really bad."

"So am I, Benny. So am I...." I thought for a moment, then said, "Tell you what, go ahead and make the call, now."

"Ah come on, Harry. That Gino will cut my nuts off if he thinks I'm workin' for you."

"You're not working for me, Benny. You are just doing as he told you. I came in. I left. You're calling to tell him. Now make the goddamn call before *I* cut them off."

I watched as he nervously punched the number into his

cell phone. I could hear it ringing on the other end, then someone answered.

"Yeah?"

"Tony?" Benny said.

"Yeah. Who's this?"

I leaned over and snatched the piece out of Benny's hand and put it to my ear.

"This is your worst nightmare, Tony, Harry Starke. I hear you're looking for me."

"Screw you, Starke."

"No, screw you, Tony, and Gino, too, and that gecko you work for. How's his hand, by the way? Never mind. Now listen, Tony, and listen carefully. I'm gonna say this only once. If you, any of you, screw with me, or anyone I know, one more time, I'll put a hollow point right between your eyes. *Capiche*?" Click. He hung up. I handed the phone back to Benny. He was staring at me, white faced, and wide eyed.

"You shouldn't aughta done that, Harry." He was shaking.

"They don't bother me, Benny."

"Hell no, maybe not, but they bother the hell outa me, especially that mother Gino. He'll know it was me what told ya, and he'll cut m' goddamn balls off."

I grinned at him, gave him my card, and said, "Nah! They come in here, you just give 'em this. Tell them I said if they lay a hand on you, I'll kill 'em. Tell them to come see me at my office. You'll be fine."

I left him staring at the card, walked out of the Sorbonne, and into the night. I looked through the darkened window and could see Benny talking into the phone, my card still in his hand. I smiled and decided to take a walk. The Walnut Street Bridge was just a couple of blocks away, and it was a beautiful evening.

Chapter Twenty-Two

I have sad memories of the bridge, and I go there often. It was there that Tabitha Willard decided to end her life, and I always felt it was at least partly my fault. So, from time to time, I walk the bridge and spend a few moments looking down into the water, remembering. That night I sat on one of the benches and stared out over the river. To the left, the city was a blaze of lights. To the right, on the North Shore, not quite so much. To the front, the vast, black bulk of Lookout Mountain was a stark but bejeweled silhouette against a moonlit sky, the lights of the homes on the crest twinkling like stars. Chattanooga is indeed the Scenic City.

I looked at my watch. It was almost midnight, and yet for some reason I had no desire to go home. For one thing, I'd had a couple of drinks, just two, but that's enough to get a man hauled off to jail around here. It wasn't worth the risk, so I decided to leave the Maxima in the Sorbonne lot and take a cab to my office.

I could have taken the cab ride home, but that would have meant fooling around the next morning: another cab to get my car. If I stayed the night at the office, though, all I had to do was have Mike take me the few blocks to where it was parked, no problem. Anyway, it wouldn't be the first time I'd slept on the sofa in my cave, and it sure as hell wouldn't be the last. I keep a change of clothes there, and there's a full service bathroom complete with a shower: home away from home.

It was a little after twelve-thirty in the morning when the cab dropped me off outside the front door of my office. I turned the key in the lock and pushed the door open. I wasn't thinking about much when I flipped the light switch, but when the lights didn't come on, I had a sudden feeling that all was not as it should be. Hell, somehow I knew what was coming. It's been said by Kate and others that I have second sight. Whatever. My reflexes kicked in, and I dived forward into the office. As I fell, I twisted hard to the right. I was quick, but not quick enough. Something hard and heavy slammed into my left shoulder. Whatever it was, must have hit a nerve, because pain seared down my arm all the way to the fingertips of my left hand.

I hit the floor hard on my right arm and shoulder, rolling, my hand inside my jacket, fumbling for the gun. Before I could pull it, BAM! A brilliant flash of red fire and something tugged hard at the sleeve of my jacket. Then I had the nine in my fist and I jerked the trigger, three times, BAM, BAM, BAM.

There was a yelp on the far side of the room, and the sound of scrambling feet. The side door opened and then slammed shut, and I could hear running feet in the corridor; there was more than one of them. I jumped to my feet, ripped open the door, and ran after them. My left arm was throbbing with pain from the whack it had received. I reached the outer door, stopped, and pushed it slowly open. Nothing. I stepped out into the street, my gun at the ready. All was quiet, the amber light of the street lamps threw soft shadows: poles, road signs, cars. Store doorways were black holes that hid... God only knew what. It was an urban jungle, dark and threatening, but nothing was moving. The animals had gone to ground. Whoever they were, they were gone... at least I hoped they were.

I closed the door, twisted the latch, took out my key fob, turned on the tiny LED flashlight, and returned to my office. I found the breaker box on the far wall next to the window that looked out onto a narrow alley, and flipped the switch. The lights came on and I dropped into the chair behind Jacque's desk and looked around. The place had been trashed. File cabinet drawers had been forced open, papers were strewn about all over the floor, and the side window was wide open, the glass broken. *So that's how they got in.*

My own office door was also wide open, the doorjamb splintered where it had been forced. I didn't need to get up and go look to know that it, too, had been trashed.

I sighed, shook my head, and fished my cell phone out of my jacket pocket. It was then I noticed the blood dripping from the tips of the fingers of my right hand.

Funny, I don't feel anything. Oh, I see. God dammit, I've been hit!

There was a neat little hole in the sleeve of my leather jacket; two holes. Entry and exit.

Oh yeah. Now I can feel it.

I slipped the jacket off. The tee shirtsleeve was soaked, so was the inside of my jacket.

Damn. I wonder if it will clean.

I was wearing a black tee shirt. It also had two holes, although it was hard to see them because of the blood. I was leaking like a rusty bucket with a hole in the bottom.

Wouldn't you just know it?

I pulled my sleeve up. It didn't look too bad. The slug had clipped the top of my arm, about four inches down from the shoulder. I say clipped. It was a little more than that. The bullet had entered the fatty tissue just west of the muscle and had gone through and through. It wasn't deep, and it had missed the muscle, but it was way more than a crease and would require a visit to the hospital.

God dammit. Shit, that thing hurts.

My left arm was also beginning to stiffen.

Geeze! I must be getting old.

I punched 911 into the phone and reported the break in and shots fired, and then I called Kate. She was still at the PD, working late, just as she said. Two cruisers arrived within minutes. I wouldn't let them into the office. Instead, I suggested they tape the door and wait for Lieutenant Gazzara. She arrived a few minutes later, a worried look on her face.

"Harry, we've got to stop meeting like this. You hurt?"

"Duh... yeah! I took one in the arm. Damn right I'm hurt."

She came around to my right side, pulled the sleeve up so she could see the wound.

"Through and through. The exit wound is nice and clean; not much there to stop it. It's leaking nicely, so it's not too bad. You'll live. Did you see who it was?"

"No, they'd flipped the breaker; no lights. There were at least two of them, though. I'm guessing they were Sal De Luca's two goons, Gino Polti and Tony Carpeta. I guess Sal was getting back at me for what happened earlier."

She nodded, grabbed some tissues from a box on Jacque's desk, and dabbed at the wound.

"I was at the Sorbonne earlier. Benny said they'd been

looking for me. He had a piece of paper with Tony's number and instructions to call if I went into the bar. I made him call while I was there, and I talked to Tony. Gave him some bullshit and told him to lay off. That may have triggered it, but it's more likely De Luca sent them, especially after what Bob and I did to him earlier this evening. Why they trashed the place, though, I have no idea."

"Looks like they were looking for something," Kate said.

"Maybe. Then again, maybe they were just waiting for me and decided to enjoy themselves while they did."

"Why would you say that? You don't stay here that often. How would they know?"

"Easy enough. I told Benny that if they were to come looking, he was to tell them to come see me at the office. I saw him call someone as I was leaving the bar. I knew he would. He said he had to, to cover his ample ass. Can't blame him for that. Wow, that hurts."

"Sorry, Harry. I need to get you to a doctor."

"Yeah, yeah," I said. "Maybe Benny told them that, about seeing me at the office, and they misunderstood, thought I was heading here instead of home. If so, they got lucky, because I was going to spend the night on the sofa. I've done it before, as you know."

"Is anything missing?"

"Hell, I dunno, but I think I may have hit one of them. I

got three shots off. Heard one of them yell. No blood, though. Shit, this hurts a son of a bitch."

She looked sideways at me. "The gunshot wound? Yeah, I bet it does."

"Yeah... the gunshot. That and this." I pulled up the left sleeve of the tee shirt and showed her the welt across my left shoulder. It was already turning black.

"Oh my God." She shook her head. "We need to get you to the hospital. I'll take you. Go get a towel and try not to leak all over my car. Go on... do it *now!* One more thing." She stuck out her hand and waggled her fingers.

"What?"

"You know what. You fired your weapon. Give it to me."

Sadly, I handed over the M&P9. "That's two. I'm gonna have to go shopping tomorrow."

She grinned, stuck a pencil down the barrel, and bagged it.

Reluctantly, I went into the bathroom, grabbed a towel, wrapped it around my shoulder as best I could, which wasn't too great. We left for Erlanger Hospital in her unmarked, blue lights flashing and the siren howling and whooping.

Damn, any other time, this would be fun.

She was right. It wasn't too bad, but the wait was interminable. It was after three in the morning by the time I was all nicely cleaned up, stitched, and bandaged, and we were finally able to get out of there.

Which one of those two goons managed to clip me, I wonder, and which one did I clip? If any. Maybe I just scared the sons of bitches.

I grinned at the thought. Chances were that if I had hit him, I'd damaged him more than he did me.

Chapter Twenty-Three

I woke early the following morning, Wednesday. Kate had dropped me home the previous evening after more than two hours at Erlanger Hospital's emergency room. Thank God for Kate's presence. Without her, I would have been in there all night, especially with a gunshot wound. Fortunately, the presence of a middle rank police officer to handle the paperwork got us in and out in a relatively short time. It was almost three-thirty in the morning when she dropped me off at my home. She left me at the door, and five minutes later, I'd stripped off what was left of my clothes, fell on the bed and went fast asleep.

I woke the next morning to the sound of my cell phone. It was Jacque. She wanted to know what the hell had happened to the office, why there were four bullet holes in the walls, and why I wasn't there.

Four bullet holes? Three of mine and one of theirs; the one that went through me. So I didn't hit one of them. Well damn.

I explained as best I could, told her to get the place cleaned up, and to send Mike over to get me.

My arms were as stiff as two short planks of wood, and they both hurt like hell, especially the bullet wound. I needed a shower.

Have you ever tried to shower with an arm covered with a dressing? It ain't easy.

I gulped down four Ibuprofen tablets followed by almost a pint of milk. Then I wrapped the dressing in plastic wrap, tried to make it as waterproof as possible, and then I hit the shower. I turned it up to hot, as hot as I could stand it. Almost took the skin off my back, but I felt better for it.

I dressed in a pair of lightweight gray slacks, a pale blue polo shirt, and black Gucci loafers. The shoulder rig was out of the question, and I was all out of guns anyway, so I clipped a leather Blackhawk holster onto my belt and topped that off with a black, lightweight golf jacket. I punched up a Yeti cup full of Italian Dark Roast coffee from the Keurig, called Kate and arranged to meet her at my office at eleven, and then I sat down to wait for Mike. He arrived just a couple of minutes later.

Carter Shooting Supply is out on Highway 58, and that was where I had Mike make our first stop. I picked up another Smith and Wesson M&P9, a couple of extra mags, and a box of shells. I fired a couple of mag fulls in their range, swapped the back strap, and fired a couple more. Satisfied that all was in order, I reloaded it and slipped it into the Blackhawk, the grip facing forward. I winced as pain speared down the arm when I lifted it to allow access to the holster. *Damn!*

From Carter's, Mike drove me to the Sorbonne. My car was still right where I'd left it. I had Mike crawl around, looking underneath it to see if the damn thing was going to blow up when I started it. As far as he could tell, all was as it should be. I unlocked it, popped the hood and gave the engine compartment the once over. Nothing. I got in, took a deep breath, and hit the starter button. The engine awoke with a growl, and I felt something akin to a great weight being lifted off my chest. Relief? I guess so.

Back at the office, Kate, Amanda Cole, and the rest of the crew were all waiting for me; even Lonnie Guest. I walked in through the front door and immediately felt like some kind of idiot; they just sat and stared at me, like I was... well. I dunno. Unnerving, is what it was.

"What the hell is this?" I growled, at no one in particular. "Some kind of convention? Bob, Kate, Amanda, Tim, Ronnie, Jacque, yeah, you, too, Lonnie, conference room. Mike, old son, coffee all round, please. Then you can come and sit in. Jacque, you need to record everything then have Margo type up the transcript and see that everyone gets copies, including Amanda."

For some reason, I was in an unusual, for me, no-nonsense kind of mood. Maybe it was the fact that I could barely move either of my arms, and that pain was coursing through them. Even my fingertips were hurting, throbbing. I went to my office, grabbed the legal pad from the desk drawer and joined everyone else around the conference table.

"Okay, people," I said. "Where the hell are we? Who wants to go first? No one? Okay, then I will."

I grabbed my coffee, sipped, nodded at Mike, took a deep breath, and flipped open the pad.

"Okay. Before we begin, I want everyone to understand that everything said in this meeting is confidential. If anyone has a problem with that, they need to leave, now. Amanda?"

She shook her head.

"Okay, let's start with what we have, and then move on to what we don't. We have Tom Sattler dead, murdered, and we have seven suspects, including Gloria Sattler's boyfriend, Richard Hollins, and Sattler's girlfriend, Wendy Brewer. Hollins has an alibi, of sorts, and Wendy Brewer is a washed out basket case. Neither one of them rank high on the list as far as I'm concerned, at least for now. Any thoughts, anyone?"

I looked around the table, rubbed my left shoulder, took a sip of coffee, and continued.

"That leaves us with Gloria Sattler, Stephanie Sattler, Sal De Luca, and the three partners, one of whom was badly beaten yesterday. Kate, how is Cassell, by the way?"

"They released him early this morning. He's at home."

I nodded. "We think, no, we *know*, that Sal De Luca was responsible for the beating, and for the break in here last night. As to which one of the five might be responsible for Tom's death, it could be any one of them, or none of them. I don't think it was De Luca. He had big money tied up in the fund. I can't see him jeopardizing that. That leaves the two Sattlers and the three partners. Now, as Kate will tell you, we're not supposed to be fooling with the missing $350 million, only Sattler's murder, but there's no doubt in my mind that the two are connected. Kate?"

'That's true," she said. "If we can find out what happened to the money, I think we'll know who killed him. My biggest concern right now is safety. Someone tried to kill Harry last night and I think they'll try again. I'm going to see De Luca when we've finished here. If I can, I'll put a stop to it right there. No, Harry, you're not coming with me. I don't trust you not to kill someone, and I can't have that."

"Kate," I said. "I'm going with you. If not me, Bob will go. You can't go and face those three bastards by yourself."

Bob nodded.

"I'm not going alone. Lonnie will go with me."

I looked skeptically at the big sergeant. Dumb as a box of rocks he might be, but he was an imposing figure; overweight, but imposing nonetheless. He grinned at me across the table. I glared back at him.

"Lonnie, if you let anything happen to–"

"Oh, for Christ's sake, Harry," she interrupted. "I've been handling assholes like De Luca all my life. I can handle him."

"Yeah, you probably can, especially the way we left him, right, Bob?" I grinned at him; he grinned back at me.

"No, Kate. It's Gino and Tony I'm worried about." Then I noticed the evil look I was getting from Amanda.

Damn, Amanda. Lighten up. I'm just concerned she doesn't get killed. Geez. Who needs women?

"Well, don't be," Kate said. "And what do you mean, the way you left him?"

"You'll see," I said.

"Oh boy," she said. "Okay. Lonnie. Let's go."

They left, and so did everyone else, leaving me alone with my thoughts.

Chapter Twenty-Four

I spent the rest of the morning with my notepad, trying to make some sense of what we knew so far, which wasn't much. *So what exactly do I know?*

1. I have five persons of interest: Gloria, Stephanie, Steiner, Cassell, Westwood.

2. I have two more of lesser interest: Hollins and Brewer. Then I have Sal De Luca and the two ugly sisters.

3. Gloria and Stephanie were both in the vicinity, but they have mutual alibis, so they cancel each other out; they don't have alibis. Do they have motives? Possibly. Child sexual abuse would give either one or both of them a very strong motive.

4. Steiner, Cassell and Westwood don't have alibis, thus they all three have opportunity. As far as I can tell, none of the three have motives, other than greed, and they are all greedy. As to means? Nope. According to their cell phone records, *none of them were there at the time Sattler was killed, but as I've said before, that only means their phones weren't there.*

5. *Sal Deluca is responsible for the attack on Cassell, the break in to this office, and for my being shot. All that being so, I don't think he has a motive to kill Sattler, nor the wherewithal to steal the 350 mil, but....*

6. *Brewer doesn't have opportunity, means or motive. She lost the most by Sattler's death. She lost her meal ticket and she's also a borderline basket case.*

7. *Richard Hollins has an alibi of sorts, but as Gloria's boyfriend he would also have a motive (the child abuse).*

8. *We have three questions:*

A. *Who out of the seven is most likely the killer? I have no earthly idea.*

B. *Who is most likely the thief? Again, I have no idea.*

C. *How many solid clues do we have? Not a one. Not a single, solitary one. The hair we found beneath the body could have been there for weeks. The gun was wiped clean, and we know there was a second shot fired from it, but we don't know what happened to it. We know why it was fired to make the killing look like a suicide, but not by whom.*

I got up from my desk, wandered into the outer office, stared at each of my staff in turn, not really seeing any one of them. I made myself a cup of coffee, went back into my office, flopped down in my chair, and stared, hypnotized, at the notepad.

Two weeks. Two whole weeks, and what have we got? Not one single damned thing that we didn't have the day after Tom was murdered. That's crazy. Geez, we need a break in the worst way!

I leaned back in my chair, put my feet up on the desk, and stared up at the ceiling; it helped not a whit.

It was right on noon when Kate called. She said she'd pick me up and we'd grab lunch at the Flatiron Deli. She walked into my office just ten minutes later.

"So, how did it go?" I said, almost before she'd set foot inside the door. "Where's Lonnie?"

"I dropped him off at Amnicola." She smiled as she said it. "As to how it went, I'll tell you over coffee and a sandwich. Let's go."

I grabbed a lightweight jacket and followed her out the door.

The Flatiron Deli is just a couple of blocks away from my office, housed in the building that bears the same name. It's a beautiful structure with a footprint shaped like... a flatiron. The food is excellent: they make the best BLT in town. We both ordered one of those. I had a cup of coffee. Kate had a Coke.

We grabbed a window seat,

The sun had disappeared behind a bank of rolling black clouds that had descended like a soggy gray blanket upon the crest of Lookout Mountain. It looked for all the world like Mount Doom. Within minutes, the rain began and the streets were soon deserted.

As soon as she sat down, she picked up her sandwich and began to eat. I looked at her like she was stupid.

"Hey. You. Miss Piggy. Are you going to tell me or do I have to beat it out of you?"

"Tell you what?" She looked up at me, stopped chewing, her mouth full. "Oh that," she mumbled through the food.

She finished chewing, took a drink from her Coke, looked at me and grinned.

"Let me say this," she began. "You, Harry Starke, are about as popular with our friend Sal De Luca as a raccoon in a chicken run. What did you do to him? His hand is all bandaged and his head has a knot on it the size of a basketball."

"I can only take credit for the hand," I said, modestly. "Bob whacked him on the head with that little bat he's so fond of. So... what did he say?"

"Not much. He swears he had nothing to do with the break-in, your injuries, Cassell's injuries, or anything else. His henchmen tell the same story, and they all have alibis for last night. They were all playing poker...."

"'With a half-dozen of their friends.'" I chimed in along with her.

She grinned, nodded, and took a big bite out of the sandwich and looked at me, chewing vigorously.

"You like that, huh?" I said, "The sandwich. You need to take it easy. You'll choke yourself."

"I'm hungry," she mumbled through a mouthful. "I didn't eat this morning."

"So, I said. We have nothing, right?"

"Yup! Nothing! Oh, by the way. He did say that if you set foot inside his restaurant again, he will kill you."

We finished our food, sat and talked for a while, mainly about how little we had to go on, and then she had to go back to the Police Department. I decided to call it a day.

I dropped back by the office, let them know where they could find me, should the need arise, and then I headed home. I needed a break, some food, a little scotch whiskey and some serious sleep.

I drove home that afternoon in a kind of daze. The situation with De Luca was bothering me more than a little, and I had an idea that things were about to get worse. Nobody likes to lose money, and De Luca was no exception. Twelve million dollars could, and probably would, sink him with the mob, and I didn't mean figuratively. He could literally end up at the bottom of the Tennessee, and I couldn't see him allowing that. He would do what it took to get his money back: more torture, even murder.

It was almost four o'clock when I closed the garage door and walked up the stairs to my living room. It was peaceful. The view across the river through the light rain had a settling effect on my turbulent mind. I dropped my document case on the coffee table – I'd brought my papers home with me for once, something I rarely ever did – went into the bedroom, stripped, and took a shower.

Back in the living room, I turned on some music, spa music. I do that sometimes, mostly when I can't see the wood for the trees. It helps me concentrate. I poured myself a stiff jolt of Laphroaig and settled down on the sofa in front of the big window, and then goddamn it, I fell asleep.

When I awoke, it was dark outside. The rain had stopped. I looked at my watch. It was eleven o'clock. I'd slept for six solid hours. I knew I wouldn't be able to sleep after that, so what to do?

I turned on Channel 7 News just in time to watch Amanda sign off from the evening news. I sighed, turned off the TV, went into the bedroom, and lay down, knowing good and well it was a waste of time.

I lay staring up into the shadows, thinking about Amanda, what she was doing. I looked at the bedside clock. It was eleven-fifty. She was probably on her way home. *Go on. Call her. It's worth a shot.*

I was right. She was in the car.

"Harry?" She sounded puzzled.

"Yes. Where are you?"

"I'm on Market, near the Choo Choo. I'm on my way home. Why?"

"I thought you might like to talk."

"Okay. Shoot."

I laughed. "That's not a good word to use right now...."

"Oh wow, yeah. Sorry, Harry. Are you hurting?"

Okay, Harry. Play it for all it's worth.

"Um. Yeah. It's really bad. I mean really bad."

She laughed. "Liar."

"Damn. Well okay. What I meant was I thought you might come over here. Have a drink. Talk...."

"Harry. It's almost midnight and I have to be at the station by seven in the morning."

"Okay. It was just a thought."

"Are you alright?"

"Yes, of course. I'll talk to you tomorrow."

"Wait.... Pour me some scotch, no ice, not yet. It'll melt before I get there. I'll see you in thirty minutes, or less." She disconnected.

I smiled.

Things are looking up.

She was still wearing her on-air clothes and makeup, and she looked great, a little pasty around the face from the foundation, but great just the same. She was wearing a short, lightweight white jacket over the simple, sleeveless, light blue dress she'd worn on the set.

I opened the door for her and took her in my arms. Her hair was stiff from the spray used to keep it in place while on the air, but I didn't care. I was just pleased to see her.

"Get away from me," she said, laughing and pushed me away. "I stink, and I need a shower. Now look. I can't stay all night. I can't go into work in the same clothes. I'm gonna have to go home... sometime."

"Hmmm. Sometime is good," I said as I pulled her in close. "Just not for a while."

She giggled, wriggled out from under my arms, and ran into the bathroom and locked the door.

I smiled, then grimaced. No, I wasn't lying. The bullet wound was hurting like hell. Funny thing, though. Thirty minutes later, it wasn't hurting at all. Well, I was by then, as they say, 'feeling no pain.'

Chapter Twenty-Five

I'd had no intention of going in to the office early that Thursday morning. In fact, I'd asked Jacque to cover for me. It was, therefore, something of a surprise when my cell phone rang at ten after nine.

"Hey, Kate. What's up?"

"Westwood's dead. They found him thirty minutes ago. You dressed? I'm outside your front door."

"*Goddamn it,*" I said, dumbfounded. "No. I'm not, not yet, but you can come on in. I'll open the door." Fortunately, Amanda had left early to get to the station in time for the early morning broadcast.

Thanks for small rewards.

All I had on when I opened the door were my boxers but she didn't seem to notice. She rushed in, headed for the kitchen and the Keurig, punched up a coffee, and then started pacing the kitchen as she drank it.

"Come *on,* Harry. For God's sake, get a grip. It'll take us at least thirty minutes to get up to Brow Road and I want to get there while Doc Sheddon is still there...." She looked around the kitchen, living room, then said, "Did... you have company last night?"

I ignored the question, went into the bedroom, threw on a pair of jeans, a pale blue golf shirt, and loafers. I went back into the kitchen, grabbed a coffee, grabbed her arm, and hustled her to the door.

She grinned. "So who was it?"

"None of your damned business. Now get in the car and drive."

She was right. The drive up the mountain took even longer than we expected. It was almost ten o'clock when we arrived at the house on Brow Road. Doc Sheddon was putting away his gear and the CSI techs were already about their business, but that all stopped so that we could view the scene.

James Westwood was a sad-looking shadow of the man he had been. The blue eyes could no longer be seen; the lids were glued shut by dried blood. The once white hair was a tangled mess, wet, streaked with red. The tan, especially on his face, was now a dirty shade of pallid gray.

Dressed only in a pair of bloodstained boxers, and seated

on a high-back dining chair, he was a pathetic caricature of the self-confident financier that had met us at the door only a week before.

Whoever it was that had done this thing had intended to get results. He was held upright in the chair by Duct Tape. His hands were taped to his thighs; his ankles were taped to the chair legs.

How long he had been like that was anybody's guess. My own was that he had suffered a long time before he gave out. I looked at Kate. Her face was pale, her eyes hard, her lips set tight, turned down at the corners, disgusted.

I felt someone come up beside me, and I turned to find a sad-looking Doc Sheddon. His hands were in his pants pockets, his chin down, almost to his chest as he looked over the top of his glasses.

"Hello, Lieutenant, Harry. It's a bad one. I've not seen anything like it since Viet Nam."

"Tortured, right?" I said, looking down at the body.

"I'd say so, and quite professionally. He must have suffered a great deal of pain."

"And then they killed him?" Kate said.

"No. I don't think so. I'll know more when I've done the autopsy, but I'm pretty sure he died of a heart attack. The cuts were not meant to kill, just to inflict the maximum amount of pain... and terror. It was torture pure and simple, and it got out of hand, I'd say."

He was silent for a long moment, and then, "The fingers... they're all broken. I haven't counted, but there must be at least thirty cuts. None of them deep, but all extremely painful, and bloody. Look at the skin under the tapes around his wrists and ankles. They're rubbed raw where he struggled. Very nasty," he said, shaking his head.

"How long, Doc?" I could barely stand to hear the answer.

"I'd say he could have lasted a couple of hours before his heart finally gave out. Look." He pointed to a bloody, half-empty salt shaker. "I guess the cuts alone didn't do it for them. Time of death? Ten, twelve hours, late last night, probably. I'll let you know for sure as soon as I have it."

"Them? You said 'them.' So you think there was more than one?" Kate said.

"Oh yes. He was a fit old fella. I'm sure he didn't let them hog tie him like this willingly. He's taken a beating to the head, too, tut, tut, tut. Bastards. I hope you find 'em. Well, I must go; let you young folks do your thing."

We said our goodbyes, and Sheddon shambled off through the house and out through the front door, his big black case almost scraping the floor.

"Christ, Kate," I said. "What a mess. De Luca has a lot to answer for."

She nodded her agreement. "So you like De Luca for it?"

"Not him personally, no, Gino. He's the guy with the knife and a willingness to use it. Tony? I don't think he has the balls for something like this. The beating? Yes. That's more his style. Why, though? This guy had nothing to do with De Luca's money. So why him? Cassell, I can understand, but this.... Well, you know what I mean."

"Doc Sheddon said 'pain and terror,'" Kate said, thoughtfully. "Terror would be my guess. De Luca wants to put the fear of God into Cassell, maybe Steiner, too, and him." She looked down at all that was left of the once handsome James Westwood.

"Lieutenant. Do you have a minute?" The senior CSI tech was holding an empty spool of Duct Tape.

"Yes, of course. What do you have?"

"Well, as you can see, the tape is all gone, but I've managed to lift a good-size partial print from the inside of the spool. It's good. I think there's enough so AFIS will be able to make a match. There are no more, at least not yet, and there are none on the tape they used on the body. I'd say they were wearing gloves, both of them."

"How did that print get on there, then?" Kate said.

He grinned. "They ain't as smart as they think they are. They always forget something, don't they? Leave something behind, take something away. Here's how I see it.

They knew what they were going to do, so they came prepared. They brought the tape with them. They wore gloves. Yes, there were more than one of them. They tore off the first few inches of each roll. There would have been prints on it, put there before they put the gloves on. They probably stuffed it into a pocket and took it away with them, but they forgot about the inside of the roll. It's nice and slick. The surface takes prints well. They used more than one roll, too, but they must have packed what was left of the others and took it away with them. This empty spool was on the mantelpiece. They must have put it down when they changed rolls and forgot about it. You've got yourself a big fat break, Lieutenant."

"Let's go back to your office, Harry," Kate said, "and see if we can figure this thing out.

Chapter Twenty-Six

O n the drive back to the office, I called Jacque and had her send Mike out to get some pizzas. It was just after noon when we arrived. Kate and Lonnie, who was waiting for us in the outer office, followed me into the conference room where the rest of my crew were already present, eating pizza and drinking Coke. No Coke for me; I grabbed a large cup of Dark Italian, a paper plate, four slices of pie, and flopped down in my chair at the head of the table. By now, I was in a foul mood. The wound to my right arm was weeping through the dressing and it hurt like hell. My left shoulder had stiffened up nicely, so nicely I could barely lift my hand to my plate. I was one sorry S.O.B., and in no mood to talk, so I gave Kate the floor.

She stood, grabbed her Coke, sucked down a big gulp, and looked at the gathering. I couldn't help but stare at her. She was wearing tight-fitting jeans, a white sleeveless top, and three-inch heels. The Glock 26 was in a holster on her right hip. Her gold badge was clipped to her belt in front of the left pocket. Her hair was tied back in a ponytail; she wore almost no makeup, just a little lipstick. Standing there at the table, at a little over six feet two in those heels, she looked stunning.

"Let's talk about Westwood," she began. "He was killed sometime late last night. He was found this morning at around eight-thirty by his Hispanic maid. He was Duct Taped to a chair. He'd been tortured. There was a lot of blood, but not enough to kill him. It looks like a heart attack brought on by the torture; we'll know later when we get the results of the autopsy. Even so, that could bring a charge of first-degree murder. The intent was to commit torture to the point where the victim died, even if by a heart attack. Anyway, CSI still has the scene under wraps, so we can only assume.... Harry, you want to take over?"

"Sure." I looked at Kate, then at each person at the table, ending with Lonnie.

"It's my considered opinion that we're dealing with two separate killers here. Someone killed Sattler for whatever reason; someone else killed Westwood, but not intentionally. There's no doubt in my mind, or Kate's, that Westwood was not intended to die. Right, Kate?"

She nodded.

"This was a botched attempt to do one of two things,

maybe both. The first was to get information from West-wood, probably about the missing money. The second was to put the fear of God into the other two partners. Maybe, as I said, the idea was to do both. It matters not. Westwood died in the process and that means murder. Does anyone have any other ideas or comments?"

Lonnie stuck his hand up.

"No need for that, Lonnie," I said. "We're not in high school. Just ask the question."

"Two killers? I don't get it. It doesn't make sense, at least not to me."

I nodded. I understood.

"Okay. Let's think about it this way," I said. "Sattler was killed without a lot of malice and forethought, but whoever killed him went to a lot of trouble to make it look like suicide. The Westwood killing was not like that. Yes, whoever did it, and I think we know who that was, also did a little upfront planning. There were at least two of them, and they took everything they thought they would need with them, including several rolls of Duct Tape. They wore gloves, both of them, all of them, as the case may be. Westwood wasn't supposed to die. They wanted either information or they wanted to set an example. These killers didn't care about covering it up. They left him there, taped to the chair. They used a knife and they made it as graphic and *scary* as possible. The fact that he died was a bonus for them, even though it was a mistake.

The intent, according to Doc Sheddon, was terror, either for the victim... or for someone else."

Lonnie nodded, so did Mike.

"I believe, and Kate agrees with me, that Westwood's demise was the work of Sal De Luca's two soldiers, Gino Polti and Tony Carpeta. The cuts to Westwood's arms and legs were done by an expert, so that would be Gino; he's the knife man. Tony was the muscle."

"If De Luca was responsible for Westwood's death, what happened to the money?" Tim said. "Do you have any idea who could have made the transfer, or killed Sattler?"

"Not a clue. Sattler is still in the wind. I have no idea who might have killed him, or who stole the cash, but I think they were one and the same. Whoever it was, they were well known to him. That means it could have been one of the three partners or one or both of the family: Gloria or Stephanie. Kate?"

"I agree," Kate said, "but as Harry said. It could have been any one of them or... none of them. We need more information. We'll have to reinterview all of them and quickly. Harry, we have to find this killer. I'm catching all kinds of heat from the chief." She looked down at Guest who was sitting beside her.

"Lonnie. I want you to go and talk to the Hollister kid and Wendy Brewer. I'm thinking it'll be a waste of time, but you never know. I need the reports as soon as you can. Okay?"

Lonnie rose heavily to his feet, crammed a last bite of mushroom and peperoni into his mouth, took a huge swig of Coke, and started for the door.

"Hold on, Lonnie. We're not finished yet. Harry, let's you and me start right now with Cassell and then follow up with as many of the other three as possible."

"Why not start with De Luca?" I asked. "We know that son of a bitch killed Westwood, or at least is responsible for it. Let's start with Sal."

"No, we don't yet know if the print on the Duct Tape belongs to Gino or Tony. All we have right now is conjecture. We need more. We'll go see Cassell, the Steiner woman, and then the Sattlers."

"I don't agree. For one thing, as you say, right now *we* don't know if that print is theirs or not, but they don't know that we don't know that. We can bluff them. If the print doesn't belong to either of them, they'll know it, then we'll know it, and there's no harm done. If it does belong to one of them, they'll show it, and we'll have them. Look, Kate, if the son of a bitch did for Westwood, we need to know, now, before they kill someone else. The interviews can wait. De Luca can't. He may already have sent them out after Steiner or Cassell."

"For once, I agree with Harry." Lonnie was serious.

Damn, Lonnie. That's a first. What brought that on, I wonder?

"If it was one of them," he continued, "and they think they're clean, left no trace, they could, as Harry said, hit someone else, or they might even leave town, go back where they came from. De Luca can't afford to take chances losing his twelve mil, so we need to get to them ASAP. If not...."

Wow, good for you, Lonnie.

"Anyone else have any thoughts?" I said.

They all shook their heads.

"Right, De Luca it is, then. Kate?"

She shook her head. Obviously, she wasn't happy, "Harry, you and I will go in my car. Lonnie, you'll follow in the cruiser. When we're done, you go and interview Hollins and Brewer. I'll call for more backup when we get there. Let's go."

Chapter Twenty-Seven

I t was almost two o'clock when we arrived outside Il Sapore Roma. Kate pulled up at the curb outside the front door. Lonnie parked just behind her, and two more cruisers pulled up behind him.

I checked my weapon, jacked a shell into the breach, replaced it on my hip, and looked at Kate. She nodded. We both took a deep breath and then exited the car. Lonnie was already waiting at the front door.

"Okay," Lonnie said, nervously. "What's the plan?"

"Harry and I will go in first," Kate replied. "You follow us, but stay back. Keep your weapon holstered and your eyes peeled. If you see anything you don't like, sing out. Okay?"

He nodded. "Okay!" He hitched his belt, flipped the strap on his holster to free his Glock, jiggled it to make sure it would draw freely, let his jacket fall back into place, and then said, "Ready."

Kate looked at me. "Ready, Harry."

"As always."

She stepped forward. I did likewise. She pushed open the door and I followed her in, Lonnie right on my heels. I could hear him breathing.

They were there, all three of them, in their usual place. Sal sat on a stool at the bar, his bandaged right hand resting on the granite top. Tony was just to his right, Gino to his left, between Sal and the kitchen door.

When they heard the door open, they all looked up. Tony got up off his stool and moved away from Sal, slightly further to his right. Whether this was to give De Luca an unobstructed view, or to provide himself with one, I don't know, but it served as a warning and the three of us stopped in mid-stride.

"Take it easy, boys," Kate said, as she laid her hand lightly on the Glock. "We don't need any accidents, now do we?"

"What the hell do you want?" De Luca said. "I told you never to set foot in here again, Starke. You lookin' to get your ass handed to you in a bag?"

I said nothing. I stood beside Kate, watching all three, looking for the first sign of trouble.

"We've come for your boys, De Luca," she said. "Step forward, boys. You're coming with us."

"Like hell they are," Sal said, reaching for his phone. "What's the charge?"

"Murder. They killed James Westwood."

"What? Murder? Westwood's dead? You're shittin' me, right?" He was incredulous. It was easy to see he didn't know Westwood was dead.

"Nope. He's dead. Now, Tony. Take your weapon and place it on the bar, carefully and slowly. Lonnie, go get it." She gave the instructions without taking her eyes off any one of them. Lonnie retrieved Tony's 9mm Glock and stepped back, out of the line of fire.

"Gino," she said. "You did a bad thing. You left your prints on the inside of a roll of Duct Tape."

He glared at her, his eyes filled with hate. He flicked them back and forth, between me and Kate, finally settling them on me.

"Put the knife on the bar, Gino," she said, "and step away."

He growled something unintelligible, but didn't move.

"You heard her, Gino," I said, quietly. "Do it now."

He screwed up his mouth in a wild grimace, his eyes still on mine, narrowed to twin slits of pure evil, and he reached down. When his hand came up, it was holding Sal's .45 and he was thumbing the hammer.

Acting on instinct alone, in one single motion, I swept my right hand across to my left side, drew the nine, swung it upward and, BAM... BAM, BAM. I got off two shots to his one. I don't know if it was because he wasn't used to such a big weapon, but whatever, he missed. I didn't. My two slugs hit him in the heart, less than two inches apart. He staggered backward under the double impact. His legs were working, but his heart wasn't. They were already collapsing under him as he slammed into the kitchen door. It was locked, and he fell in a heap in front of it, dead before he hit the floor, the .45 clattering beside him.

Even I was stunned by the suddenness of it. It had taken less than three seconds and a man was dead, and I had killed him. I didn't see how De Luca and Tony reacted, but they both raised their hands. I only know that because I saw them do it by my peripheral vision. I was still staring dumbfounded at what was left of Gino Polti. The next thing I was aware of was Kate taking the weapon out of my hand, and the restaurant filling with cops.

Damn, that's three! I remember thinking as she took the gun, and yes, it was a stupid and unwarranted thought, but what the hell. I'd just shot a man dead.

The aftermath was a blur. I sat alone in Kate's car for what seemed like hours. Everybody and their mothers arrived on the scene, including Chief Johnston and DA Jack McClure. I was in the shit. That was for sure.

Tony and Sal Deluca were hauled away in handcuffs, on what charges I had no idea. Doc Sheddon arrived and pronounced Gino dead, duh, and they zipped him into a black vinyl bag and took him away to Sheddon's lair.

Me? My ears were ringing from the gunfire. Every time someone spoke to me, the words echoed. You know, just as you can sometimes hear yourself when you're talking on the phone. My head was aching, my eyes watering, but more than that, I was filled with an overwhelming sense of the enormity of what had just happened. It wasn't the first time. It wasn't even the second, but I had just shot a man to death, and I couldn't get the look in his eyes out of my mind.

Other than that, I guess I was okay. They dug the .45 slug Gino had sent my way out of the wall by the front door. It wasn't until later, when I was seated alone in the unmarked police car, that I remembered feeling the wind of it as it passed by my right ear. He'd meant it for me, that was for sure.

Kate returned to the car. She got in, didn't say a word, and then drove to the Police Department on Amnicola. The next three hours were filled with interrogations, statements, and a whole lot of stupid questions asked both by the chief and the DA. Finally, they let me go, and Kate drove me back to my office.

I didn't go in. I didn't want to talk, to anyone. I just wanted to go home.

"It's okay, Harry," Kate said, quietly as we sat together in her car. "It's self-defense, clear and simple. Both Lonnie and I saw what happened. There'll be no charges. By the way, De Luca and Carpeta were released before you were. Sal's lawyer was at the PD waiting when they were taken in. We have nothing on them, unless the print on roll of tape belongs to Tony, which I doubt."

"Yeah. Why am I not surprised? No charges for me, either, huh? That's something. Thanks, Kate. See you tomorrow?"

"Of course. Will you be all right?"

"Yeah. I'll be fine. Thanks. I love you." I don't know why I said that, it just came out. I felt pretty foolish, but what the hell.

She smiled, nodded, leaned over, and kissed me lightly on the cheek. "You sure you'll be okay?"

"Yep... yep. No problem."

I got out of her car, said goodnight to her, climbed into the Maxima, and headed home. Somehow, being in my own car was kind of calming. To this day, though, I'm not sure how I managed the drive home; everything was a blur. I remember starting the car, and the next thing I knew was hitting the garage door opener on the sun visor. I remembered nothing of the eight miles or so between my office and Lakeshore Lane. I parked the car in the garage and headed up the stairs into the kitchen. I looked at the clock on the wall. It was still early, not quite seven-thirty. I went to the bedroom, stripped, took a long, hot shower, and put on sweats. It was going to be one of those nights.

I made myself a grilled cheese sandwich, poured three fingers of Bombay Sapphire gin into a tall glass, added ice, tonic, a slice of lime, and then sat down on the couch in front of the big window.

The view across the Tennessee River was, as it always is, spectacular, even in bad weather, and it was deteriorating rapidly. The sky was the color of dirty snow. The light was dropping quickly and the Thrasher Bridge away to the west was already ablaze with streetlights and the lights of cars heading home from the city. The raindrops began to fall, slowly at first, and then harder: giant droplets that turned the surface of the river into a rippling blanket of tiny waterspouts. It was good to be home, even if I was alone.

For some reason, though, I couldn't settle. I was antsy. It had been a tough week. Too much information, most of it worthless, and what little of it did have some meaning was hard to separate. On top of it all, I had Gino's death to cope with. Killing a man, even when there's no other option, is one thing; living with it is quite another.

I need someone to talk to, maybe....

I dialed the number and waited. "Hello, Harry. Now's not a good time. I'm kind of tied up, and I have a meeting scheduled shortly. Can I call you back?"

I heaved a sigh. Senator Linda Michaels always seemed to be busy these days.

"Yeah, Linda. Sorry I bothered you. I just wanted to talk for a minute." I wasn't about to tell her I'd just killed a man.

"Harry, I'm sorry. I have to go. I'll call you as soon as I can, I promise. Okay?"

"Sure. Any time." I disconnected, stared at the iPhone screen, and then tossed it onto the coffee table. I don't think I'd ever felt quite as alone as I did at that moment.

I wasn't really hungry, but I ate the sandwich anyway, drank the gin and, with the empty glass still in hand, I sat and stared, unseeing, out across the water. The rain was coming down in sheets. Visibility was down to just a few yards. I sat alone in the dark with only my thoughts for company. It wasn't pleasant. I got up, poured another very large gin, sat down again, and stared some more.

I must have dozed off because the next thing I knew it was after ten o'clock and my cell phone was buzzing.

"Hello, Amanda. It's kinda late, don't you think? Yes, I'm alone. I dunno. I'm bushed. I don't want to talk. I just need to relax.... You're already here?"

Geez, I really don't need this tonight.

"Okay. I'll come down."

I opened the front door. She didn't have a coat on, just a thin cotton sundress. She was holding an open newspaper over her head. She was soaked to the skin, shivering and laughing, both at the same time. As bad as I felt, I couldn't help it. I laughed, too. I grabbed her arm and pulled her inside, out of the rain.

"I should have known better," she said, shivering. "Jack's forecast said only forty percent rain. Look at me. I'm soaked."

I did look at her. Even with her hair stuck to her face, she was beautiful. The thin dress was pasted to her body, and it outlined every curve; she was perfection.

"You know where the bathroom is. Go take off those wet clothes. I'll find something for you to wear."

"Do you mind if I take a shower?"

"Of course not. Help yourself."

Ten minutes later, she was out of the shower and dressed in one of my long-sleeve shirts. Her hair was wet. Her makeup was gone. She held her arms out for me to look at her, and she laughed. I did, too. All of a sudden, I was feeling better.

"I hope my dress dries. I have to be out of here by seven."

"Oh. I see. You're planning to spend the night, then?"

She looked at me through her eyelashes. "Yes, please."

I nodded, smiled. "What would you like to drink?"

I poured her a vodka tonic and we sat down together on the sofa to watch the rain.

"It's beautiful, Harry."

"It always is," I said. "Amanda?"

"Hmmm?"

"No shop talk. Okay? I need to relax, clear my head."

She nodded, slowly. "Harry... I heard you killed Gino today."

"I don't want to talk about it, okay?"

"But...."

"Leave it, Amanda."

She snuggled in closer. "I'm sorry, Harry. I can't even begin to imagine."

I didn't answer. I squeezed her tightly and stared out over the water.

"Harry...."

"It was his eyes," I interrupted her. "I can't get them out of my head...."

She put her hand to my chin, pulled my face to hers, and kissed me gently. I looked at her. There were tears rolling down her cheeks.

Chapter Twenty-Eight

Amanda had left my place before seven and headed straight to Channel 7. She had slept like a baby, I not at all. I still had Gino on my mind. She brought me coffee before she left, kissed me, and looked into my eyes.

"Will you be all right?"

"Hah! Oh yes. How about you?"

"Well. I need to go. Can I call you later? Just to see how you are?"

"Of course. You can call me whenever you like. Amanda...."

"What?"

"Thank you."

"For what?"

"For being there when I needed someone."

"Any time, Harry. Any time. Later... okay?"

"Yeah, later."

She left. I lay in bed watching the sun rise over the river. The rain of the night before had ended. The sky was a deep cerulean with vast banks of billowing white clouds, ever changing shape as they scudded across the heavens. It was going to be a beautiful day, and I was going to be a part of it, despite the worst intentions of the now deceased Gino Polti.

I drank my coffee, got out of bed, and stretched.

Ouch. Dammit that hurt.

The wound in my arm was still sore, and my left shoulder was still stiff. No matter. I had to work it off. I dropped and did six pushups. I'd planned on fifty, but it was too much for my arms. I did some crunches, just a few, but my heart just wasn't in it. I lay there for maybe ten minutes, staring up at the ceiling. When I finally made it into the shower, I was hurting like the devil. The hot water helped, but I still felt like death warmed over.

I dressed: light gray slacks, black golf shirt, loafers, and then swallowed five Ibuprofen tablets. I felt the empty Blackhawk holster at my hip.

*Awe hell. I can't keep on buying guns. They're gonna
have to let me have at least one of them back.*

I called Kate.

"Heeey, Harry. How are you feeling this morning?"

"I'm good. Listen. How about you get one of my guns
released? I can't keep on replacing them. It's ridiculous."

"I'll see what I can do. I'll bring it with me. You at the
office?"

"No. I'm still at home. I'm about to leave. I should be
there by nine."

"See you at nine then."

I slipped the phone into my pants pocket, grabbed a Yeti
full of Italian Roast, and headed out into bright sunlight.

As I drove south in heavy traffic across the Thrasher
Bridge on 153, I became lost in thought, not about Gino,
or the past couple of days, or even the investigation. I was
thinking about Amanda, and the other women in my life.

There were now three of them.

Kate, with whom I'd had an on again off again relationship for more than ten years, currently off.

Senator Linda Michaels, one of the gods of Washington
DC, who rarely had time even for herself, let alone
for me.

And now the lovely Amanda Cole, star of local TV. I didn't know whether to count myself extremely lucky, or a stupid fool for pressing my luck. I didn't believe in love, at least not until six months ago when I first became involved with Linda. Even now I'm not sure if such a thing even exists. Lust, yeah. Love? *I ain't so sure.*

Visions of all three of them flashed in and out of my subconscious. It was like a slideshow: one beautiful image after another. What it all meant, I had no idea. I think, in a way, I loved them all. In another... none of them. I was still trying to figure it out when I pulled the Maxima into my parking space outside my office.

The looks I got from the staff when I walked into the outer office were odd. Except for Bob, who grinned at me and winked, a combination of sympathy and concern. I waved them off, walked over to the Keurig and made myself a cup of coffee.

"Okay, everyone." I looked around the office. "Grab your notes, coffee, and let's do it."

Kate and Lonnie arrived just after nine o'clock. My scheduled Friday morning status meeting was all but finished.

"Hey, Kate, Lonnie," I said. "Grab some coffee; take a seat. We're almost done here."

"How are you feeling, Harry?" Kate asked.

Oh hell, here we go again.

"I'm good," I said, impatiently. "If you're talking about Gino, it's over, done with. He was a piece of garbage. I can live with it. Let's move on. I was saying before you came in, that even though De Luca admitted nothing, we can take it to the bank that he was responsible for both the attack on Cassell and Westwood's death, which was an accident. Well... you know what I mean. I don't think De Luca killed Sattler, and I don't think he had anything to do with the theft of the 350 mil. Does everyone agree? Any comments?"

"Just one," Kate said. "Doc Sheddon called me earlier this morning. He did the autopsy on Gino. Guess what? Gino had a bullet wound, on his left forearm, a crease, seven or eight days old. It must have been him you shot in Sattler's home that night."

"Well, that's good to know, I suppose. We can only guess why he was there, though. De Luca's not talking, neither's Tony, and Gino certainly isn't." *So, I nailed the bastard twice.*

"Anything else?" I looked around the table. They were all shaking their heads.

"No? Okay, so let's get the interviews done. Lonnie is going to see Hollins and Brewer, right?"

"Yes. He'll meet us back here when we're done. You good with that, Lonnie?" Kate asked.

He was.

"Good." I looked at Kate. "So you and I will start with Cassell. If you need coffee, now's the time to get it. Let's go."

Marty Cassell was not pleased to see us. In fact, he was downright pissed off. At first, he wouldn't even come to the door.

"We just need a minute of your time, Mr. Cassell," Kate yelled at the glass door panel. Then she pounded on it with the side of her fist. Finally.

"*Clear off!* I don't want any more trouble. You're gonna get my ass killed! I got nothin' to say to you."

The door opened a crack and a bloodshot eye appeared. "I said, *clear off.* Now go."

I put my shoulder to the door, winced as pain coursed down my arm. Now I was mad.

"Goddamn it, Cassell," I shouted. "We just want to talk. Open the goddamn door or I'll smash it open."

"Piss off!"

I stepped back and kicked the frame. The chain tore away from the frame, the door flew open, and Cassell staggered backward.

"Ow, ow, you piece o' garbage. You busted my nose again. I'll goddamn sue you. I'm callin' my goddamn' lawyer right now. Goddamn it, ow, my nose!"

He was right. Well, maybe it wasn't broken, but it was bleeding. I felt a wave of remorse wash over me.

Oh shit. I need this like a hole in the head.

"Marty, I'm sorry," I said, helping him to his feet. "You should have opened the damn door; we're not going to hurt you."

"You already did, you son of a bitch. Where's my goddamn phone? I'll have your ass locked up." It was then he noticed Kate.

"What the hell are you grinning at, Goldie Locks? You're a goddamn cop. Handcuff this son of a bitch. I want him charged with assault."

"Calm down, Marty," she said. "I wasn't grinning at you. It was Harry. You should be honored. He never apologizes, to *anyone*. Look, we're here to help you. Did you know James was dead?"

He stared at her, his mouth wide open, and put his hand to his wounded nose.

"Dead?" he whispered. "Oh my God. How? When?"

"Wednesday night, late. He died of a heart attack as a result of extended torture."

"Torture," he whimpered. "Like me? What... who?"

"You know who, Marty," she said. "Look at what they did to you."

In fact, he was looking a whole lot better than he was four days ago. The eyes were both black, but the swelling had gone down. His lips were almost back to their normal size. His ears were hidden by a bandage wrapped completely around his head from under which he stared out at us with bloodshot eyes. He looked like the manager at the sleazy motel near the airport.

"De Luca," she said. "Not him personally. Gino and Tony. James Westwood wasn't supposed to die. The idea was to scare him, and you, and Ms. Steiner. He wants his money back."

Cassell looked wildly around him, then over Kate's shoulder.

"It's okay," she said, placing a calming hand on his shoulder. "Gino Polti is dead, and I don't think De Luca will bother you again, okay?"

"Gino's dead? How?"

"I shot him."

That brought a huge smile to his face, which, considering his injuries, was downright scary. It also hurt him, because it lasted only a second, and then he winced, and closed his eyes.

"Hell, Starke," he said. "Maybe you ain't such a goddamn jerk after all. Okay. You'd better come in, I suppose."

"We won't be long, Marty. Just a few questions."

He nodded, and we sat down at the same table as the first time we met him.

"When they were beating on you," she began, "what did they want? What were they after?"

"The money, of course. The week was up. I was supposed to deliver it to De Luca, but I didn't have it."

"Has De Luca contacted you since then?" I asked.

"Every goddamn day. What he's gonna do to me is.... He said he's gonna cut my balls off, an' that's just for starters. He'll do it, too. You don't know him."

"Now think about this carefully, Marty," I said. "Could he have killed Tom Sattler?"

Slowly, he shook his head. "I don't know; I don't think so. I don't think he even knew him. I handled his money. Why would he go after Tom?"

Yeah, why indeed? For the same reason he went after James Westwood, and you, maybe.

"Look, Marty," Kate said. "We know you and Jessica were both at Tom's house on the day he died. Did you go back later?"

We both watched him carefully, looking for some sort of reaction. We got one and it wasn't pretty. He stood up, pushed his chair back, and pointed toward the door.

"Screw you, both of you," he snarled, wincing. "Get the

hell out of my house. Tom Sattler was a friend, so was James... and Jessica. You think any one of us could have killed Tom? You're crazy. No, I didn't go back. Now get the hell out of my home and don't come back."

He sniffed through the splint on his nose, gave us a withering look, shook his head, and stalked out of the room. I looked at Kate. She rolled her eyes and stood up.

"Let's do as the man said."

I nodded, got up, and followed her out to the car. As I did so, I turned and looked back at the house. Marty Cassell was watching from one of the windows.

The interview with Jessica Steiner didn't go any better. Fortunately, or unfortunately, depending upon how you view these things, she was fully dressed in shorts, a tank top, and sandals.

Oh well.

She was stunned to hear about Westwood, and she stared at me with what could only have been open admiration when Kate told her that I had killed Gino Polti. Yes, she knew De Luca, had met him several times. He'd made passes at her twice, both of which she had rejected. She hadn't seen or heard from him for several weeks.

When Kate asked her if she'd returned to Tom's house

the evening he died, she maintained eye contact and simply shook her head.

As we left, she caught my eye, put her left hand to her ear, her thumb and little finger extended, and mouthed, "Call me."

Two down, two to go.

Chapter Twenty-Nine

By three-thirty that afternoon we were back on Stony Mountain Drive in the Mountain Shadows subdivision, outside the home of Gloria and Stephanie Sattler.

"How do you want to play this?" I asked.

"We need to talk to them separately. You take Stephanie, I'll take Gloria. What do you think?"

"I think we need to find out exactly what was going on between Tom Sattler and Stephanie. If he was abusing her and what part the mother played in it all. She did, after all, use the abuse card to get her divorce settlement."

"Okay. Let's do it."

Gloria opened the door. The passing days had not treated her kindly. It was mid-afternoon and she looked like she was dressed for bed in a T-shirt at least two sizes too big for her with the words, *"You Can Have It If You Want It,"* emblazoned across the front. A pair of old and sweaty spandex yoga pants clung to her thighs and ass and emphasized every extra pound.

Er... no. I don't want it, but thanks anyway.

She didn't give us a chance to speak. She simply looked at us, from one to the other, with dull, tired eyes, shook her head, shrugged, and then turned and walked from the foyer into the kitchen, leaving the door open behind her.

We followed.

She waved a listless hand in the general direction of the stools arranged along the outside of the breakfast bar. I supposed it was an invitation to sit. I looked at Kate. She rolled her eyes and sat. I dropped onto the stool next to her.

"Mrs. Sattler–" Kate began.

"Yeah, yeah," she interrupted, "I know, you want to ask more questions. Gimme a minute, will you? You want some coffee?" She was already pouring herself a cup. Neither of us did.

"So what do you want this time?" she asked, parking her spandex-covered rear on a stool on the opposite side of the bar.

"We'd like to talk to you, and Stephanie, if you don't mind. We need to ask a few more questions about Mr. Sattler's death. Is she here?"

She reached for an iPhone a couple of feet away on the bar top, punched something into it, hit send and put it down again.

"She's upstairs. She'll be down, whenever. Look, I'm not feeling so good, as you can probably tell. Is this going to take long?"

"We need to talk to you individually," Kate said. "If you don't mind."

"Yeah, yeah, whatever." She looked over my shoulder.

I turned and looked, too. Stephanie Sattler was coming down the stairs.

"They have more questions for us," Gloria said, then looked at Kate. "Who goes first?"

"If you don't mind," Kate said. "Mr. Starke will talk to your daughter while you and I have a chat. Is that okay?"

She sighed. "Whatever. Steph, why don't you take him into the den? I can't be bothered to get up."

She nodded. "Please, come with me, Mr. Starke."

This time, she wasn't quite so lovely. Her eyes were red, and she looked as if she'd been crying, nervous. She was wearing jeans, a tank top, and slippers. She led me through the foyer and down two steps into a comfortable, though cluttered, family room. She sat down on the sofa; I sat on the edge of the seat of a huge, leather easy chair. There was a heavy, tile-top coffee table between us.

"If you don't mind, Miss Sattler, I need to record this conversation." I set my small digital recorder on the table and looked at her.

"I don't mind. So, what would you like to know, Mr. Starke?"

"First, I'd like to ask you about the day your father died. Did you have occasion to visit him that day?" She quickly raised her hand to her mouth, and then put it down again. There was a slight flicker of her right eye, but she answered immediately.

"Yes, I went over that morning for coffee, and I dropped by after lunch on my way back from town. He had company so I didn't go in. I didn't see him again."

"Look, Miss Sattler...."

"Please, call me Stephanie."

"Right. Look, Stephanie, there's no easy way for me to do this, but I need to talk to you about your father."

"Okay. Go ahead."

"What, exactly, was your relationship with him like?"

"Like? He was my dad. What do you think it was like? I loved him. He loved me."

I stared at her, leaned back in the chair. I almost disappeared; it was so big and deep. She smiled. I sat up again.

"Yes, I'm sure you did, and I'm sure he did, too, but how well did you get along with him?"

"Mr. Starke. You asked that question the first time you were here. I told you then that my sisters and I loved our father and got along well with him. There's nothing I can add to that. He was our... dad."

Okay, this is going nowhere. Let's try a little shock and awe.

Stephanie," I said, quietly. "I know about the charges that were brought against him during the divorce proceedings, for child abuse. Would you like to tell me about that?"

Her face went white. She swallowed, blinked rapidly, looked away, and then back again. Her eyes were watering.

"You *bastard.* How dare you? *How dare you besmirch my father's good name?* My dad was a good man. He never laid a finger on me, on any of us."

"So why were the charges brought against him?"

"No charges were ever brought against him. That was my bitch of a mother. She threatened him. Had her goddamn lawyers threaten him. She screwed him out of almost everything he owned. Said she would expose him, that he sexually abused me."

"Did he? Did he abuse you?"

"*Hell, no, you asshole.* I told you he loved me."

"How about your sisters?"

I thought she was going to come across the table at me, but she didn't. She shook her head. Her eyes were watering; a tear ran down her cheek. She sat there, trembling, her hands twisting together in her lap. She looked away, unable to hold my stare. I wasn't sure. If it was an act, it was a good one, but there was something....

"Stephanie. You can tell–"

I didn't get the chance to finish. She jumped to her feet and ran from the room. I sighed, picked up the recorder, turned it off, and went back to the kitchen. Kate was just wrapping up her interview with Gloria, who looked angry. We said goodbye to her. Stephanie was nowhere to be seen.

"So," Kate said when we were back in the car. "I wonder if you got any more out of Stephanie than I got out of her mother, which was nothing."

"I didn't get a whole lot either. Stephanie is very sensitive about the sexual abuse thing. She became very upset when I brought it up; stormed out of the room at the end. I do believe that it might be a case of 'she doth protest too much.' I can understand her being upset, but to fly off the handle like that... well, it could all have been an act. How about her mother?"

"From what you've just told me," she said, "I think it was more of the same. I thought she was going to slap me when I asked if he'd been abusing Stephanie. If something was going on, and I think it probably was, Gloria knew about it, and she did nothing to stop it."

"Well, that's typical. It happens all the time. The child complains to the mother. The mother goes into denial, and the child continues to be abused until she grows too old. Hell, it's not unusual under such circumstances for the child to fall in love with the father, and then suffer all of the rejection and jealousy any other lover experiences when she gets dumped. If that's the case, and Stephanie did kill him, there could be all kinds of defenses, including justifiable homicide, insanity, you name it."

"Yeah, I suppose so," she said, thoughtfully

"What makes you think the mother knew what was going on?" I asked.

"She's a liar, that's why. Oh, I can't pinpoint any one thing, but you and that fancy degree of yours know what I'm talking about. It's a look, a twitch of the mouth, body language; she kept playing with her hair and looking away as she answered the questions. She's a liar. I think that at some time in the past Tom Sattler was indeed abusing Stephanie. Now what the result of it all might be, I have no idea. What I do know is that it gives both of them a strong motive."

I nodded. "That and the estate. Stephanie was of the opinion that, as Sattler's next of kin, she and her sisters will split it. If that's true, we're talking millions of dollars.

Tom was very good at what he did, and he had ten years after the divorce to rebuild his wealth."

"I wonder what Gloria thinks about that," Kate said, thoughtfully. "About all that money going to the kids. Oh, and by the way, I forgot to tell you. Richard Hollins is in the clear. He was out with three of his pals. Lonnie interviewed all four of them. Hollins said he got home just after midnight. His buddies backed that up. His alibi is good and tight."

"Yeah, well. Somehow I never really figured him for it."

I looked at my watch. It was after five. The weekend was upon us. I was tired, thirsty, and hungry.

"You want to go eat?" I said.

She shook her head. "I'd like to, but I can't. Raincheck? I'll take you back to your car. I have to go to the office, and I don't want to be there all night."

Just like that, huh? No explanation, no.... Ah, screw it.

She dropped me off at my car, and I headed for the Sorbonne.

Geez, even Benny Hinkle is better than no company at all.

Chapter Thirty

I don't usually work on weekends, but with the state of the Sattler investigation, I made an exception. More than that, though, I had a bug up my ass, so I called Kate and arranged for her to meet me at the office.

"Kate, there's something been bugging me for days, about Sattler's murder. That second shot from the murder weapon. We never found it, and we haven't given it much thought; and then there's the hair. What about that?"

"Oh you can forget about the hair. It's no help at all. It was Stephanie's, and there's no reason why it shouldn't have been there. She was in and out of the house almost daily and forever. The second shot, though... I must admit, it's not even crossed my mind this last week or so. Does it really have any significance, now we know he was murdered?"

"I don't know. It might. I'd like to find it. If not, I'd at least like to figure out what happened to it. Somebody went to a whole hell of a lot of trouble to hide it, make it look like suicide. That must mean something, right?"

"I suppose. It's not going to tell us who did it, though.... Is it?"

"Kate, there are two things I think we need to know. One is what happened to that second shot, the other is how the hell the money was transferred using Sattler's laptop... unless.... Kate, you don't suppose we're on the wrong track, do you? That Sattler did it himself?"

"What? Transfer the money? He... yes, he could have. We've assumed all along that he didn't, just because he was killed, but that could have been the reason *why* he was killed."

"Okay, so let's for a minute assume that he stole the money. That brings up a whole new set of questions, the most important of which is, why? And if that is indeed the case," I mused, "then who can we eliminate?"

"The family?" Kate said. "No, I don't thinks so. Hollins is out anyway. He has an ironclad alibi. Brewer? Maybe, but I never really liked either of those two for it anyway. That leaves the two surviving partners. It couldn't have been De Luca, could it? So Steiner, Cassell, Gloria, or Stephanie...."

I waited for her to continue, but she didn't. She just sat with her elbows on her knees, and stared into her cup.

"Is that it?" I said.

"I don't like Sattler for it, Harry. He's worth millions, and he would have known that he couldn't get away with it, and even if he did, why would anyone want to kill him and kiss the money goodbye, forever? It just doesn't make any sense."

"So who *do* you like for it, Kate? If Sattler didn't steal the money, we're looking for two separate perps. Who do you think killed him?"

"I'm thinking Steiner. She could have done both: killed him and made the steal. We have only her word for her sexual encounter with Sattler. She has no alibi for the time of death. She was there earlier in the day, as late as five o'clock, so we know she was in town. As you said before, the cell phone records only tell us her phone wasn't there. She could have pulled the chip and returned later, and she has the knowhow to make the transfer and... well, I just don't like her. What about you? Who do you like for it?"

"You don't like her? What the hell kind of thinking is that for an experienced detective?"

She laughed. "I'm a woman, right? Anyone who looks that good.... Okay, okay. So who?"

"I don't like Steiner for it, or Cassell; he's in too deep with De Luca. He would have been committing suicide by Sal. I'm thinking possibly Stephanie Sattler, but it's a real stretch. The only alibi she has is her mother, and there's something about the interviews that tells me that they, or at least she, are hiding something. Then there's the alleged child abuse. If Sattler had been abusing her all these years, well.... That's a huge motive. She also had the expertise to make the transfer, and... she had access to his codes. Maybe she's not such a long shot after all."

"Dammit, Harry. He was her father. She loved him."

"True, well, she *said* she loved him... but it happens all the time, and for less. Look at what the Menendez brothers did to their parents, and that was just for money. Sexual abuse is something else again, and most juries would look sympathetically on it. Sure, she said she loved him, but did she?"

"Whew. Who the hell knows? Only her mother, I suppose, and that's a dead end," she said. "And what about her mother, Gloria? Any thoughts about her? Stephanie is her alibi, and that sexual abuse motive works both ways, for both of them. Hey, they could have done it together."

"You're right," I said. "That one motive fits either one or both of them, and neither of them has an alibi, except for each other. Pity the boyfriend, Hollins, wasn't home. Right now, I suppose Gloria's as good a choice as any of the others. I dunno; I just don't know."

I looked at her, she seemed as mystified as I was. We were more than two weeks into this thing and neither one of us seemed to be any the wiser.

"Kate, let's just suppose that the wire transfer has nothing to do with the murder, that Sattler did make it himself, and I don't think he did. I don't see that it would make anything any easier."

"So what do we do, Sherlock? I need a solution to this mess and quickly."

"We need to go back to the scene, see if we can figure out that second shot. It may help; it may not, but right now we have nowhere else to go, and we'll never know unless we try."

"Okay. When do you want to do it?"

I looked at my watch. It was almost noon.

"No time like the present, Kate. Tell you what. Let's go see what we can find. We can grab lunch on the way and then, later this evening maybe, I'll buy you dinner. Sound good?"

She looked at me skeptically. "You know, Harry... nah."

"What? What were you going to say?"

"Well, I was thinking. I missed dinner with you the night I had to work, and you are a good cook...." She looked down at the table, blushing.

I reached over and took her hand. "You got it. What do you fancy?"

"Right now I fancy something I can't have, at least not here. Now look. Don't read anything into this. I still haven't forgotten Olivia Hansen, and I know you've been screwing Amanda Cole. There's also the senator to consider. My God, Harry, you do put yourself about. For now, let's just plan on having a nice evening and let it go at that. Okay?" She took her hand away, leaned back in her chair, and smiled at me.

"Cool," I said. "My car or yours?"

"Yours, of course. It's nicer than my unmarked, and it's also nice for someone else to do the driving for a change."

Chapter Thirty-One

We stopped at Arby's on the way and ordered roast beef sandwiches and iced tea to go. We arrived outside Tom Sattler's home on Royal Mountain Drive at one o'clock in the afternoon. The crime scene tapes were still up, and someone had put sign-in sheets on both doors. We both signed, put on gloves and boot covers, and Kate unlocked the side door.

"Whoa," I said, as a gust of hot, malodorous air hit us in the face. "What the hell is that about? Someone must have turned the air off."

"Yeah." Kate flipped the light switch just inside the door. "Someone must have turned everything off at the breaker box. That's not good."

The place stunk. Black fingerprint powder covered every surface.

Damn. I should've known better than to wear light-colored pants and shirt.

We made our way through the kitchen to the foyer and living room. The smell was worse in there. The blood-stained section of carpet had been removed, but the wooden particle board floor below was black and crawling with life. The blood had soaked the wood composite, putrefied, and the flies had taken full advantage of it. It might not have been so bad if the air had been left on. As it was... it was disgusting.

"Hell," Kate said. "This is no fun."

She was right. We looked around the room. The silence was almost palpable. It hung over everywhere like a pall of invisible fog.

"We know he didn't use one of the cushions," she said. "If he had, he would have had to have taken it with him, but they're all there. You can see them in the photos on the piano."

"Okay," I said. "Let's not screw around. Let's get on with it. Come with me."

I walked over to the bare patch of floor and stood at the right side of it, to the right side of where Tom's head had been, the side from which he'd been shot.

"Come and stand behind me," I said. "Okay. Good. He was lying here, facing the foyer. The killer had to have been where I am. So Tom is on his knees, and the killer fires one shot into the side of his head, like so." I pointed my right index finger to indicate the direction.

"What if the killer was left-handed?"

"He wasn't," I said. "If he had been, the shot would probably have been even further back than it was, or he would have shot him in the other side of his head. So, from here, what do we see?"

I looked at every inch of the room I could see from where I was standing. I shook my head. *It has to be here somewhere. Come on, come, come on.... What the hell am I not seeing?*

She leaned in close and looked over my right shoulder. I could smell her perfume. Nice, but distracting. I took a step away from her.

"What?" she said.

"Nothing. What do you see?"

"CSI checked all the walls, the woodwork, the ceiling, floor, nothing. He sure as hell didn't shoot it out of the window. That would have meant dragging the body over there and back again. Sorry, Harry. That was a stupid thing to say."

"Yeah." I laughed. "It was. Hey...." I said, thoughtfully. "Come over here."

I stepped over the bloodstained patch of floorboard and over to the bookshelf beside the fireplace.

"A book," I said. "How about one of the books?"

She was nodding, her eyes wide open, excited.

"You take that one," she said, pointing to the shelves to the right. "I'll do the one to the left. Start as close to the where the body was as you can. He wouldn't have reached far. Ignore the thin books; it would have to have been a thick one, like this one." She dragged out a huge copy of *War and Peace*, scanned the cover, and put it back.

"Hey, wait," I said. "We need to look inside. You never know."

She grabbed it again and riffled through the pages. Nothing.

It didn't take as long as I thought it would. In fact, I had pulled only a dozen or so books from the shelves when I found it. It was inside a copy of Dostoyevsky's *Crime and Punishment. How appropriate.* It was an expensive book, cloth bound. The killer had opened it, as I had thought he might, and not just the cover; he'd gone inside to page thirty-two. The small hole, surrounded by a scorch mark, was right in the center of the page. The slug was still in there, smashed almost beyond recognition. It had penetrated less than 100 pages.

"Here you go," I said, showing it to Kate, and then handing it to her. "You need to get this over to forensics, have it processed. I don't think the slug will do us any good, but you never know. We've got what we came for, now let's get the hell out of here. The stink of this place is making me sick."

I took one last look at the bloody floorboards, all that was left of Tom Sattler, and followed her out into the fresh air. After the house, it was intoxicating. I never knew anything could smell so good.

Chapter Thirty-Two

I drove her back to my office where her car was parked.

"Okay, Kate. You need to take that book to forensics. The weekend is upon us. I am tired. My arms, both of them, are sore. It's been a long week and I need a break, a large drink, a good meal, and some good company, in that order. You still up for it?"

She looked hard at me, thought for a moment, then slowly nodded.

"Good." I looked at my watch. It was just after four-fifteen. "I need to stop along the way home to get some food. What do you fancy?"

She grinned and looked sideways at me.

"Just make sure you have a couple of bottles of nice red

wine... and a thick, juicy filet would be nice, with... oh, I don't know. You figure it out."

I did. She left to take the book in to get it processed. That done, she said she would head home to change clothes. I spent a few moments in my office with Jacque. What the hell she was doing there on a Saturday afternoon, I had no idea, and she wouldn't tell me. I suspected she figured that if I was at work, she needed to be there too. Great gal, that Jacque. I hustled her out to her car, made sure the office doors were locked, got into my car and headed home. I stopped off at the Fresh Market. I bought two huge filets, a dozen large sea scallops, a nice bunch of asparagus, some romaine lettuce, and a couple of tomatoes. From there, I went to Huey's on Highway 58 and persuaded him to let loose of two bottles of Cakebread Cabernet Sauvignon 2012 from his own private reserve. The man is a treasure.

I arrived home at five-thirty. The sun was already low over the crest of Lookout Mountain, and the sky was tinged with pink. It was going to be a beautiful evening, in more ways than one, I hoped.

I put the car away, poured myself a couple of fingers of Laphroaig, sipped, showered, shaved, put on a pair of white, lightweight slacks and a navy golf shirt, and then went into the kitchen to start cooking. I was already feeling better. My left shoulder was no longer stiff, and the pain from the bullet wound had subsided almost to nothing.

A couple more stiff jolts of Laphroaig, and I'll be feeling no pain at all.

You have to love scotch whiskey to appreciate the subtleties of that finest of malts. They say it 'gives you a big, peaty slap in the face.' Hah. I wouldn't put it quite like that. For sure, it's an acquired taste, and one I spent many a happy hour and no little cash acquiring. That being said, I duly acquired two fingers more of the said 'big peaty, slap in the face,' and then I went to work.

It was just after seven-thirty when she arrived. She let herself in. Yes, she still had her own key, although she hadn't used it in more than six months.

She slipped quietly up behind me, slid her arms around my waist, and pulled me tightly to her. I could feel every curve of her body. She was warm, soft, like a cashmere blanket. I turned to face her, kissed her gently, and then pushed her away to arm's length so that I could look at her.

"It's been a long time, Kate."

She nodded. "Too long. Pour me some wine, please."

I was holding both of her hands, and I didn't want to let them go, at that moment, or ever. She looked stunning. She was wearing a white, sleeveless translucent top, a glittering black mini-skirt, and black sandals with three-inch heels. Her hair was down. It cascaded around her face like a dark, golden cloud, all the way to the tips of her breasts. She wore only a hint of makeup, a little blush and a soft rose lipstick. For more than a minute, we stood eye-to-eye. Me? I must have had the most stupid look on my face.

"Come on, Harry. You can't eat me. Please, I want some wine."

I grinned and shook my head. She was the most perfect thing.

How in God's name did I ever let her get away from me?

The sad part is I knew exactly how. I dropped her hands and did as she said.

It was almost six o'clock the next morning when she left. I had thoughts that our relationship had finally turned the corner, for the better. Boy, was I wrong. I heard nothing from her all the next day, Sunday. She wasn't answering my calls or texts. I spent that day, moping around the house, watching football, and reading my notes. By the time I went to bed, I was truly and totally depressed.

Chapter Thirty-Three

When Kate arrived at my office at eight o'clock on Monday morning, she was all business. It was as if that evening had never happened.

Wow, what the hell went wrong?

We grabbed cups of coffee. I told Jacque that we were not to be disturbed and went to my office and closed the door.

We sat down together in two of the guest chairs with a coffee table between us. I tried; God help me I tried, but I couldn't let it go.

"Kate, about Saturday night–"

"No," she interrupted. "Let's not go there. It was a wonderful evening, one I needed more than I'm prepared to say, but please, let's not talk about it."

"Okay... but, I have to know: what about... well, what about us?"

"Harry, there is no us. There hasn't been since Olivia Hansen.... I don't know if there ever will be again. I need time. Saturday night was wonderful. Please take it for what it was worth. Oh, don't worry. I didn't say we couldn't spend time together; just not...."

I heaved a huge sigh. I knew it was no good arguing with her. She'd made up her mind, and I would have to live with it. We sat together in silence; she staring into her cup; me lying back in the chair, eyes closed. Then I felt her lips on mine, just a quick brush, and then they were gone. I opened my eyes. She was back in her chair, smiling at me.

"Come on, Harry. Please don't mope. We'll get through this. Okay?"

I smiled back at her, took a deep breath, leaned forward and grabbed my pad from the table.

Geez, Harry. Grow up. Get a grip of yourself. You pissed her off, big time. Let her get over it, for Christ's sake.

I looked at her, smiled, and said, "I know we will." I looked at my watch. It was almost 8:45. I got to my feet, offered her my hand to help her up, and said, "Let's get to work."

"Right," she said, taking my hand and pulling herself up. I winced as pain coursed through my upper arm.

"Listen," she said. "We're not due to meet until nine. I have a few calls to make, check in with the office, and such. I'll do it from my car, if you don't mind. I'll join you all when I'm done, okay?"

By nine o'clock, we were sitting at the table in my conference room, along with Jacque, Tim, Ronnie, and Mike. Amanda had arrived fifteen minutes earlier, looking like a million bucks. Kate had walked in a few minutes after her, followed by the inimitable Sergeant Lonnie Guest.

"Hey, Kate, Lonnie, take a seat; nice to see you both," I said, dryly.

What the hell is he doing here?

"Lonnie is here," Kate said, "because I thought we might be able to use an extra hand. Talking of hands, how's yours, Harry? Your arm, that is?"

There she goes again, reading my damn mind. She knows damn well how my arm is. She spent the goddamn night with me, for God's sake. Extra hand? Lonnie? Yep, nice, but it would be even nicer if he had a brain to go with it.

"Which one?" I asked. "The gunshot has scabbed over but still hurts like the devil. My left shoulder is black and feels like it has a clamp screwed down tight on it. Ah... they're both okay. I've had worse."

I flipped open my legal pad, looked around the room, and said, "Anyone need coffee before we start?"

Kate and Lonnie held up their hands.

"Hey, buddy," I said to Mike. "I hate to ask, but would you mind?"

He grinned, left the room, and returned a couple of minutes later with two cups.

"Okay, let's get started," I said. "Kate, you go first."

"First, let's get the Westwood killing out of the way," she began. "As you know, De Luca and Tony Scarpeta have been arrested for his death, but both are back on the streets again. No evidence; no charges.

"Second, the $350 million is still missing and we don't have a clue as to who stole it.

"Third. On Saturday, Harry and I went back to Sattler's home. Harry was of the opinion that the second shot fired from Sattler's Ruger was important, and that we needed to find it. We did find it. The killer had fired it into a book. The book was then replaced on the bookshelf. CSI missed it, which is not surprising because there are more than eight hundred volumes on the bookshelves. Good job, Harry."

"So, you took it to forensics? What did they find?" I asked.

"Not a whole lot, just two partial prints; one on the spine, the other on the inside of the cover. Neither have enough detail to make an ID. The cover itself is cloth bound, so they found nothing else, either on it, or the pages inside.

The bullet, of course, is no help at all. In short, it's a washout."

"Goddammit," I said. "So we're no farther forward, then? We have nothing, other than a half-dozen suspects, most of whom have dubious alibis, or no alibi at all, a hole in a book, a couple of smudges, a deformed .22 slug, and a few prints we have yet to identify. Come *on*, people. Talk to me. Give me something to work with, dammit."

"Tim," Kate said. "Is there any way you could enhance the two partials, make them more readable?"

"I can try, but–"

"Yes," Amanda interrupted, "but even if you had a clear print on the book, if it belonged to someone that was supposed to be there, it wouldn't help, right?

"Right," I said. "Geez, Kate, what the hell does it matter? Even if we identify them, unless they belong to either Steiner, Westwood, Hollins or Cassell, it would be inconclusive. It's like that damned hair. It belonged to Stephanie and could have been left there for weeks or even months before he was killed. Same goes for the prints. Even if they belong to one of the suspects, they could have been there for years. It's a wash. The second shot means nothing; nothing at all."

"Er...."

"What, Lonnie? Speak up, if you have an idea. Anything is better than nothing."

"Well, actually," he said, hesitantly, "I was reading in one of the tech mags in the office. I read a lot. There was an article about fingerprinting. It said how it's now possible to determine the age of a fingerprint...." He trailed off, blushed, and looked away, embarrassed.

"Go on, Lonnie," Kate said. "I missed that."

He took a deep breath. "There's a new sensor available to CSI units that can age fingerprints; tell them how old they are. I didn't understand the tech, but it says that it's very accurate. It measures the electrostatic charges on the surface of a print."

He looked around the table. Everyone was watching him, even me.

"Not only that," he continued, "they can also find and photograph a print that would otherwise be invisible. The sensor detects and measures the gradual deterioration of the electrostatic charge as the print ages. It's kinda like Carbon 14 dating, only... different."

I had to smile at that one.

"That's new one on me. Did it say how accurate it is?" Tim asked.

"Yeah, they say it's pretty accurate. It can get as close as a couple of hours, if it's done fairly quickly, say within a couple of weeks, while the electrostatic charge is still hot. Beyond that, gets a bit iffy, several hours, half a day, maybe."

I looked at Kate, who shrugged.

"Is there any way we could get our hands on one of those sensors?" I asked. "Chattanooga PD doesn't have anything like that, I suppose?"

She smiled. "Not hardly. If it's that new, I doubt even the TBI has one."

"Damn!" I said. "If we could get our hands on of those...."

"Yeah, well. Good luck with that. I bet they cost the earth," Kate said.

"You're right," I said, "but let's think about it for a minute. We have a fairly accurate idea of when Sattler was killed. To within maybe thirty minutes, right?"

Everyone nodded.

"So if one or both of the prints on the book could be aged to within that time period, we'd know that they must belong to the killer, right?

"But that wouldn't help any because we can't identify the prints," Mike said.

"That's true," I said, "but the killer doesn't know that. Nor does the killer know that we don't have one of those electrostatic sensors. So maybe we can use that to catch him; run a bluff. Yeah?"

"How do you figure?" Lonnie said.

"Let's think about it," I said. "We know the gun was

wiped, because there were no prints on it but Sattler's. Other than that, there is no indication that the room was wiped for prints which, to me, indicates that the killer figured he didn't need to because... well, for a couple of reasons.

"First, because he thought Sattler's death would be classed as a suicide and there would be no investigation. Second, and most important, because he knew his prints were already present, not just at the crime scene, but all over the house, at least in the living room, dining room, kitchen, etcetera. That being so, we can assume it had to be one of our seven suspects. If it was Westwood, we're screwed. We'll never know, but I don't think it was."

Geez, I ain't even sure of that.

"To catch this killer, we have to put that book into his hands. The only way we're going to be able to do that is to set a trap for him, make him think we can identify it and time-stamp it; we have to employ a little subterfuge."

"All of that sounds good," Kate said, "but how do you plan on doing that? We already know that the killer is no fool. We've been at this now for more than two weeks and we still have no idea who it is, or who stole the money."

"First," I said. "We need to put the book back where it was on the shelf. Then we have to persuade the killer to make a try for it."

I looked at Amanda. "That's where you come in. Can you put the word out that the police are convinced that a second shot was fired from the murder weapon, but as yet have been unable to find it?"

"Yes. I can do that. What do you need me to say?"

"That's going to take a little figuring out. We can work on it. You also need to say that they are using the latest in fingerprint technology to date and time-stamp any fingerprints they may find, and that they think that if they can find a print that was made at the time of the killing, they will have their killer, but as yet no such prints have been found."

Amanda nodded. "So you think the killer will see the broadcast and realize that he or she may have left fingerprints on the book, and will have to do something about it; grab it, maybe?"

"That's what I think. I think the killer will panic. He, or she, as you so rightly said, didn't use gloves, so he will think about what he did that night, go over it in his mind. He won't know if he did or didn't leave prints on the book, but he sure as hell will want to make sure he didn't. He'll want to get the book and either take it away or at least wipe it clean. He *has* to make a try for it. If he does, we'll be waiting for him. Amanda, can you get something out on the news tonight? The six o'clock news first, and then, if need be, do an update at eleven."

"Okay. I can do that. How about I write something up and run it by you? It'll take but a few minutes?"

"Sounds good. Kate? Is there anything you want to add?"

She didn't.

"Anyone?" I looked around the table. No one did.

"Okay, I suggest we break for coffee, let Amanda write her piece, and then we'll discuss strategy."

Ten minutes later, Jacque handed copies of Amanda's proposed broadcast to everyone. There was a moment of silence while we read it.

It's now been more than two weeks since local hedge fund manager, Thomas Sattler, was found murdered in his home on Royal Mountain Drive. Sources close to the investigation tell me that the police are optimistic, and that they anticipate making an arrest soon. They know that in order to make the murder look like a suicide, the killer placed the murder weapon in the victim's hand and fired a second shot, thus putting gunshot residue on his hand. The police are looking for that second bullet, but as yet they have been unable to find it. When they do, and they are confident that they will, they are certain that it will lead them to the identity of the killer.

My source also informed me that they are using the very latest in fingerprint technology, a new technique that enables them to age latent fingerprints; to literally time-stamp the print. The technology is said to be accurate to within one hour, and can place a suspect at the scene of a crime at the time it was committed. We'll have more on this developing story on Channel 7 News at Eleven.

I looked up at Amanda and smiled. "One hour? Not

exactly accurate, but hey, it should work. Kate, what do you think?"

"It looks good to me. Will you be able to run it tonight?"

"Yes," Amanda replied. "I'm going to need to clean it up a little, flesh it out, but I've already given the news director the heads up, and he's agreed to run with it. If it doesn't work the first time, they'll run the clip again at eleven." She looked at her watch. "I'd like to be at the station by no later than five o'clock."

"Okay, great," I said. "So here's what we'll do...."

Chapter Thirty-Four

W e all ate lunch together at the Pickle Barrel in the Flatiron building, my treat. We were all there, even Amanda. Kate, to her credit, made every effort to be nice to her. I'm not sure how well that worked, but we got through it. The group included all of my office staff, and Lonnie Guest.

Is he beginning to grow on me? Nah!

There was an air of excitement during the meal. Everyone was aware that things could be coming to a head. We ate, chatted lightheartedly, about nothing in particular. Yes, the conversation was contrived, because no one wanted to jinx the op. Finally, I arranged for us all to meet back at the office by five o'clock, all but Amanda, and then we all went our separate ways.

I went home. It was just after two o'clock that afternoon when I flopped down on the sofa to nap. I set the alarm on my iPhone for four o'clock, and then the next thing I knew was an unearthly chiming when it woke me up. The two hours, so it seemed, had gone by in a blink.

I stripped, showered, shaved, dressed in what Kate called my "bad boy gear", black T-shirt, black jeans, black Bruno Magli Ernelio sneakers. It was then I realized I didn't have a gun. Chattanooga PD had all three. I called Kate and asked for at least one of them to be released. She said she'd do her best, and that if she could, she'd bring it with her.

That, my girl, is just not good enough. I ain't going on a jaunt like this naked.

I looked at my watch. It was 4:45. *Damn!* I grabbed the rest of my gear and ran down the stairs to the garage. If the traffic was light, I might just have time....

It was, but I made a call to Carter's to get the paperwork started and that I was on my way. When I got there, the weapon and the paperwork were ready for me. I was in there less than twenty minutes, and only ten minutes late to the office.

We wasted no time. I gathered the crew together: Kate, Lonnie, Bob, and I had Mike drive us all over to Royal Mountain Drive in Bob's Pathfinder. It was a bit of a squeeze, but we made it. When everyone was inside the house, I had Mike drive three blocks and park, as far away from the Sattler family residence as he could but still be handy if we needed him.

I walked into the house and the stink hit me like a solid wall. The air was still off and the rot had continued. I hoped Amanda's broadcast would stir the pot, and that the killer would move quickly. If not, we were in for a long and nauseating night.

We sat in the kitchen, around the breakfast table and watched the *Channel 7 News at Six* on our iPads. I was beginning to think it was a bust. At 6:15, Amanda still had not appeared. Finally, at 6:25, they showed her outside the house, mike in hand, and she made her pitch. It wasn't quite what we'd discussed in my office, but it was close enough, and she was damned good. Even I believed her.

I looked out of one of the front windows, but there was no sign of her or her Channel 7 car. They must have recorded the piece earlier.

Great job, Amanda.

And we settled down to wait, talking almost in whispers, though there was no reason why we should. I didn't expect anything to happen until well after dark, and it didn't, and so we waited, and we waited.

Everyone had taken cover, hiding in other rooms. I was just inside the den, just off the hallway that led from the living room to the master bedroom. Kate and Lonnie were on the floor in the kitchen, behind the counter, seated on cushions from the sofa in the living room. Bob was at the top of the stairs on the landing.

Finally, after several calls from Mike and Amanda, I turned on my iPad and we watched the clip again on *News at Eleven*. This time, it was the first thing up.

Thank you, Amanda.

It was well after midnight. I was sitting there in the den, in the dark, eyes closed, daydreaming, going over what we'd learned during the past two weeks, when it hit me. Suddenly, I thought I knew who the killer was.

Oh... my... God. No. It can't be....

It was at that moment when I heard a noise outside the French doors in the living room, and I was immediately drawn back into the land of the living. It must have been the sound of a key in the lock that I heard. Then I heard the door open. I crept out of the den on my hands and knees. Slowly, I crossed the couple of yards into the foyer where I had an uninterrupted view of the big room.

Shrouded in darkness, I could just make out a shadowy figure, obviously dressed from head to toe in black. Whoever it was, was on one knee, scanning the books in the right-hand shelf with a tiny LED flashlight. Finally, it found what it was looking for, pulled the book from the shelf, opened it, nodded, closed it, and turned toward the open French door.

"Hello, Wendy," I said, rising to my feet and turning on my flashlight. "Find what you were looking for?"

She gasped, turned, and ran straight out of the open door.

I didn't have time to react before Kate hurtled past me. The girl was no match for the long-legged, ultra-fit cop. She caught her in the middle of the lawn, less than a dozen yards from the house, and brought her down with a flying tackle that Aaron Donald would have been proud of. She dragged her to her feet, snapped the cuffs over her wrists and steered her back inside.

Surrounded by a ring of flashlights, Kate dragged the ski-mask off the girl's head. Even then, I still wasn't sure who was under that mask, but I had a good idea. It came to me while I was sitting there in the dark, in Tom's den. Up until that moment, I'd thought it was probably Stephanie Sattler.

Well, I'll be damned. I was right. Wendy Brewer. Shit. This girl has no motive....

But she did.

Kate called for backup and within minutes a half-dozen cruisers arrived, lights flashing and sirens howling.

Why do they do that?

Unfortunately, I wasn't allowed to attend her interrogation, but the upshot of it all was that Wendy was charged with second-degree murder. There would be a plea, of course, but for now, Wendy Brewer was a guest of the State of Tennessee, and would be for many years to come.

I didn't get home until after four o'clock that morning. Mike dropped us all at the office, and I left a note for

Jacque telling her I wouldn't be in until after lunch, and that I wasn't to be disturbed, by anyone, for any reason. Then I drove home and went to bed.

I must have died, because the next thing I knew it was almost seven o'clock, and I wouldn't have woken even then if it hadn't been for the warm, naked body that slipped under the covers and spooned me.

"Kate, I'm gonna have to get that key back from you one of these days."

"Not a chance, big fella," she said, sliding her hand down my belly. "Ummm, nice. You really are a big boy. Can I have some, please?"

She could, and she did. In fact, she had a lot, and so did I.

We didn't go in to work at all that day. We lay in bed until well after noon. It was *the* most pleasant of mornings I'd experienced in many a long month. I think Kate must have enjoyed it, too, because she made no effort to leave.

Finally, after we'd showered together, and... well... we got around to talking about Wendy Brewer.

"I always liked her for it," Kate said, as she sipped her third cup of coffee and gazed out over the river. We were seated on loungers on the patio, enjoying what probably would be the last of the summer sunshine. I was wearing boxers, she only her bra and panties.

"Oh, bull," I said. "You had no more idea who it was than I did. Hell, I didn't figure it out myself until a few minutes before she arrived."

She laughed. It was that throaty gurgling laugh that turned my stomach inside out, and that was not all it did.

Geez, how I'd missed that laugh.

"No," she said, "I didn't. I thought for sure it was Stephanie. She had the motive. I'm certain Sattler had been screwing her for years. She also had access to the gun, so she had the means, and she lived less than two hundred yards away, so she had the opportunity. I didn't think Brewer had any of those."

"So, you conducted Brewer's interview, right?"

She nodded.

"So did she confess? Why did she do it?"

"She did. She's a whole lot smarter than we gave her credit for. She caught him with his pants down, literally. She said she had a doctor's appointment that afternoon, and she did, but she got back early and saw that Cassell's and Jessica Steiner's cars were still in Sattler's drive."

She took another sip of coffee.

"She left without going into the house, but she came back later that afternoon, much later and found Cassell's car was gone, but Steiner's was still there. She drove around the block, parked the car, came back to the house through the backyard, just as she did last night, and let herself in the French door. She had keys to all the doors. She saw Tom and Steiner doing the nasty in the master bedroom, and she left again without them seeing her.

"She came back later. Steiner was gone. Tom was alone. There was a confrontation. She grabbed the gun out of the desk drawer, made him get down on his knees, and she shot him, then she realized what she'd done. In a panic, she wiped the gun, put it in Tom's hand, then she grabbed a book from the bookshelf and fired a second shot into it, leaving gunshot residue on his hand, and put it back on the shelf. I asked her why she didn't take it with her. She said she didn't know; just didn't think to do it. Her final act was to replace one of the two empty casings with a live one from the desk drawer, leaving only one spent cartridge in the cylinder. She was even smart enough to make sure the empty was in the firing position."

She paused and took a sip from the glass of iced tea.

"The perfect suicide," Kate continued. "At least it would have been, if she hadn't done it on the spur of the moment, and without thinking. If she'd taken her time, given it a little thought, shot him in the temple instead of behind his ear, we never would have known.

"She wasn't worried about prints or any other forms of trace. Shit, Harry, they all watch too much *CSI* on TV these days. She knew her prints, hair, skin cells, whatever, were all over the house, and couldn't be used as evidence, even if they were on the book, because she'd been virtually living there for the past ten years. She opened the book and fired into the pages, thinking it would never be found, and she was right. If you weren't looking for it, you'd never would have found it."

She took another sip of the drink.

"When she heard that broadcast, that we could accurately age fingerprints, she panicked. She knew she'd handled the book less than two minutes after she'd killed him. So she figured she had to do something about it, just as you said. Now then, smart-ass. You tell me how you figured it was her."

"Oh, that was easy. All I had to do was think it through. The problem was, before I was able to relax, in the dark, in Sattler's den, I couldn't think straight at all. I had too many other things on my mind."

She grinned, impishly. "And that would have been?"

"You know what it was.... Oh forget it."

If you think I'm going to admit that it was you I was thinking about....

"How did I figure it out? I realized when I was sitting in the dark back there, that Brewer had told me during her first interview that she left Sattler's place at around one o'clock that afternoon, and that was the last time she saw him. She said she had a doctor's appointment, and she did. I checked the same day as the interview, made a note of it, and then filed it away somewhere in the back of my mind and forgot about it.

"Last night, however, daydreaming in the dark, I realized that her cell phone records put her back at Sattler's home from just after four-thirty that afternoon until almost five. I realized then that she had lied to me. Why would she do that? When I thought about it, the answer was obvious. She did it because she caught Sattler screwing Steiner; she saw them. What almost threw me off was that her cell records didn't place her there at the time of Sattler's death. Then I remembered what I'd said to Mike. Do you remember?

"I do," she said. "You told him something to the effect that the cell phone records only tell us when someone *was* there; not when they weren't, right?"

"Yeah, and that's the way it was. She was smart enough to know that cell phones can be tracked. So she left hers at home that night. I checked...."

For several moments, we both sat quietly, staring out into space, and then Kate said, quietly, "You do know it's not yet over, right?"

"Right... the money. She didn't do it, did she? How do you feel about a little action?"

"Fine. Why?"

"Trust me. Get dressed. We can come back here later, if you want to." I dressed in a pair of lightweight tan slacks, a black shirt, and loafers. Two minutes later, Kate walked out of the bedroom. Her hair was swept back in a pony-tail, and she was wearing skin-tight jeans, flip flops, and a gaudy, Tennessee Orange tank. Hardly work-related attire, but what the hell; she looked fantastic.

"Grab your clutch," I said. "It has your cuffs and Glock in it, right?"

"Harry, I can't arrest someone dressed like this, like a hooker."

Wow, some hooker.

"Hooker? I hardly think so, but why not? You look great to me."

"Yeah, right. Now I feel so much better. Where are we going?"

"Patience, girl. You'll see."

Chapter Thirty-Five

We arrived outside the Sattler home on Stony Mountain Drive at two o'clock.

"You're kidding, right?" Kate said.

"No, I'm not kidding."

"Momma Sattler? Stephanie? I don't think so."

"Bear with me, Kate. Just stay quiet, and follow my lead, okay?"

She nodded. We got out of the car and walked to the front door. I thumbed the bell push, and we waited.

Gloria Sattler was dressed to kill. That is, to kill any chance of arousing even a hint of desire. Her hair was a mess. She wore no makeup. Her backside and thighs strained against the dirty, light-gray spandex yoga sweats over which she wore a similarly colored sweat shirt, several sizes too big. Both bore the stains of housework and at least one meal and were in dire need of laundering.

"Lieutenant Gazzara, Mr. Starke. What do you want?"

"We'd like a word with you and Stephanie. Is she in?"

"Yes, she is. Come in."

Stephanie Sattler was a completely different story. She came downstairs, stepping slowly, her right hand on the rail, reminding me of Audrey Hepburn in *Breakfast at Tiffany's*. She was barefoot, wearing a short, gray leather skirt, and a white blouse; simple, sophisticated.

"Please, sit down," Gloria said, waving her hand at the chairs around the breakfast table. "Can I get you something to drink? Coffee? Tea?"

We declined and sat down together at the table. The two Sattlers did likewise, on the opposite side.

"So," Stephanie said, as she looked at Kate. "What is it you want to talk to us about? You caught the killer. It was Wendy. So it's over, right?"

Kate looked sideways at me, nodded, and said, "Go ahead. It's your party."

"No, Miss Sattler," I said. "It's not over. Not yet. We still have to find out what happened to the money."

"That shouldn't be a problem," she replied. "It had to be one of the partners."

I stared hard at her. She held my gaze, her face expressionless. We must have sat looking at each other like that for thirty seconds or more, neither one of us blinking.

"You want to tell us about it, Stephanie?"

"*What?*" Gloria exploded, and started to rise from her seat.

Stephanie put a hand on her mother's arm, pulled her down, and sighed, resignedly.

"It's okay, Mom. They know."

She sat with her head down, looking at the table top, her hands clasped together in front of her.

"I went to see my father that Tuesday afternoon. I wanted his laptop. He was there. So was Jessica Steiner. They were together in his bedroom, screwing like a couple of dogs, literally; it was fascinating to watch." She was staring off into space, as if she was replaying it again in her mind.

"Please, Stephanie. Don't do this. They'll lock you up...." Her mother was now sobbing quietly.

Stephanie sat back in her chair, ran her fingers through her hair and looked sideways at her mother, then back at me. There were tears welling up in her eyes. I couldn't help it. I felt sorry for her.

"I wanted him dead," she said. "I wanted to kill him myself. In fact, I made up my mind to do it months ago, when I saw how he was looking at Nicola, but I didn't; I couldn't. I tried once. I took Mom's Glock, but when it came to it, I just couldn't pull the trigger."

She sniffed, got up from the table, grabbed a box of tissues from the breakfast bar, and sat down again, wiped her eyes and nose, sighed heavily, and continued.

"He'd been abusing me for years, since my eleventh birthday. He was screwing Wendy at the same time, since she was fifteen. She liked it, the little bitch; she thought she owned him. For some reason, I don't know what it was, he never bothered with Julie, but Nicola: oh yeah, I saw it coming. I could see it in his eyes when he looked at her, and I couldn't allow it. She's almost eleven; the same age as I was when he started molesting me. He was about to dump Wendy, I could tell, and he'd been fooling around with the Steiner woman for a couple of months, but I knew by the way he watched Nicola it wouldn't last. The filthy bastard." She was crying now. "He destroyed me, turned me off men, forever. I can't stand to be touched."

"Why didn't you tell someone?" Kate said.

"Oh I did... I did." She looked sideways at her mother, tears streaming down her cheeks. "I told you, didn't I, Mother? But you didn't, you wouldn't, believe me. But you did in the end, didn't you? You caught him, screwing me. You caught him in my bed, naked, on top of me."

She got up from the table again, went to the kitchen sink,

poured herself a glass of water, drank deeply, and then returned to her seat.

"That's when she divorced him, screwed every damned dollar out of him she could. But it didn't stop, even then, and she wouldn't do anything about it. She just looked the other way and pretended it wasn't happening. Finally, it just stopped. He never said a word; never said why; nothing. He just stopped. I guess he decided he'd had enough of me. I was too old. He was still screwing Wendy, but not me. I thought it was all over, and for me it was, but by then I hated all men, and him in particular.... If he'd have laid a finger on Nicola, I don't know what I'd have done. I guess I would have had to go through with it and shoot his sorry ass."

I looked at her mother. She had her head down, sobbing into a handful of tissues. I looked at Kate. She was slowly shaking her head.

"So why did you steal the money, Stephanie?" I asked, quietly.

"I knew I couldn't kill him, but maybe someone else would. Maybe I was being stupid, but I thought that if I stole the money maybe that sleazy mobster might do it, or one of the partners, or maybe even one of the investors, anyone... anyone.... Never for a moment did I think Wendy would do it."

"How did you do it, Stephanie?" Kate asked.

She sniffed, looked at Kate through her tears, and smiled. Her cheeks were wet, glistening.

"That was the easy part. From time to time, I helped him with the accounts. He paid me, not much, the tight bastard, but I had access to the fund, and I knew his codes. I was there when they decided to liquidate the bulk of the assets, and that's when I decided to do it. It was so easy. I set up the holding accounts in advance, from my own computer, and I knew to the minute when the funds were available. I had no trouble taking the laptop. I just grabbed it while they were at it, him and Steiner. He rarely ever used it. All I had to do was wait until the banks were closing. I wired the money just before five-thirty. I'd been planning it for days."

She smiled, wanly. "The money is in an account in Grand Cayman. It's intact, all $350 million. I never intended to keep it. I just wanted to bring him and his whole corrupt network down, give someone, anyone, a reason to kill him. I was going to wire it back into the fund, but.... Dammit, they locked it. I couldn't get into it."

She sat quietly for a moment, thinking. Kate leaned forward and was about to say something when Stephanie said, seemingly to no one but herself, "Isn't life funny, ironic? I went to all that trouble and I didn't need to. Wendy did it; she killed him, and it had nothing to do with the money. All I had needed to do was wait."

She stood up and looked at Kate, questioningly. "Shall we go?"

Kate nodded, took the cuffs from her clutch, and looked at me. I shook my head. She put them back, and took Stephanie by the arm.

Later that evening, back on the sofa, Kate and I sat together watching the lights moving slowly over the Thrasher Bridge. I had no real sense of accomplishment. Stephanie's story had hit us both hard. I was completely washed out by it, and I know Kate was, too. Unfortunately, it wasn't unique. Incest in some areas of the Deep South is fairly commonplace, but to run into it firsthand like that....

Tom Sattler, the star of McCallie wrestling. I never would have believed it.

"How did you know it was Stephanie?" Kate asked.

"I didn't. Not until we sat down in front of them. I just went back to basics. You've called me Sherlock several times. You know what he said to Doctor Watson, right?"

"Oh yeah," she said. "When you have eliminated the impossible, whatever remains, however improbable, must be the truth." She looked at me, the question unasked.

"Kate, how many times did we discuss the possibilities that it could have been one of the partners, and then discarded the idea? Dozens, right? The same for De Luca. It just wasn't possible."

She nodded.

"And we knew it wasn't Brewer. If it had been, she would have confessed. Hell, she's going down for murder. A little theft, even $350 million, wasn't going to make a whole hell of a difference, now was it? Hollins didn't have the know how. That only left the mother and daughter, so it had to be one of them. When she met us at the door, looking like some flophouse custodian, I didn't think Momma had it in her. Stephanie, however...."

"Well, it all worked out," Kate said. "The cash is back where it belongs, the investors will get every penny they are owed, even De Luca. The DA will go easy on her, seeing how rough she had it, her father abusing her, and the fact that the money was all recovered. There's not a lot of harm done. She'll cop a plea; maybe even get off with probation."

"You think? I hope so. She had it tough all right.... Well, you got your solution and the chief is happy, right?"

"Yep. Good one, Harry. Can we take it easy for a little while? I know..." She sat up, excited. "How about we go spend a few days up in the mountains, at your cabin?"

"Now that sounds like a plan."

And we did.

Thank you.

I hope you enjoyed reading this story as much as I did writing it. If you did, I really would appreciate it if you would take just a minute to write a brief review on Amazon (just a sentence will do).

Reviews are so very important. I don't have the backing of a major New York publisher. I can't afford take out ads in the newspapers and on TV, but you can help get the word out. I would be very grateful if you would spend just a couple of minutes and leave a review. You can jump to the page by clicking the link below.

Amazon U.S. http://amzn.to/1MRsdmo

Amazon U.K. http://amzn.to/1KlQk6n

If you have comments or questions, you can contact me by email at blair@blairhoward.com, and you can visit my website http://www.blairhoward.com.

If you haven't already read them, you may also enjoy reading the other novels in the series, Harry Starke and Hill House:

Harry Starke

It's almost midnight, bitterly cold, snowing, when a beautiful young girl, Tabitha Willard, throws herself off the Walnut Street Bridge into the icy waters of the Tennessee. Harry Starke is there, on the bridge. Wrong time, wrong place? Maybe. He tries, but is unable to stop her. Thus begins a series of events and an investigation that involves a local United States congressman, a senior lady senator from Boston, a local crime boss, several very nasty individuals, sex, extortion, high finance, corruption, and three murders. Harry has to work his way through a web of deceit and corruption until finally.... Well, as always, there's a twist in the tale, several in fact.

You can grab your copy here:

Amazon U.S. http://amzn.to/1K8zCrl

Amazon U.K. http://amzn.to/1RUx5XW

As always, if you're a Kindle Unlimited member, you can read it for free.

Hill House - Harry Starke Book 3

For more than ten years, she lay beneath the floorboards of Hill House. For more than ten years, she waited. Who was she? Who put her there? Why? Harry Starke vows to find the answers to those questions, but to do so he must embark upon an investigation that will put him and those close to him in deadly danger, take him deep into the underground city, the Dark Web, murder, organized crime, prostitution, and human trafficking. One by one, he peels back the layers, and with each one, he sinks a little deeper into the morass, the seamy underbelly of a world few know of, and even fewer want to be a part of. Hill House has many doors. None of them lead anywhere but into darkness and despair.

You can grab your copy here:

Amazon U.S. http://amzn.to/1P7KFYU

Amazon U.K. http://amzn.to/1ZbMqY3

As always, if you're a Kindle Unlimited member, you can read it for free.

Checkmate – Harry Starke Book 4

They found Angela Hartwell lying in the shallow waters beside the golf course. There wasn't a mark on her, yet she was dead, strangled. How could that be?

Once again, it's up to Harry Starke to find out. The investigation takes him into a world he's very familiar with, a world of affluence, privilege and... corruption.

To solve the mystery, he must deal with three murders, a beautiful used car dealer, her lovely twin sisters, and a crooked banker. Not to mention Burke and Hare, two crazy repo men who will stop at nothing to protect their employer's interests. There's also the matter of an ingenious, sadistic killer. But nothing is ever quite what it seems....

You can grab your copy here on Amazon U.S. http://amzn.to/1SQhf4q

In the U.K. This is the link: http://amzn.to/2oAVnc7

As always, Kindle unlimited members read for free.